The Lighthouse

Luna's Light

Pacific Ocean

LIGHTHOUSE WAY

Lighthouse Pizza

Whalers Gallery

FERNGULL DRIVE

CHAPEL BEND

Gordy's Diner

Little White Chapel

SEASIDE LN.

Huckleberry Delight

Three Sisters Kitchen

Crush

Books on The Bay

Huckleberry Bay

The Grind

Wolfe's Workshop

MAIN ST.

SHELTER COVE DRIVE

Lighthouse Way

A Huckleberry Bay Novel

Kristen Proby

Ampersand Publishing, Inc.

Lighthouse Way
A Huckleberry Bay Novel
By
Kristen Proby

This book is dedicated to my grandfather,
Bill J. Beller.
First, thank you for inspiring me with your letters home
from WWII.
Second, thank you for passing your incredible love and
passion for the Oregon Coast on to me.
I miss you every day.

Prologue

Luna

J ANUARY 1, 2000

DEAR DIARY,

WE FOUND THE COOLEST THING TODAY! SARAH, JUNE, AND I WERE IN THE LIGHTHOUSE, IN OUR SECRET PLACE, AND THE FLOORBOARD CREAKED. JUNE WAS ABLE TO PRY IT UP. THERE WAS A DIARY INSIDE! A REALLY, REALLY OLD ONE THAT STARTS IN 1871. SO, IT INSPIRED THE THREE OF US TO START DIARIES, TOO. AND WHAT BETTER DAY TO START THAN THE FIRST DAY OF A NEW MILLENNIUM?

SO FAR, WE'VE ONLY READ THE FIRST ENTRY. WE DECIDED THAT WE WOULD READ ONE AT A TIME, AND WE ALL HAVE TO BE TOGETHER WHEN WE DO. TODAY'S WAS

SAD. THE WOMAN WHO WROTE IT, ROSE, TALKS ABOUT HOW SHE MISSES HER MAN. HE SET SAIL AND PROMISED TO BE HOME IN THREE MONTHS, BUT HE'S BEEN GONE FOR ALMOST A YEAR. SHE SOUNDED SO HEARTBROKEN.

I GUESS THEY COULDN'T JUST CALL EACH OTHER WAY BACK IN THE OLDEN TIMES.

I SAID IT REMINDED ME OF ONE OF THE ROMANCE NOVELS I JUST READ. OF COURSE, I HAVE TO HIDE THOSE FROM MY MOM. SHE'D SAY THIRTEEN ISN'T OLD ENOUGH TO READ THOSE BOOKS, BUT THEY'RE SO GOOD!

ANYWAY, THE DIARY IS TOTALLY AWESOME. WE PUT IT SAFELY BACK IN ITS HIDING SPOT SO WE CAN JUST PULL IT OUT AND READ IT WHENEVER WE'RE UP IN THE LIGHTHOUSE. IT'S BEEN REALLY RAINY AND STORMY LATELY, SO WE HAVEN'T BEEN UP THERE VERY MUCH. DAD SAYS IT'S TOO DANGEROUS. BUT WHEN WE GET A BREAK IN THE WEATHER, WE'LL GO BACK UP AND READ SOME MORE.

I WONDER IF ROSE IS THE GHOST I SEE HERE SOME- TIMES. I SEE HER UP ON WHAT DAD CALLS THE WIDOW'S WALK, AND OTHER TIMES, I FEEL HER NEXT TO ME LIKE SHE'S TRYING TO TELL ME SOMETHING. ONCE WHEN I FELT HER, I SAW THAT WOLFE WAS UP IN A TREE, AND HE ALMOST FELL. IT WAS SO WEIRD! BUT I'M NOT SCARED OF HER. I HAVE TO LIVE HERE, AT THE LIGHT- HOUSE, WITH MY PARENTS, SO IT'S GOOD THAT SHE DOESN'T SCARE ME. THAT WOULD SUCK.

OKAY, I THINK THAT'S ENOUGH FOR MY FIRST ENTRY. I'LL WRITE MORE WHEN THERE'S SOMETHING

GOOD TO TALK ABOUT. I CAN'T WAIT TO READ MORE OF
ROSE'S DIARY!

    LOVE,

    LUNA

Chapter One

Wolfe

"It's my distinct pleasure to introduce a man who needs no introduction at all," Mayor Rebecca Schlinger says with a wide grin as she looks over at me. "Our own hometown pride and joy, Wolfe Conrad!"

It seems that all two thousand and nine citizens of Huckleberry Bay are in the crowd, cheering and waving their arms and flags as I take the stage and smile out at them.

It's the Fourth of July Festival in my hometown of Huckleberry Bay, and I'm here as a celebrity guest—and to drive in the dirt races for charity.

I'm used to loud crowds and exuberant fans, but this hits a little differently. Okay, a *lot* differently.

Because this is home, and the crowd cheering right now is full of friends and people I've known for most of my life. I lit out of here as fast as I could after high school, obsessed with cars and driving fast. Hell, I haven't even been back home since my parents died almost two years ago, within months of each other. My dad died from cancer, and my mom passed from what I'm sure was a broken heart.

Yet, still, the people here are proud of me.

And there's nothing like the Oregon coast in the summertime.

"Thank you," I call out into the microphone, and the crowd starts to quiet so they can hear me. "It's always good to be home, and I'm glad I could be here for this. You know, when I was a kid, this festival was my favorite time of year. We're going to put on an exciting race for you all today and raise some money for the local food bank while we're at it."

I let my gaze skim over the familiar faces, pausing when I see Luna Winchester. I lift a brow at her, and she smiles.

It's been a lot longer than two years since I saw Luna.

I send her a wink and then get back to the task at hand.

Racing. My lifeblood. It's always a thrill to drive, but doing it in my hometown? Well, there's an added layer of adrenaline in that mix.

"I hope I see some familiar faces tonight at the pub crawl."

The famous *pub crawl* in a town the size of Huckleberry Bay consists of roughly three bars, but it'll be fun to unwind after the race.

I hurry down the steps at the side of the stage to where my best friend, Zeke, is waiting.

"Why don't we come here more often?" he asks as we hurry toward the track. I slip my sunglasses onto my face and try to ignore the unfamiliar nervousness that's set up residence in my stomach.

I never get nervous.

Except, apparently, when I'm racing in my hometown.

"This town is fun. And beautiful. A little cold for being on the beach, but there are some good-looking women here, Wolfe."

"The race starts in thirty," I remind him. "Stop ogling the women and focus. You can ogle tonight."

"Oh, I plan to. There's a blonde who's caught my eye. Hopefully, she shows up later."

"Hopefully, she isn't married like that chick in Daytona."

I give my friend the side-eye, and he sighs, rubbing the back of his neck.

"Yeah, well, that wasn't entirely my fault. She didn't say she was married. Wasn't wearing a ring."

"Might be something you want to ask before you get them naked," I suggest as we approach the car. "Now, let's work on winning this race before we shift focus to other activities, shall we?"

"Of course, you're going to win," Zeke points out. "This is a dirt track. You're a stock car *champion*. These guys all do this as a hobby, and you've won more cups than I can count on two hands."

"Thanks for reciting my resume."

"You've got this in the bag. It's all to show off for your

hometown and raise some money," he says with an arrogant grin. "But I'm not complaining. We needed some R&R."

"And we can start that after we finish *this*."

Twenty-six minutes later, after the national anthem's been sung and I've waved to the crowd some more, we're ready to go.

Ten laps in, the car is warming up nicely, and I'm pumped full of adrenaline and in the lead. Someone pulls up beside me on the straightaway and tries to cut me off, drifting around the corner. But they're too close. Way too damn close.

"Back off," I mutter, eyeing the other car in my mirror as I grip the wheel harder. "You're going to kill us, asshole."

The next thing I know, they've clipped my bumper with theirs, and I'm spinning, then rolling—at almost a hundred miles an hour. I see the wall coming for me.

And then I don't see anything at all.

"You've only been in therapy for a few weeks," my doctor, Amaryllis Lovejoy—who was also my senior prom date—says with a scowl. "You have a *lot* of work to do, Wolfe."

"I'm not leaving town," I reply in resignation as I tie my shoes. My head is pounding again. The migraines are the worst part of what's left over from the accident, even worse than the leg injury. I feel like I'm in a tunnel with someone pounding a sledgehammer on the top of my head, and I can't hear or see well. "But coming in every day is a waste of time. I'm walking fine."

I may be able to walk, but the career I built over the course of fifteen years is over. Just like that, in the literal blink of an eye, it's all gone.

"I'd like for you to come in three times a week."

"The leg is healed," I reply impatiently. "I don't even walk with a limp anymore, and you said yourself that that's impressive, given the accident was only a month ago. The bruises are faded, and there's nothing you can do for the headaches."

She frowns and then sighs, lifting a shoulder in resignation. "What are you going to do, Wolfe?"

"I'll figure it out." If my head would stop pounding long enough for me to think straight.

"I want to see you in a week," she says sternly. "If the leg starts to give you any issues, we'll need to work on more therapy."

"Okay." I sigh and set my hand on her shoulder. "I'm sorry. I don't mean to be a jerk. Thanks for everything, Amy."

I want a dark room and some ice. And I don't want to be in a damn hospital every day anymore. Sure, it's outpatient, but it's still a pain in my ass.

And now that we know the therapy won't put me in the cockpit of a race car ever again, I'm over it.

I don't know what comes next, but it's time to figure it out.

* * *

"This house is fucking falling apart," I mutter, and with my hand on my hip, stare at the cabinet door that just fell off in the kitchen.

I opened it to get a coffee mug, and the whole thing just came off in my hand.

I lean the old, out-of-date oak door against the bottom cabinets, make my coffee in a different thermal mug, and set off for outside.

It's summer in Huckleberry Bay, but it's a nice sixty degrees this morning even with the sun high in the sky. The air is heavy with salt from the ocean, and if I have to take a walk to exercise this leg, I'd rather do it outside than on a damn treadmill in a hospital.

Besides, I've found the less time I spend in my parents' house, which is crumbling around me, the better.

It's been two months since the accident. Aside from some soreness in my leg once in a while, usually warning me that rain is coming in, I'm physically healed.

If you don't count the screaming migraines that appear out of nowhere and knock me on my ass. Amaryllis calls them *crash migraines*.

And isn't that just appropriate?

So far today, I'm headache-free, so I start out down Lighthouse Way, the street I grew up on, just a few blocks from the cliffs. I've been taking this walk daily, though at different times. It clears my head.

Being out here always did.

I loved my parents, but they fought a lot. Whenever

they had a particularly bad one, I'd sneak out of the house and wander up the road toward the cliffs, where the lighthouse sits.

Where Luna and Apollo lived.

The three of us played together all over this area from the time we were barely in kindergarten to middle school. We rode our bikes, played in the trees, and spent one hell of a childhood together. You would think I'd have been the closest to Apollo, but it was Luna I enjoyed being with the most. Apollo was fun, too, but there was something about the connection I had with Luna that I craved. She was so smart. Always so kind. And she had a soothing personality, even as a young kid.

But then we got older. Luna started playing with her girlfriends, and I shifted my attention to learning about cars. Eventually, we grew apart the way kids do. Apollo and I hung out in high school, but I rarely saw Luna.

It's just the natural way of things.

But, man, I loved those years when we played together here in the neighborhood. We knew every tree, every hill. But we never went near the cliffs. That was off-limits, and it was well known that our parents would have our heads if we played on them. It wasn't until I was a teenager and *dying* to get out of town to race that I started climbing down the rocks to sit closer to the water.

It still smells the same, like saltwater and crisp trees. And, as I walk around the bend that leads to the lighthouse and the Winchester homestead, I have to admit that it looks pretty much the same, too. Sure, the house has had a coat or two of paint added over the years, but the lighthouse hasn't changed at all. It still stands tall and proud on the cliffs as the waves crash below, sending up misty sprays of water. It must be high tide because the seawater flies over the horizon, reaching almost as high as the house

The property has other outbuildings that Luna's family hasn't used, leaving them mostly in disrepair. As far as I know, no one ever used them in our lifetime.

We always thought they looked haunted with their weathered, gray wood and broken windows.

Luna swore she saw a ghost, but I always shrugged it off as a fanciful story told by an imaginative little girl.

Who knows? Maybe it was true.

The grass is green set against the big, blue sky, and the wind is relatively calm today, making for a nice late-summer morning.

Just before I turn toward the cliffs, I see someone walk out the side door of the house and start toward the old barn. I raise my hand to wave when they glance my way, and I see that it's Luna.

Luna smiles, and I take that as an invitation to cross over to chat with her.

"I wondered when I'd see you around," she says as I approach, opening her arms in an invitation for a hug.

"I've been here and there." I briefly wrap my arms around her and then sip my coffee to hide the jolt of awareness that shoots through me. Luna was always cute but damned if she didn't grow into a *gorgeous* woman. Her long, dark hair shimmers in the sunshine, and her dark eyes aren't just brown. They're like whiskey. "How have you been? It's been a long time."

"Oh, I'm good. Mom and Daddy moved to Florida, so I'm taking care of things around here now."

"Really? By yourself?"

She arches an eyebrow in annoyance, and I hold up a hand in defense.

"Not that you're incapable of it. I imagine it's a lot of work. If anyone can do it, though, it's you."

"Yeah." She sighs and then shrugs, glancing around. "It is a lot of work, but you know I've always loved it here. I never planned to do anything else, even when I went away to college. Apollo's an electrician and busier than a cat in a room full of rocking chairs. He loves it. And I love the light."

Luna's parents named her and her older brother, Apollo, after gods of light. Isn't it fitting that they both dedicated their lives to it?

"So, here you are." I nod and take a long, deep breath, looking around. "It's a special place, Luna. It always was."

"And it's about to get better."

My gaze returns to hers at the excitement I hear in her voice. "Oh? How so?"

"You know the old barn?" she says and points to the big structure behind her.

"Sure."

"I'm going to make it into a bed and breakfast. We start renovations next week."

"*We?*"

"Well, yeah. I can swing a hammer. I have blueprints and a general contractor. Demo starts today."

I turn in a circle and then smile at her. "I don't see anyone else here."

"I'm gonna tear some stuff apart myself before June gets here," she declares with a wide, excited smile.

"In the haunted barn."

"It's all haunted, not just the barn," she says with a careless shrug, then narrows her eyes on me. "Do you have somewhere you need to be?"

"Me? No, I was just out getting some fresh air."

"Come on. I'll put you to work. We can break some stuff. It helps get the aggression out."

"Who says I need to work out aggression?"

Luna rolls her eyes and waves for me to follow her to the barn. "After the couple of months you've had, I think it's probably a safe bet that you could stand to swing a hammer at something. How's your parents' house, by the way?"

"Falling apart around me. They never mentioned that it needed so much work."

She nods and works on the padlock of the door. "Well, that happens when a building sits empty for years, Wolfe."

Was she always this sassy? This bossy?

Probably.

I never found it sexy before.

Of course, I never looked at her like this before, either.

Her body is curvy now with hips and breasts, and the

14

V-neck T-shirt she's wearing could bring any man to his knees.

Especially *this* man.

Luna is definitely no longer a child, but she *is* maybe the sexiest woman I've ever seen—and that's saying something.

She pushes open the sliding door, and we both cough as dust rolls out, clouding the air around us.

"How long has it been since anyone opened this?"

"About a week," she says with a laugh as the sun shines into the big space, making the dust glitter. "It's just dirty out here. But it won't always be. There will be eight guest suites, a library, a dining room, and a kitchen."

"What are you going to call it?"

"Luna's Light," she says immediately and sets her hands on her hips as she takes in the vast space.

There's not much in here now. Some debris and tarps cover things here and there, but for the most part, it's empty.

"It looks mostly like a shell right now."

"Yeah."

"So, what do you have to tear apart?"

"The floor."

She walks over to where a sledgehammer leans against a post and picks it up.

"The *floor?*"

"Yeah. It's not sound, so it has to come up. And there are some boards on the walls that are rotten and need to be torn out, too. Probably most of them, honestly. I'm hoping the support beams under the floors are sound. Otherwise, we'll have to replace those as well."

"Why don't you just bulldoze the place and start over?"

"We could, but I like the idea of building it around the old stuff, you know? Like, you're sleeping in a building originally built in the eighteen hundreds."

"Should you even be *walking* on this floor?"

"It's okay. I'm going to start in the far corner and work my way out. In fact, I think I'll start with the walls."

"You can't just start tearing things apart, Luna."

"Why not? It's mine. I'm the boss around here."

"You don't have a hardhat on, although I'm sure your hard *head* would protect you. You need eye protection. Gloves. Long sleeves, for God's sake."

"Who are you, the Occupational Safety and Health Administration?"

"Maybe." I cross my arms over my chest and narrow my eyes at her, not willing to back down. "You're not starting demo until you're protected. I won't have you out here getting hurt."

"You know, you're not the boss of me."

I don't answer, and I also don't move a muscle. I just stare her down until her shoulders slump, and she mutters, "*Killjoy.*"

I want to kiss her more than I've ever wanted anything else.

Well, except maybe to race again. But that's never going to happen.

"I probably wouldn't get hurt."

"There are old, rusty nails sticking out all over in here," I say, shaking my head. "The last thing you need is tetanus."

"I've had my shots," she says but then sighs. "You're right. I'm just excited to get started. I've wanted to do this for a long time, and I'm impatient."

"I understand impatience," I reply. "These days especially."

"How do you feel?" she asks quietly.

"Fine." My voice is curt, but I'm sick of having conversations about how I feel. It's time to move on.

"Can I ask one question?" She turns to me and tilts her head to the side.

"Ask away."

"What are you going to do now that you can't race?"

It's a blow to the chest, just like *every* time I'm reminded that I can no longer do what I love.

"I don't mean to be insensitive. It just occurred to me, that's all."

"I'm going to live my damn life." I pace away and watch the sun shining through a window. "Try to work through the anger that doesn't feel like it will ever go away. And I'm going to open a garage."

"Car repair?"

"Yeah. But a little more than that. We'll be restoring classics, too. High-end stuff. I'm trying to talk my best friend, Zeke, into moving to town and going into business with me."

"That's really cool, Wolfe."

"If I can get it going, it'll be awesome. I have to keep

my hands in a car, and if this is the only way I can, then that's fine by me."

Maybe if I keep saying that out loud, I'll start to believe it. Because, as of right now, it's not *fine*. Nothing is *fine* about this goddamn situation.

"I have to take the business plan to the city board to get it approved. Huckleberry Bay is very particular about the businesses they allow to open up around here."

"Don't I know it. I can probably help you with the business plan," she offers. "I had to write one for the bed and breakfast, so I have practice."

"I would *not* turn down that offer." This is the best news I've had in a while. "I'm afraid I'll screw something up, and they'll tell me to take a hike."

Luna smiles softly. "We need a repair shop. I hate driving an hour away just to get my oil changed."

"You don't know how to change your own oil?" I demand.

"Why would I know something like that? There are experts who know how. And now, I'll have one close by."

"I'll take a look at your car," I say immediately. "I can change the damn oil and do anything else you need."

By the smile on her face, you'd think I just proposed marriage.

"You don't have to do that."

"Trust me. I have the time on my hands. It'll give me something productive to do."

"Okay, I won't complain. Listen, I know it's not under the best of circumstances, but I'd be lying if I said I wasn't glad you're home for good, Wolfe. Huckleberry Bay just wasn't the same without you."

"Thanks. I have some mixed feelings if I'm being honest. I love the town, but—"

"But you lost a lot."

"Yeah." I blow out a breath and drag my hand down my face. "Let's go find some supplies, and I'll help you out in here. You shouldn't be pulling up a hundred-year-old floor by yourself."

"I have to buy gloves and stuff," she says with a resigned shrug. "So, I probably won't get to it until tomorrow. But you're welcome to come back anytime. I can pay you in food and whatever you'd like to drink."

Before I can take her up on that offer, someone calls out from outside the barn door.

"Where are you? I've been banging on the front door for ten minutes!"

We turn just as a pretty woman with a crop of shockingly red hair, currently stuffed under an old trucker hat, walks through the doors.

She stops short when she sees me.

"Well, well, well, if it isn't Wolfe Conrad."

"Juniper Snow," I reply with a smile and take her in. I move my gaze from that cap and red hair down her gray coveralls to her steel-toed boots. "Now, *you're* dressed correctly to demo a building."

"Just June," she says and pops a stick of gum into her mouth. "Only my mom calls me Juniper. I'm sorry for what happened, Wolfe."

"Yeah, thanks."

"He's living in his parents' old place down the road," Luna says to her best friend, and I realize that I'm looking at two of the three musketeers.

Luna, June, and Sarah. Thick as thieves.

"Where's Sarah?" I ask out of the blue, and both women frown over at me. "Wherever there are two of you, the other isn't usually far away."

"You haven't heard?" Luna asks.

"Heard what?" My heart stops. Jesus, she didn't...?

"She's in California," June says, and I blow out a breath. "Married some rich asshole right out of high school and hasn't been back since."

I scowl and shake my head. "That doesn't sound like her. Granted, I didn't know you guys *that* well, but you were attached at the hip."

"Until she married Mr. Moneybags," June agrees. "I usually get a Christmas card from her, but that's about it. I think Luna talks to her more often."

"We try to talk every few months," Luna confirms. "But I haven't heard much since last Christmas either."

Luna looks concerned, but before I can ask more questions, June points to a big tarp in a corner and asks, "What's under there?"

"I have no idea," Luna says. "I've always avoided this building, and I haven't started digging around yet."

"She thinks it's haunted, and she's probably right, although I've never seen anything," June says to me and, with a smile, saunters over to the far corner. I let out a long, low whistle when she pulls back the tarp.

"Holy moly," June whispers.

"I had no idea that was in here," Luna says as I pull the rest of the heavy tarp off the old car, and we all stare in silent awe.

"What is it?" June asks and reaches out to touch the faded red paint.

"This, my friends, is a 1927 Ford Model A."

Both women look at me in surprise.

"Wow, that's very specific," June says.

"I know my cars."

"It's a convertible," Luna says. "And the top's not torn all to hell."

"It's original," I mutter, examining it closely. "This is a freaking *gold mine*, Luna. It's dirty, and I'm sure it needs a lot of work, but my God, she's beautiful. Cherry-red with the whitewall tires. Look at these fenders. Just look at them."

"Nice fenders," June agrees, sarcasm dripping from her tone, and I whip my head around to glare at her. "Hey, you're the car man. If you say it's a big deal, then it's a big deal."

"This automobile—and that's what it is, it's not simply a *car*—would have cost up to about a grand brand-new. That was a *lot* of money back then. In the shape it's in, with some work...man, I can only guess what it might get at auction now. Maybe close to six figures."

"Shut up," Luna says, shaking her head. "No way."

"Way. You don't understand. There might be less than a hundred of these left in existence. Far less than that in this condition."

"Oh, my gosh. Luna, wouldn't it be cool if you had

21

this restored and it was the official car for the B&B? You could offer rides into town and stuff in it. I'll drive."

"You have a job," Luna reminds her but bites her plump lower lip, clearly thinking it over. "Although, that's a really good idea."

"It's a *damn* good idea," I agree. "I'll restore her for you."

"I could be your first customer," Luna says with a bright smile on her gorgeous face.

"This isn't a job. This is pure pleasure."

"Mm-hmm," June says, giving us both the beady eye. "I'm sure it is."

June hasn't changed a bit.

"I think it sounds like the coolest thing ever," Luna says at last. "If you're willing to do it. I can't wait to find out who it belonged to and why it's been sitting here in the barn all these years. How do we get it out of here? The floor isn't sound enough to pull a tow truck in."

"Good question," I mutter. "Let me figure that out."

"I'll happily leave it up to you," Luna says. She grins and then does a little happy dance. "This is already so much fun!"

Suddenly, I hear a loud slam from up in the loft, and we all look up.

"Is there a door up there?" June asks.

"Yeah, a small attic," Luna says with a sigh. "And something made her mad."

"Who?" I ask.

Both women turn to me and, in unison, reply. "The ghost."

Chapter Two

Luna

"So, let me get this straight," Wolfe says, shaking his head slowly as he sets his hands on his lean hips—his *very* trim hips. Not that I noticed or anything. "You're going to build a hotel around a haunted barn. Aren't you afraid it'll be bad for business?"

"One," I reply as June snickers, "as I told you before, the whole property is haunted, not just the barn. And two, it could actually be *good* for business."

"A lot of people are into that stuff," June agrees. "And there are plenty more who don't believe in it at all, so I don't think it'll be bad for the pocketbook. Oh! Maybe you could offer ghost tours."

I raise an eyebrow at the thought. "Hey, that's not a bad idea."

"Halloween would be a *blast*," June continues.

"I don't know," I reply, thinking it over. "Maybe it's not something I want to advertise. I don't want it to become a cliché or scare people off, you know? Plus, I don't want to miss your grandma's party. It's too epic."

"True," June says, and we both turn our attention to Wolfe as he laughs at us.

"What's so funny?" I demand.

"You two. I'm glad I came up here and got to see you both." He shakes his head and then turns to my friend. "Oh, hey, June?"

"What's up?" she asks.

"My parents' house is falling apart. Literally. Would you have time to come look things over and give me an estimate on some repairs?"

June nods thoughtfully. "Sure. I can pop over later this week to see what's going on. It's been a killer summer for my schedule, but I should have some time this fall if you can wait a month or two."

"Nothing's urgent, just things falling apart around me," Wolfe says to her. "I'd appreciate the help."

"Why don't you just sell it and buy something else?" I ask him.

"Yeah, you did well with racing," June points out. "You could buy something a *lot* nicer."

"I could," he says but shakes his head and then pins me with his dark blue gaze. "But I can't imagine living in Huckleberry Bay and *not* being on this road. The house will be fine with some repairs." He looks in the direction of his property. "I'll see you both soon."

But it's me that he winks at before turning to walk out of the barn. My eyes immediately fall to his backside.

Wolfe always did have a nice butt. Somehow, it's only gotten better.

"I'm going to go figure out how to get that automobile out of here," he tosses over his shoulder. "I'll be in touch."

"Wait, you don't have my number."

That stops him in his tracks. He turns and walks back to me, holding out his phone.

"Just send yourself a text."

"I feel like I'm watching a rom-com unfold before my very eyes," June says, but I ignore her as I type in my number and send myself a simple *hi*.

The phone in my back pocket dings.

"Now I have your number." Wolfe winks at me and turns away once more to leave. His sneakers are quiet on the old wood floor, but they stir up a bit of dust as he walks away. "You'll hear from me soon."

June bumps my shoulder with hers after he's out the door and several seconds have passed.

"I bet you hear about more than that old car."

"What are you talking about?" I walk over to the far wall and inspect some rotten boards. "Boy, the salty air really does a number on buildings, you know?"

"Of course, I know. I'm a *builder*. And you just changed the subject."

"Wolfe's always been good-looking," I reply with a shrug. "That hasn't changed. I'm sure you noticed."

"As I'm not currently dead, yes, I noticed."

Another slam comes from the loft.

"I guess the dead lady noticed, too," June says. "And I saw the way you looked at his ass."

"That's not against the law."

June laughs. "No, definitely not. And if it makes you feel better, he was checking you out, too."

"We haven't seen each other in a long time," I remind her. "So, it makes sense that we were sizing each other up."

"Right. Yeah, it was only normal. If lusty eyes can be considered *normal*."

"Okay, I admit it. Wolfe's damn hot." I laugh and then turn to my friend with a shrug. "With a capital H."

"Did you see the way his muscles strained against that shirt?"

"Maybe he needs a bigger shirt."

"It would be a shame to cover those muscles," June says with a smirk and turns to the old Ford. "He was crazy excited about this car. How did we not know that it was out here?"

"No one ever mentioned it," I reply. "I'll have to call my dad and ask him about it. The idea of using it as a guest shuttle is awesome."

"Hell, I'll book a room just so I can ride in it," June adds.

"You don't have to do that." I grin over at her. "Hey, I wanted to talk to you about Sarah, and since Wolfe brought her up, now's as good a time as any."

June's phone rings, and she immediately reaches for it. "Saved by the bell."

But then she frowns.

"Just a spam call." She shoves it back into her pocket. "I don't really want to talk about Sarah."

"I know. But, damn it, I'm worried about her, June. I've never gone this long without hearing from her. I only have the post office box address, and she hasn't replied to my last letter."

"Don't you think it's weird that she's never given you a phone number to call? An email address? Why is she so damn secretive?"

"I think her husband is a controlling ass who doesn't want her to have anything to do with any of us—or Huckleberry Bay."

"Clearly. And if she's willing to live like that, I say let her."

"June."

"Listen, I get that you're the peacekeeper, okay? You always were. You're a really nice person. But she left us behind without even a backward glance. She *left us*. So, no, I'm not worried."

I just stare at her silently until June frowns and blows out a breath.

"Okay, I admit that it's weird. But damn it, Luna, she made it clear that she doesn't want us in her life. If she won't reply to you, there's a reason for it."

"I guess so. I can't help but worry about her, though. She was our best friend."

"*Was*," June says. "And I hate that as much as you do, but I'm not one to beg for attention from someone who doesn't want me."

June was always the most stubborn of us all. But she's also fiercely loyal.

Until you shove that loyalty in her face—the way Sarah did. Then, June is more likely to write a person off.

Not that I blame her. Sarah hurt us both.

She hurt everyone when she left, including Sarah's younger brother, Scott.

But we took Scott under our wing. Despite some rocky moments, he's doing well now and even owns his own home.

"I know Sarah did a lot of damage when she left," I admit softly. "And I'm not making excuses for her. I'm just worried."

"I'm sure she's fine," June replies. "She's just...busy. Now, I need to get started on some demo in here. And you can't be in here because you're not dressed right."

"That's what Wolfe said."

"Sexy *and* smart." June's mouth relaxes into a playful smile. "That just doesn't seem fair."

"Well, if you're sure you have this handled for now, I have some errands to run."

"Go." June waves me off, already focused on the job. "Have fun. I'll see you later."

"See you later."

I leave the dusty old barn and walk across the grass to the house attached to the lighthouse. I've lived here my whole life. Well, except for the years that I went away to college, and when June and I were roommates here in town until my parents decided to retire and move to Florida. Once they did, I moved back in—after making some minor improvements and decorating the place to my tastes.

I don't think I could have moved in and left it exactly how Mom and Daddy left it. It wasn't in bad shape. It was just...outdated.

And now I have an updated kitchen with white cabinets and black granite countertops, perfect for baking and cooking. I had the floors refinished and stained to a light honey color. With white walls, the house is bright and inviting and not at all cold, thanks to beautiful local artwork and plenty of pillows and throw blankets.

I love it here. It's the perfect mix of familiar and fresh.

After I quickly change out of my dirty clothes and into a pretty, yellow summer dress with a light pink cardigan and sandals, I walk out to the car and fire it up.

My ten-year-old Mazda has seen better days, but she usually gets the job done. If Wolfe is good to his word and takes the time to give her a once-over, she'll last quite a while longer.

The lighthouse is perched on a hill, high on the cliffs so the beacon can be seen many miles out into the Pacific Ocean. I'm only a couple of miles outside of town, so the drive is relatively short, even on the twisty road by the sea.

I never tire of seeing the blue of the Pacific. I went to college inland and felt like a fish out of water. I couldn't wait to get back.

Whether the ocean shimmers with sunlight as it does today, or churns gray with a storm, it fuels me the way nothing else ever has.

Because it's still summer, it means we're still in the

heart of tourist season. I don't allow tours of the light-house—not yet, anyway—so it stays pretty quiet at my place. Our little town, however, is hopping with visitors. Finding a spot near Three Sisters Kitchen is a challenge, and I end up parking about a block away.

But I don't mind the short walk in the warm sunshine to the front of the adorable establishment. Three Sisters is a farm-to-table restaurant that has quickly become a favorite in Huckleberry Bay. I'm not here for a meal today, though. Instead, I'd like to pick Cordelia's brain.

"Well, it's good to see a familiar face," Cordelia says when she sees me walk through the door.

"You're busy," I reply, glancing around at the full tables. "I can come back another time."

"Don't you dare leave me," she says, shaking her head. "Do you want a table? I have a delicious corn chowder in the kitchen for lunch."

"Actually, I'll take some of that to go, thanks, but I'm really here to ask you a couple of questions. But it's not urgent. I can come back when there aren't so many customers in here."

"That probably won't be until October." She laughs. "Come on back to the office where it's a smidge quieter, and we'll talk. Phoebe, honey, just call if you need somethin'. Oh, and have a bowl of the corn chowder packaged up to go for Luna, please."

Phoebe, the young woman working the cash register, gives a thumbs-up, and I follow Cordelia to her office.

"How's business been this summer?" I ask as she shuts the door behind us.

"More than we can handle," she replies. "It's both a blessing and a curse if I'm being honest. A blessing because our tables are full from the time we open until we close, but a curse because we're all exhausted around here. But on the upside, this busy season will get us through the lean ones when the tourists go home and leave our town quiet for a while."

I love listening to this woman talk. She and her sisters moved here from South Carolina a few years ago to open this incredible restaurant, and I'm so glad they did. Scoring something new in a town like ours is refreshing. And it doesn't happen very often.

"But enough about us, how are you doing out there on the cliffs all by yourself?" Cordelia takes a seat in the chair next to mine rather than behind her desk and tucks a stray piece of dark hair behind her ear. She's poised and always perfectly dressed, the epitome of what I've always pictured a southern woman to be.

"Oh, I'm great. But, based on what you just told me, I think your answer will be no. And I understand."

"Well, honey, you won't know unless you ask. What do you need?"

I press my lips together and then smile at her. "I'm opening a bed and breakfast."

As I tell Cordelia about my plans, her face changes from surprise, to interest, to pure excitement.

"This all sounds absolutely wonderful," she gushes and pats me on the arm. "And it's exactly what our little town needs. I know folks are curious about your lighthouse, me being one of them, so inviting guests in to experience it all firsthand is just fantastic. Maybe you could do an open house just for the citizens of Huckleberry Bay to come inside and snoop around before you're bombarded with guests."

"I think that's an *excellent* idea," I reply, already loving the thought.

"Now, what do you need from us?" Cordelia asks.

"Well, I'll be providing breakfast and an all-day snack bar for the guests. I would love it if I could work with you and your sisters on some baked goods to offer. I know you're not a bakery, but your desserts are some of the best in town."

Cordelia grins. "I know we can work something out. Mira would likely enjoy coming up with special items just for you. A Lighthouse Menu, if you will."

"Mira is a genius in the kitchen."

"That she is. And she loves coming up with new things. She'll probably offer to do sack lunches with sandwiches and salads for you, as well."

"Oh, that would be perfect."

"When will you need us to start?" she asks, and I feel my cheeks heating with embarrassment. "That soon?" She raises an eyebrow.

"No." I laugh a little and shake my head. "I haven't even broken ground yet. But we should be underway by next week, and I hope to open for the summer season next year."

Cordelia's eyebrows climb into her perfect hairline. "That is fast."

"I know it's ambitious. Trust me, I know. But I'm

crossing my fingers. Still, we have time to nail down the specifics. I just wanted to reach out to people I'd like to work with now, in case I'm told no and have to go to plan B."

"And who was plan B for this?"

"I didn't have one, so I'm relieved you said yes."

She laughs, and a knock sounds on the door. Phoebe pokes her head in.

"Mr. Lovejoy is here to pick up pies, but Mary Beth accidentally sold one to another customer, and I'm pretty sure there's about to be a riot out here."

"I'm coming," Cordelia assures her as we both stand. "Thank you for thinking of us. I'll talk to Mira and Darla tonight after we close."

"No, thank *you* for taking the time. I won't take any more of it. Good luck with Mr. Lovejoy."

"That man's a teddy bear."

I wave at Darla behind the pie counter and then hurry out of the restaurant to get out of everyone's way. It's an adrenaline rush in there.

Pleased with my first meeting, I sit in my car and pull my phone out of my purse to dial my brother's number.

"Yello," he says. I can hear a saw in the background. "Sorry, let me step out. Hold on."

I grin and wait for a few minutes, watching a family walk down the sidewalk, all four of them eating ice cream from Huckleberry Delight. Maybe I'll swing by there on my way home.

"Sorry," Apollo says again. "We're wrapping up a

33

build, and it's a madhouse in there today. What's up with you?"

"It's okay. I just have some good news and needed to share it. Three Sisters is going to work with me on the food side of things for the B&B."

"We don't even have walls yet, Luna."

"I know." I laugh and shrug, even though he can't see me. "But I'm excited, and it doesn't hurt to have things figured out. I'm organized."

"I'll say you are. Is the contractor there yet?"

"He's coming tomorrow. June's over there now, ripping out some rotten wood and cleaning things up. Hey, did you know there's a super old car in the barn? It was in the corner, covered up."

"No, I didn't know that. How did we miss it?"

"I don't know, but Wolfe is excited about it."

I hear a pause on the other end of the line. "Wolfe Conrad was in the barn?"

"He was out for a walk and hung out for a bit. He's going to fix it up for us so we can use it as a shuttle vehicle. Anyway, we'll talk more about that later. Are you coming over for dinner?"

"Yeah, I'll be there around six. I want to see this car. If June's still there, I guess I could give her a hand, too."

"Right, you'll tear each other up rather than the rotten wood. Besides, she probably won't still be there that late."

I hear him pull the phone away from his ear and say something to someone.

"Hey, I have to go. I'll see you tonight. Good job on the restaurant thing, sis."

"Thanks. See you later."

I toss my phone back into my bag and pull out of my parking space, headed toward home. When I pass the ice cream shop and see the line down the block, I decide against a treat.

I'll just bake some cookies or something.

It's a gorgeous drive back home, and I roll down all the windows so I can enjoy the fresh air. Tonight's sunset will be spectacular. The stellar sunsets are something I absolutely *have* to advertise on the website and social media. I already have the perfect viewing spot from the gazebo fifty yards from the lighthouse. But most of the rooms in the barn will have water views, as well.

There will be whale-watching opportunities in the winter, and no one will even have to get on a boat.

I don't know why my family didn't do this sooner. It just feels like a no-brainer.

I park my car by the house and notice that June's already gone for the day. I know she had another job to check in on. She's been so busy, and I'm grateful that she's making time for me and this project.

I quickly check the mail and sigh in defeat when I see there still isn't anything from Sarah.

What's going on with her?

FEBRUARY 10, 2000

DEAR DIARY,

OKAY, SO I DIDN'T GET OFF TO A GOOD START WITH THIS DIARY THING, BUT IT'S BEEN REALLY BORING AROUND HERE. THE WEATHER HAS SUCKED. I DON'T THINK WE'VE SEEN THE SUN IN ALMOST TWO MONTHS, BUT THERE HAS BEEN PLENTY OF RAIN. WE EVEN HAD SOME SNOW LAST MONTH, AND THAT NEVER HAPPENS. I SUPPOSE I COULD HAVE WRITTEN ABOUT THAT, BUT I FORGOT.

I'VE BEEN READING A TON. I GO THROUGH A BOOK EVERY COUPLE OF DAYS. DAD SAYS I HAVE TO START CHECKING THEM OUT OF THE LIBRARY RATHER THAN BUYING ALL OF THEM BECAUSE IT'S TOO EXPENSIVE. BUT I LIKE HAVING THEM ALL ON MY SHELF! I WISH I WERE OLD ENOUGH TO GET A JOB SO I COULD JUST BUY THEM MYSELF. APOLLO SAYS HE'LL GET ME ONE A WEEK SINCE HE'S SIXTEEN AND HAS A JOB AFTER SCHOOL AND ON THE WEEKENDS. I GUESS HE'S NOT ALWAYS A BIG JERK.

BECAUSE OF THE WEATHER, WE HAVEN'T BEEN ABLE TO SPEND MUCH TIME READING THE DIARY WE FOUND IN OUR SECRET SPOT, AND I'M DYING TO READ MORE! I WANT TO KNOW MORE ABOUT THE WOMAN AND THE MAN SHE LOVES. I HOPE HE WAS ABLE TO COME HOME TO HER. MAYBE HE WAS CAPTURED BY PIRATES! THAT WOULD SUCK.

I HAVEN'T BEEN HANGING OUT WITH WOLFE AS OFTEN AS I USED TO EITHER. WE WERE ALWAYS SO

CLOSE WHEN WE WERE KIDS, BUT NOW HE'S MORE INTER-
ESTED IN CARS AND TOOLS AND PROBABLY GIRLS. GIRLS
PRETTIER THAN ME, ANYWAY. AND THAT'S OKAY
BECAUSE I DO **NOT** LIKE HIM LIKE THAT. EW. NO. BUT
HE'S ALWAYS BEEN MY FRIEND, AND I MISS HANGING
OUT WITH HIM. MAYBE I'LL SEE HIM MORE THIS
SUMMER. THAT WOULD BE COOL.

SARAH AND JUNE ARE COMING OVER THIS WEEKEND
FOR A SLEEPOVER. I HOPE THE WEATHER GETS BETTER,
AND WE CAN READ MORE OF ROSE'S DIARY. WE'RE
GOING TO HAVE PIZZA AND ICE CREAM AND RENT SOME
DVDS. IT'LL BE FUN. SARAH'S BEEN HAVING A HARD
TIME AT HOME...WORSE THAN USUAL...SO I'M GLAD SHE
CAN COME HERE WITH ME FOR A DAY OR TWO. I WISH
SHE COULD JUST LIVE WITH ME. HER PARENTS ARE THE
WORST EVER. HER BABY BROTHER SPENDS A LOT OF TIME
WITH HIS FRIENDS, TOO. IF PEOPLE DON'T WANT TO BE
NICE TO THEIR KIDS, WHY DO THEY HAVE THEM IN THE
FIRST PLACE? SEEMS STUPID TO ME.

ANYWAY, I SHOULD SIGN OFF FOR NOW. I'LL TRY TO
BE BETTER ABOUT WRITING STUFF DOWN, BUT I WON'T
PROMISE.

LOVE,
LUNA

Chapter Three

Wolfe

"The drama around here is something you'd expect to see on daytime TV," Zeke says and rolls his eyes.

"You don't usually pay attention to it," I remind him, but he shakes his head.

"I don't have you here to distract me anymore."

"Aw, you miss me."

Zeke smirks and then shrugs one shoulder. "It's not the same without you."

This is the perfect segue into why I video called my best friend today.

"Well, then, how about this? Why don't you quit the drama club there and move here to Huckleberry Bay? You can be the co-owner of the garage I want to open, and restore cars with me."

His brows draw together as he frowns. "You want me to move in with you?"

"No, smartass. You can't live here. But you *can* live in town. You liked it here. You said so yourself."

He looks like he wants to be even more of a smartass, but then he thinks twice. "A garage, huh?"

"Yeah. A garage. And I already have a customer."

I tell him about Luna's Ford and watch as Zeke's pupils dilate.

"You're fucking kidding me."

"I'm not, no. It's a honey of a car, and we can make it purr like a kitten."

"Hell, yes, we can. That's like finding a needle in a haystack. A once in a lifetime find. Any gearhead would give their eyeteeth to work on that car."

"Then move here and go into business with me."

The truth is, I could do it alone, but I've been working on cars with Zeke for close to two decades. It would feel weird not to have him be a part of it. And, yeah, I miss him.

"It's damn tempting, man."

"Okay, give it some thought and let me know. I'm going to look at a building for sale tomorrow. It's on the edge of town. If it's in good condition, it might be the ticket. I want to be up and running before the holidays."

Zeke's eyebrows wing up. "That's damn fast, Wolfe. You need equipment, tools—"

"I can get it. I know people."

"You're rich," Zeke replies dryly. "That doesn't hurt."

"That, too." I grin at him. "Come on. You know you want to."

"Yeah, it's *damn* tempting," he says again. "Give me a

couple of days to figure some stuff out, and I'll get back to you."

"Great."

We end the call, but a knock sounds on my door before I can do anything else.

The doorbell doesn't work.

When I open it, Luna and June grin back at me.

"Hey," Luna says and holds a yellow plate in the air with a bright smile on her gorgeous face. "I know I'm late, but I brought welcome-home carrot cake."

"My favorite."

She smiles, her cheeks flushing with pleasure, and I can't help the fleeting picture in my head of me making her blush just like that in very different ways.

That's new when it comes to thinking about Luna, but this isn't the little girl I used to play with as a kid.

The woman before me is gorgeous.

And I'd be lying if I said I didn't think of her so often it surprises me.

"I'm glad it's still your favorite," she says. "It would suck if you were suddenly allergic or something. June thought she'd come with me and take a look around your house."

"Come on in." I step back and usher the women inside, taking the cake out of Luna's hands, my hand brushing over hers as I do. She bites her lip as her eyes meet mine, and I offer her a wink.

Yeah, she's damn beautiful.

"I've only seen the outside," June begins as she pulls a measuring tape off her belt and measures the doorway that leads into the kitchen. I have no idea why, but I'm not the construction expert here. "This place needs a lot of work, Wolfe."

"Don't I know it?" I set the cake on the kitchen counter and sigh as we all look around. The paint, once a bright yellow, is dull. My mother hung a strip of floral wallpaper to border the ceiling in the mid-1990s, and it's begun to peel and hang down in places.

The Formica countertops have chips. The sink has a slow drain and plenty of stains.

And I still haven't gotten around to putting the cabinet door back on its hinges.

"The foundation is crumbling," she continues as she walks around, taking everything in. "The siding is warped and falling off, likely from the elements. I'm sure the roof needs to be replaced."

"Based on the water damage in the guest bedroom, I'd say you're right."

"Why did you let it just sit here?" June demands and turns to me with her hands on her hips, her green eyes blazing with the temper that comes with that riot of red hair. "Without even having a management company hired to keep an eye on things."

I blow out a breath and lean against the wall, crossing my arms over my chest. "I knew I'd have to come and take care of their things eventually," I confess. "And have the house fixed up. Part of me thought I should just go ahead and sell it."

"But you didn't," Luna says softly.

"I can't," I admit with a shrug. "Yeah, it needs a *lot* of

work. But it's only a ten-minute walk to the cliffs, and it's in a great spot."

"I won't disagree with that," June says. "You could get half a million just for the lot."

"I should tear it down and build something new here." I rub my fingers over my chin, thinking it over. "It's not the house that I'm attached to. It's the location."

"I haven't seen all of it yet," June says, "but I can tell you that it would cost just as much to renovate this place as it would to start from scratch. If you're not sentimental about the building, I say take it down and start over. You could even build something similar to this one. How big is the property?"

"A few acres, most of it wooded."

"Well, then, you can do just about anything you want. You're not within the city limits, so there are no ordinances out here. You could build a bigger house, add a nice garage..."

"That's a must," I agree, nodding. There's no existing garage now, just the carport, and it drives me nuts. "I have a few cars that I don't want sitting out in the elements—especially being so close to the ocean. They'd rust right out."

"What kinds of cars?" June asks.

"Fast ones," I reply with a wink. "And when they all get here, you can come check them out anytime."

"What *are* you going to do with all your stuff?" Luna asks with a frown. "Everything in here belonged to your parents. Where's your stuff?"

"It's all being shipped from Monaco."

Both women just blink at me, and I can't help but smile at them.

"You lived in *Monaco*?" June demands.

"A lot of the drivers do," I reply. "It's private."

"Sure," Luna says as she nods. "Private. It's also damn expensive."

I just continue smiling at her.

Damn, I miss Monaco.

I'll take her there. I'll show her the most beautiful country I've ever been to.

Make love to her there.

I mentally shake my head. I might be getting ahead of myself.

"Okay, fancy pants," June says with a gusty breath. "When will it all be here?"

"In a couple of weeks."

"Well, we won't have this place either renovated or rebuilt by then. Are you sure you want to live here in the interim?"

"Yeah," I say. "For now, anyway. I know the house is small, and there's no storage to speak of on the property. I'll rent something."

"I'd offer my buildings," Luna adds, "but I don't think they're in good enough shape to hold your things. Not yet, anyway."

"No, you don't want a Ferrari to fall through the floor of one of your outbuildings," June says.

"How did you know I have a Ferrari?"

June just barks out a laugh. "You're totally the Ferrari

type. Plus, you raced in one. Did they give you a car for free? Was it part of the sponsorship?"

"One of them was. If I'm sponsored, which I was by Ferrari, I'm expected to be seen driving their cars."

"Wow," Luna says under her breath. "I drive a Mazda."

I laugh and reach out to tug on a strand of her dark hair. "Nothing wrong with that, sweetheart."

She grins, and I want to lean in and kiss her so badly I can taste it.

"Ahem," June says, clearing her throat. "Good God, the chemistry is ridiculous between you two. I'd say get a room, but I'm not convinced the ceiling wouldn't cave in on you here."

"Were you always this blunt?" I ask her.

"Oh, yeah. I have a filter now." June winks. "Okay, you make heart eyes at each other. I'm going to look around a little bit more."

June leaves Luna and me alone in the kitchen.

"She's just trying to be funny," Luna says.

"So, you're *not* making heart eyes at me, then?" I ask and step just a little closer to her.

She doesn't back away.

"Pfft. No. Of course, not." She licks her lips and stares at my Adam's apple.

"Thanks for the cake," I murmur as I lean closer, smelling the sweetness of her. Not only does she look like sunshine, but she smells like it, too.

"You're welcome."

"Okay, break it up," June says as she walks back into

the room. "I definitely recommend a rebuild here. Your plumbing and electrical are crap. Unfortunately, I don't think you'll find a builder that can get started until at least the spring."

"Will this place hold up until then?"

"If you're lucky," she says with a grin and then keeps talking, but it suddenly feels like I'm in a tunnel, and my head is in a vise. The women's words are muffled, and all I see is what my doctor refers to as an *aura*.

Jesus, why do the migraines come on so damn fast?

I need Luna and June to go so I can grab an ice pack and lie down.

"...see you later."

"Thanks," I manage to reply. "I'll be in touch."

I hope I'm responding correctly. I don't even know what they said.

Or who said it.

Finally, when they're out the door, I stumble to the freezer for the ice pack and then make it to the couch in the living room before I fall down, pressing the pack to my pounding head.

And, just that fast, I'm reminded why I've lost everything that matters to me. Why I can't be home in Monaco. Why I can't race.

Why I'm in this shithole my parents left to me.

"Wolfe?"

Shit.

I crack open one eye and make out a figure, but I don't know who it is.

"Go away."

45

"June forgot her tape measure, and I—God, Wolfe, what can I do to help?"

Luna. Jesus, I don't want her to see me like this.

"I'm fine."

"You're not fine."

She touches my shoulder, and it's agony. I can't be touched. Everything hurts.

"Go." I don't know if I yell or whisper it. "Just go the fuck away."

She must do as I ask because she doesn't touch me again. Suddenly, the house is quiet around me as I writhe in agony, willing the pain to stop. Battling not to throw up.

* * *

It lasted three hours. By the time the headache cleared, I was so exhausted, I just fell asleep and didn't surface until this morning.

I'm still foggy from it, but at least the pain is gone, and I can function again.

The scariest part of these damn migraines is that they come out of nowhere.

But I absolutely hate that Luna was there. I couldn't do anything in that moment, and in the light of a new, pain-free day, I feel bad for how I spoke to her.

It's another beautiful day as I walk up the road to the lighthouse, and I'm relieved to see Luna's car in the driveway when I approach the house and ring the doorbell.

The door opens a few seconds later, but Luna's instant welcoming smile immediately falls.

Yeah, I hurt her feelings.

"I brought flowers," I begin and hold up a bouquet of yellow roses. "They reminded me of you."

She eyes the blooms and then looks up at me. She still hasn't smiled, and that's not like her.

"Are you okay?"

I swallow hard, take a deep breath, and nod. "Yeah. Yeah, I'm okay."

"Good." Her expression doesn't change, but she takes the flowers from me, and I don't feel like such a big jerk. "I'm glad you're okay. You didn't have to buy me flowers."

"Yeah, I did. I didn't mean to be so short with you, and I'm sorry."

She sighs, and if I'm not mistaken, she softens just a bit.

"Come in," she says and steps back to let me inside. "I was just making coffee. Want some?"

"Do you have decaf?" I ask her.

"Sure."

"Then I'd love some."

I follow her through the house to the kitchen, surprised by how different it looks from when we were kids.

"What happened yesterday?" Luna asks as she pulls two mugs out of her upper cabinet and gets to work making the coffee. As a cup brews, she arranges some cookies on a plate and sets them on the table. "Have a seat."

"Do you mind if I stand?"

She shakes her head. "No, I don't mind."

"I get migraines out of nowhere," I say as Luna passes me a mug. "A result of the accident. They're called crash migraines. I can't predict them, and they're a son of a bitch."

She pours some cream into her mug, gives it a stir, and takes a sip before turning to me.

"I'm so sorry, Wolfe."

"Yeah, me, too. But I'm mostly sorry that I snapped at you yesterday. I was just desperate to be left alone."

"I would have helped you," she says, and it makes me smile.

"I know." I can't help it. I have to touch her, so I reach out and fiddle with her hair the way I've suddenly become accustomed to doing any time I'm near her. "But there's really nothing to do except breathe when it happens. That's about all I can do, anyway."

Before she can ask more questions, I change the subject.

"I think I have a plan for getting that gorgeous car out of your barn."

Luna raises an eyebrow. "Really? How?"

"Well, I have to go out and look around a bit, but if June's going to take down a good portion of the wall behind it, that might be the best route. I can bring out a flatbed truck and pull it up behind the car. With a couple of extra hands, we'll get it out of there."

"Here's hoping it doesn't fall through the floor while you're at it," she says.

"If the floors in all the buildings are so bad, why don't you replace them?"

"We will. I just haven't been out in any of them. From what I know, no one has in more than thirty years."

"Don't go out there snooping around alone, okay?"

"Snooping?" she asks with a smile. *Finally,* a smile! "That would imply that I'm doing something wrong. Given that I own this place, I can look anywhere I want. I don't have to *snoop*."

"Okay, then don't go looking alone."

"Why are you so bossy?"

"Because I don't want you to get hurt."

"I'm not usually a clumsy woman," she reminds me. "I won't get hurt. There's no need to worry. Do you want to go out there and look at the back of the barn now?"

No, I want to pin her to the kitchen counter and kiss her into next week. As I pause to answer her, those gorgeous eyes fall to my mouth.

When her tongue brushes over her bottom lip, I know I'm a goner.

"Luna," I whisper as I move in closer to her. "If I don't kiss you, right here and now, I might die a slow, painful death."

Those eyes dart back up to mine in surprise.

"If you don't want that, tell me now."

"I don't think I would say no to that," she says, and that's all the invitation I need to close the last of the gap between us. I splay my fingers on her ribs, just under her arms, as I lower my lips to hers.

She gasps as my hands move to cradle her face, and I

feel her grip onto my T-shirt, fisting it as I take us from soft and gentle to firm and hot in less than three-point-two seconds.

God, she's fucking sweet.

She plunges one hand into my hair, and I boost her onto the counter so she's closer to me.

She wraps her legs around my waist, and I dip my head to the side so I can kiss her neck.

"You smell damn good," I growl into her ear.

"Is this just how it's going to be now?"

I pull back, and we look over to the doorway where June's standing, her arms crossed and a smirk on her face.

"Do I have to yell out whenever I'm around so I don't have to watch this? Maybe I should just wear a bell like a cat."

"That might help," I agree but don't pull away from Luna as I turn back to her and grin. "Raincheck to resume this later?"

"I'm good with that."

I kiss her forehead and then step away before helping her to her feet. When she wobbles and reaches for me to steady her rather than the countertop, I take that as a huge win.

"Let's go look at the barn," Luna suggests.

"Lead the way."

Chapter Four

Luna

Wolfe can kiss. Like, *really* kiss. Who would have thought the kid I used to climb trees and run around the neighborhood with when we were children would turn into a man who makes me feel as if I'm the only one in his universe? Even if it was only for a few minutes.

Not to mention, his hands are just...dreamy. That's the only word I can come up with right now because my brain is still scrambled from that lip-lock in my kitchen.

Wolfe is dreamy.

That's something that the sixteen-year-old me would have written in my journal. Okay, I wouldn't have used *dreamy*.

As the three of us walk toward the barn, Wolfe slips one of his magical hands into mine as if he does it every day and squeezes without even looking my way. He doesn't even have to think about it. The chemistry has been there since he walked up my road the other day, and it's only grown thicker in the few moments we've spent together.

It's like there's suddenly a direct line of electricity that moves between us pretty much constantly—which is a completely new experience for me.

One I'm not sure what to make of.

But it's also kind of nice. Or a *lot* nice.

"I hate to tell you this, Luna," June says as we round the outside of the barn, her words pulling me out of the kiss haze. "But I think we're going to have to take down most of the exterior walls."

"Given that there aren't many *interior* walls to speak of, that basically means tearing it all down. Wolfe might not be sentimental about his place down the street, but I *am* attached to this one, Juniper. I don't want to tear it down."

"I didn't say you had to, drama queen," June replies and rolls her eyes as she pulls her hat off and shakes out her curly red hair before twisting it back up under the cap. "We can probably keep some of it, but the outside is completely lost to the elements. It has to be replaced, and some internal boards have rotted out, as well."

"Does that mean you'll take down most of this exterior wall?" Wolfe asks, pointing to the back of the barn. "The car's sitting in this corner. If you take down most of this wall, I can pull it out that way."

"We can make that happen," June confirms. "Come on, let's go check it out from the inside again."

"I definitely want another look at that baby," Wolfe says with excitement.

The three of us circle back around to the front of the barn, and I grin when I see my brother and his best friend, Tanner, walking toward us.

Apollo's gaze falls to my linked hand with Wolfe's, and his eyes narrow.

"Well, look who it is," June says with a sneer. "Apollo and Hermes."

"Damn it, June, you know that's not my name," Tanner says and reaches out to playfully steal June's hat, but she dodges out of his grasp.

"And yet, it just fits so well," June replies and then turns her glare on my brother. "What are *you* doing here?"

"We came to check out the car," Apollo says easily. My brother never shows any sign that June gets to him, but I know she does. She always has. He turns to Wolfe and holds his hand out in welcome. "Hey, man, I haven't had a chance to say welcome home yet."

"Thanks." Wolfe grins and shakes hands with Apollo and then does the same with Tanner. "Not much has changed up here on the cliffs, even in a dozen years."

"Not yet," I remind everyone. "We're working on it. Be careful in here; the floor has some rotten boards."

I push open the sliding barn door, and we walk inside, spreading out so we don't put too much weight on any one spot.

"The car's back here," Wolfe tells the other men, and they all set off in that direction in eager anticipation.

"Boys and cars," June says as she rolls her eyes.

"I seem to remember a woman I know asking Wolfe

53

about his fast cars," I say and glance her way. "You wouldn't happen to know who that was, do you?"

June just wrinkles her nose at me as we follow the three men to the far corner of the barn.

"How is it possible that this was out here all these years, and we had no idea?" Tanner asks Apollo.

"No one ever came out here," Apollo replies with a shrug and then turns to me. "Were you able to reach Dad and ask him about this?"

"Yeah, I spoke with him this morning." I shake my head. "He didn't know it was here either, which I find really weird. I'm about to start looking through the filing cabinet in the office to see if there's any paperwork on it. All the lighthouse documents are in there, so I hope I get lucky."

"Did anyone ever think to try looking in the car?" Apollo asks as he opens the passenger side door and leans inside.

"Be careful on those seats," Wolfe warns. "I don't want anything to crumble."

June and I exchange a look as the guys carefully rummage around in the car. Apollo eventually comes up with an old, faded envelope.

"Jackpot."

"It could just be seventy-five-year-old junk mail," June points out, and without looking her way, Apollo reaches over and tugs her hat farther down her forehead. "Hey!"

"Why do you always have to be so pessimistic?" my brother asks her.

"Okay, kids, no need to argue—like you always do." I hold out my hand, and when Apollo passes over the envelope, I frown. "It doesn't feel like anything's in here."

"Well, open it," Tanner says. "Put us all out of our misery."

"There's no mold in here," Wolfe mutters as he continues looking around inside of the car. "Incredible."

I open the unsealed flap and pull out a single piece of paper.

"What does it say?" June asks.

"You guys." I scan the document and then look up, directly into June's eyes. "This was Rose's car."

"Rose who?" Tanner and Wolfe ask at the same time.

"*Rose?*" June echoes, her green eyes widening in surprise. "But she would have been, like...in her seventies when this car was built."

"It's hers," I repeat and show June the paper. "This is an old registration. It was registered to Rose Winchester in 1927."

I look up at Apollo, whose eyes have narrowed.

"I think it's time to start doing some family tree research," I tell him.

"Why didn't we do it before?" June asks. "We've had her diary since we were, what, like twelve?"

"You have her diary?" Wolfe asks and pokes his head up from the back seat.

"Yeah." I grin at June. "That's right. I don't know, time passed, and I forgot."

A door slams upstairs, making us all jump.

"I'm sorry!" I toss up to the loft.

"Uh, what was that?" Tanner asks Apollo.

"Ghost," my brother replies.

"So, the car belonged to Rose," I continue and pace away from the group. "But she would have been elderly by then. And from everything I know, which isn't much, she wasn't wealthy. How would she have afforded this car?"

"Maybe it was a gift," Tanner suggests.

"Maybe," I reply and then shrug. "Well, one more thing to look around for, I guess. In the meantime, you have my go-ahead to knock out that back wall and get the car out of here."

"I'll get started on it tomorrow," June says with a smile. "Demo is my favorite."

"Shocker," Apollo says and earns a glare from June.

"You're just jealous," June says.

"And what would I be jealous of?" Apollo demands.

"That I get to do the fun stuff, like demolish things. All you get to do is run wire through the buildings that I've already built."

"Yeah. Definitely jealous." He rolls his eyes.

Before June can snipe back, I shake my head. "Nope. We're not doing this today. I have too much to do. I can't play referee with you two. Wolfe, are you going to sleep in there?"

"Just looking at something," I hear him mutter from inside the car. "About done here until I can get her to a garage. I guess I'll have to *buy* the garage first, huh?"

"Wait." June stops and blinks. "If you don't have a place to haul this thing, I'll hold off on demo."

"Just give me a couple of days," Wolfe says as he comes out from inside the car and wipes his hands on a handkerchief that he pulled out of his pocket.

He carries a handkerchief?

That's kind of hot.

The three men discuss Wolfe's plans for a repair garage as we walk to the barn door. Once everyone is out, I pull the door closed and lock it.

Only the five of us know the car is in there, but I don't want to take any chances.

I've just turned around when June says, "Luna."

She gestures toward the road with her chin, and I follow her gaze, feeling my heart stumble in my chest.

"Oh, God."

None of us moves as we watch Sarah walk up the road, pulling two large rolling suitcases behind her. She stops at the end of the driveway when she spots us and pushes her sunglasses up onto the top of her head.

"Don't give her shit," I say as I grab onto June's wrist.

"She needs us," June says softly. "Look at her face."

"Yeah. I see it."

We take off in a brisk walk toward our old friend. I hear the guys behind us. Apollo murmurs something I can't make out to Tanner.

"Hey," I say as I reach Sarah. "Honey, are you okay?"

"Yeah, I—" She swallows hard as she looks over my shoulder at Tanner. "Hi. Hi, everyone. Gosh, you're all here."

Her eyes fill with tears, and I instinctively reach out to wrap my arm around her shoulders.

"I'm sorry to interrupt and just show up out of the blue. I tried to call, but—"

"Potential spam," June says. "Sorry, it showed up as a telemarketer."

"I figured." Sarah sighs. "I don't know what to say."

"My mom always says it's best to start at the beginning," I say and look over at my brother, who clearly hears my unspoken request.

Take the guys and go.

"I have work to do," he says and offers Sarah a kind smile. "It's good to see you, kiddo. Hey, guys, let's go figure out this car removal thing."

"I'll call you later," Wolfe says to me and then smiles at Sarah. "It's good to have you home, Sarah."

"Thanks," she says, her voice breaking before she can clear her throat.

Tanner hangs back as the other two leave. He and Sarah were high school sweethearts, and I see that his face has gone ashen.

"We'll have you guys over for lunch tomorrow. Or dinner. Whatever works for you," I tell him softly.

"Yeah. Yeah, okay." He nods and turns away, then looks back at Sarah. "Call me if you need me."

She just nods as he leaves and gets into Apollo's car.

When the three of them are gone, June takes Sarah's hand in hers, and the three of us just stand in the late summer sunshine for a minute, the way we'd done countless times in our childhood.

"Luna," June says quietly. "Let's gather up some snacks and drinks and take this to our secret spot."

"Good idea."

* * *

We got all of Sarah's bags into the house, and while she used the bathroom, I loaded up a tray with molasses cookies, chips and salsa, and Cokes.

Our favorites.

Then we climbed up the lighthouse steps to our special place in the tower room. Sometimes, when the wind was calm and the weather nice, we'd sit out on the widow's walk.

But we're inside today.

"Okay," June says as she dips a chip into the salsa and pops it into her mouth. "Talk to us."

"Who, me?" Sarah asks innocently and bites into a cookie. "I want to hear about what you've been up to."

"No way," June replies. "What happened?"

Sarah sighs and closes her eyes. "You know, I dreamed of this place. So often. Whenever things got really bad, I'd just close my eyes and come here. To our place. I'd listen to the water, and for those few moments, I'd feel safe."

June and I share a glance but don't say anything. We just wait for Sarah to tell us what's going on.

"Let's just say that Anthony decided to trade me in for a newer model." She sips her Coke. "Pretty cliché, right?"

"He's having an affair with a younger woman?" I demand.

"Oh, I'd say it's more than that. He's engaged to, and having a baby with, a twenty-one-year-old."

"Ew." June scrunches up her nose.

"He likes them young," Sarah says. "I was nineteen when I married him."

"And he was thirty-four," I remind her.

"Cliché," she says again. "I got too old for him. So, he discarded me."

"But where's your car?" I demand. "You bought a brand-new car as a graduation present to yourself. It's only like...thirteen years old. Where is it?"

"Oh, he made me trade that in as soon as we got to California," she says with a humorless laugh. "No wife of Anthony's was going to drive anything but a luxury car. He got me a new Mercedes every other year."

"So, where's your fancy ride, then?" June asks her.

"Well, I was stupid enough to sign a prenup, so I didn't get to leave with anything that didn't have my name on it. And he made damn sure that literally *nothing* had my name on it."

"What in the actual fuck?" I ask as molten-hot blood roars through my veins. "How did you get here?"

"The bus," she says and shrugs one slim shoulder, reaching for another cookie. "I just have what's in those suitcases. But I managed to squirrel away a few thousand dollars over the years, so I'm not penniless. Just poor."

"I have so many questions," June says, shaking her head.

"Me, too," I add.

"Can we not today?" Sarah asks softly and stares

down at her cookie. "I know you deserve to know more, and I will tell you. I never *didn't* want to talk to you. I just didn't have a choice. You're my sisters in every sense of the word, and I'll tell you everything. But for today, can we just...not?"

"You've got it," I reply and give June the side-eye when she looks as if she might object to Sarah's request. "You'll be staying with me."

Sarah's gaze flies to mine, and her eyes fill with tears.

"You don't have to do that. I can stay at a hotel for a while."

"And eat up your savings? That's ridiculous. I have a great guest room that never gets used. Trust me, it's fine."

"Thanks. Really. Also, I need a job. I thought I'd go ask Gordy for a job at the diner. I used to wait tables there back in the day, and I was good at it."

"I bet he would hire you back," I reply with a nod. "We're always so busy with tourists now. Pretty much everyone is hiring."

"I'll go make the rounds through town tomorrow," Sarah decides.

"Sarah," June says as she pulls her hat off and sets it on the floor next to her. "Did that asshole hurt you? I mean, he obviously did mentally and emotionally. But physically?"

Sarah blows out a quiet breath. "Not until the end," she finally says and then looks up at both of us. "Not until the very end."

"Okay." I take her hand in mine and give it a squeeze. "We'll save the rest for later."

"How's Scott?" she asks.

"He's great," June says. Two days ago, she would have followed that up with something like, *"No thanks to you."* But I can see that the resentment has melted away, and the loyal, loving friend is back.

June's tough, but when she loves, she does it big. She would do anything for us.

"He has to be so mad at me," Sarah says. "But I'd like to see him."

"You should see him," I encourage her. "It'll be tough at first for both of you, but it'll get better with time."

"And I have all the time in the world," Sarah whispers. "I can't believe I'm finally home with you two. I also can't believe that when I got here, you were coming out of the barn with Wolfe, Apollo, and *Tanner.*"

"Tanner and Apollo were always best friends," I remind her.

"I know, but...it was weird. Isn't Wolfe a race car driver?"

"We have so much to catch you up on," I say with a grin. "It might require margaritas and tacos."

"I'm full on cookies," June says but then grins. "But I'm always down for tacos."

"I have to use the bathroom," Sarah says and holds up her Coke bottle. "Too much of this."

"Then let's go down to the house," I suggest. "But first, I want to grab this."

I lift the loose floorboard and reach in to retrieve the old diary.

"That's still in there?"

"Of course. But it's time to take it inside where it's a little safer. And I need to give it a read-through because I have some questions."

"Do you guys still keep a personal diary? The way we did after we found this one?" June asks.

"Yes," Sarah and I answer in unison.

"Me, too," June says with a grin. "That's pretty cool."

June follows me into the kitchen when Sarah heads to the bathroom.

"She's hiding a whole trunk full of stuff," she says with a whisper.

"More than a dozen years' worth of baggage," I agree and cross my arms over my chest as I look toward the bathroom. "But we can't unpack it all in an afternoon with Cokes and snacks."

"I know. But, damn it, I'm impatient."

"No." I clutch my invisible pearls and gasp as if shocked. "*You?*"

June just narrows her eyes at me.

"It's going to be okay," I assure my friend and rest my head on her shoulder. "She's home where she's supposed to be. The rest will figure itself out."

"Yeah. I guess you're right."

DECEMBER 27, 2007

DEAR DIARY,

I RECEIVED A CHRISTMAS CARD FROM SARAH TODAY. SHE'S BEEN GONE FOR ALMOST SIX MONTHS, AND THIS IS THE FIRST TIME I'VE HEARD FROM HER. I MISS HER SO MUCH! THE CARD DIDN'T SAY MUCH, JUST MERRY CHRISTMAS.

JUNE SAID SHE DIDN'T OPEN HERS, JUST TOSSED IT IN THE FIREPLACE. SHE'S SO MAD! AND I DON'T BLAME HER. WE BOTH MISS SARAH, AND I DON'T UNDERSTAND WHY SHE LEFT SO FAST WITH THAT ASSHOLE. OR WHY WE CAN'T EVEN HAVE HER PHONE NUMBER. IT JUST DOESN'T MAKE ANY SENSE.

OTHER THAN THAT, CHRISTMAS WAS NICE. IT'S BEEN A MILD WINTER, SO THE WEATHER HASN'T BEEN TOO BAD. I GOT TO HELP DAD CHANGE ONE OF THE LENSES UP IN THE LIGHT, AND IT WAS SO COOL. I NEED TO KNOW HOW TO DO THAT WHEN IT'S MY TURN TO BE THE LIGHTKEEPER.

I HAVE TWO WEEKS UNTIL I GO BACK TO COLLEGE AND LEAVE HUCKLEBERRY BAY. HOW DO PEOPLE LIVE AWAY FROM THE OCEAN? IT'S SO QUIET. SO DRY.

I'LL BE MOVING BACK TO HB AS SOON AS I GRADU-ATE. DAD'S RIGHT. IT WILL HELP TO HAVE A BUSINESS DEGREE. BUT, MAN, I'M READY FOR SCHOOL TO BE OVER ALREADY.

I MISS HOME.

ANYWAY, MERRY CHRISTMAS.
LOVE,
LUNA

Chapter Five

Wolfe

"I'll take it."

Indigo Lovejoy, the real estate agent I hired, raises his eyebrow in surprise. "Just like that?"

"Yeah, just like that."

I wander through the empty garage and breathe in the leftover smell of oil and *car*. It's on the other side of town from my place, but other than that tiny inconvenience, it's perfect.

"Do these stairs lead to an apartment?" I ask, pointing to a set of exterior steps that I see through the window.

"They do. There's a tiny two-bedroom above. It's not pretty, but it's functional. Let's go have a look."

I follow him out the big bay door and around the corner to climb the wooden steps that lead to a mint-green entrance. Indigo unlocks it, and we step inside.

It's empty. The carpet is stained, and the place smells musty. There's a tiny galley kitchen, a simple bathroom, and two small bedrooms.

"You're right, it's not pretty."

Indigo smiles and shrugs a shoulder. "I told you. But you could always use it for storage or replace the carpet, paint the walls, and use it as a rental."

I shake my head. "No rental. I'll figure it out."

"Amaryllis told me you're still the same old stubborn Wolfe," Indigo says with a grin. "I see she wasn't wrong."

"Your sister's rarely wrong about anything," I reply. "Not only is she an excellent doctor, but she's also a good judge of character. But this time, I'm not buying this place because I'm stubborn. I'm buying it because it's perfect for what I need. The garage already has the lift and the space I need for tools. The front desk area is great. When did Old Man Barranger retire?"

"Last fall," he replies. "It hasn't sat here long. I can get the offer sent over this afternoon and arrange for an inspection."

"When can I move my stuff in and get started?" I ask, crossing my arms over my chest. "I already have a project."

I can't wait to get my hands on that old Ford.

"We can work it all out relatively quickly," Indigo replies. "There are no other offers on the table. Let me make some calls, and I'll get back to you right away."

"Great." I shake the other man's hand. "I like it."

"It's small for a custom shop," he muses.

"Yeah, well, I think I'll build another custom garage on my property for some of the more intricate work and use this in the meantime. Later, we can still work on general repairs and such here."

"Good idea." He nods as we walk outside. "We need a car repair place here in town. Getting down to Newport is a pain in the ass."

Newport isn't the nearest town, but it's the closest *big* town, and it's almost an hour away.

"I hear Luna's building a B&B up at the lighthouse. Have you seen her?" he continues.

"Yeah." I smile, thinking about having my lips locked on hers just this morning. I can't wait to do it again. "I've seen her. The renovations on the inn should start in just a few days."

"Good. We need a place like that in town, too. Anyway, I'll keep you posted on everything and let you know when I have the paperwork for you to sign."

"Appreciate it, man." I wave at him and get into my car, shooting an email to my financial guys, alerting them of the purchase of the garage. Before I can pull out of the small parking lot, I get a text from Apollo.

Apollo: *You home?*

Me: *Headed there now.*

Apollo: *I'll meet you there.*

Ten minutes later, I pull into my driveway and see Apollo sitting on the rickety front steps, waiting for me. He stands when I get out of the car and walks toward me.

"What's up?" I ask the other man.

"Listen, this is going to be awkward, okay?" He looks...frustrated. Not angry, not scared, but frustrated.

I narrow my eyes and lean back on the car, shoving my hands in my pockets.

"Okay."

"I know she's an adult and can take care of herself. Hell, she's one of the strongest people I know." He starts to pace in front of the porch, and I watch him for a moment before replying.

"I assume we're talking about your sister?"

He rubs the back of his neck in agitation. "Of course, we're talking about my sister. I saw you holding her hand and the way you look at her."

"How do I look at her?" I'm more than intrigued now. I do believe we're having the protective-older-brother talk.

Fascinating.

"Like you want to eat her alive," he says and shakes his head, muttering as he walks away from me.

"Well, that's an accurate assumption."

He fists his hands and firms his chin as he walks back my way. "Maybe this won't be awkward, after all. I know your reputation, Wolfe. You always have a different woman draped on your arm. You're used to women who know the score. Whose only ambition is to snag the attention of a rich driver like you. That's not who my sister is."

He's not wrong, so I calmly nod in agreement. "No, that's not who she is. And thank Christ for it. Because if she *were* that person, I wouldn't be the least bit interested in her."

"I don't want you to play with her while you're here and then toss her aside when you're done with both Luna *and* this town."

"Okay." I blow out a breath and stare at the other

man. "I'm not going to punch you for that, but I want it noted that I want to."

He simply raises his eyebrows, not intimidated by me in the least.

"I'm not going anywhere," I say at last. "I can't race. Ever again. So, this is where I'm staying. And as far as your sister is concerned...you're right, she's a grown woman. I understand that I just got here and haven't seen her in more than a decade. I definitely don't know her anymore. But I took one look at her, and there was just something there. A click. As if something shifted into place. And I'm not going to ignore it. She's the one thing that makes me feel *good* in this shitshow of a life. And if she wants to see me, I'll for damn sure keep seeing her."

"If you hurt her—"

"You'll kill me and make it look like an accident?"

He just nods, and I can't help but smile.

"I haven't worked out how I feel about her yet—not all the way. But I can tell you this: I'm damn smitten. If anyone's going to get hurt here, it'll be me. Because I'm completely taken with her, and I want to see where it goes."

He sighs. "Yeah, okay. How long has this been going on, anyway?"

"About a day," I say and watch as he tips his head back and laughs. "I just got here, remember? And, yeah, I get what you said about my reputation. But just remember that not everything is as it seems in photos. I've been a jerk, sure, but I didn't leave a long line of pining women behind me."

"Good to know."

Apollo turns and takes in the house, the conversation apparently satisfactorily finished.

"So, what are you going to do with this heap of a house? No offense."

"None taken, it *is* a heap. I think I'll tear it down and start over," I reply as I step up beside him and examine the house along with him. "But I'm impatient. I really want the garage to be built first so I have a place to store my cars and work on some custom projects."

Apollo nods slowly. "You could build a nice, big barndominium behind the house and then live in that while the house is being rebuilt."

I stare at him with a frown. "What the fuck is a barndominium?"

"All the rage," he says and pulls his phone out of his pocket, tapping the screen. "I did all of the electrical on one about thirty minutes from here this past spring. Here, check it out."

He shows me photos of a big building that looks like an old barn from the outside, but inside, it's a beautiful home.

"You could make yours into a garage and add a loft apartment that you can turn into a viewing area for clients later."

"No one can get started until next year."

Apollo scoffs. "Come on, man, you have plenty of money, and money talks. This custom company I worked with out of Washington would probably be able to work you in. I'll get you the information."

"I appreciate it." I nod, thinking it over. "Yeah, if I could get the garage done, it's okay if the rest takes some time."

"Well then, let's get your garage done."

He shares the contact information for the company with me and then gets into his truck and leaves. I immediately call Zeke.

"Hey," he says. "I was just going to call you. I can be there next week."

I raise my eyebrows in surprise. "Okay, that's great. I bought the garage this morning."

"We don't do anything slow, do we?" he asks with a laugh.

"Never have," I confirm. "Also, there's an apartment above the garage where you can live if you want until you figure out your living situation."

"Dude, I already bought a house. Sight unseen. I have a rental until I can move in."

"You bought a house?"

"Well, a condo. New development just went up south of town. I'll have a view of the water, and I don't have to mow any grass."

"Yep, we move fast," I reply and immediately feel better that Zeke is coming to Huckleberry Bay for good. "If all goes well, we can start getting the garage ready for business when you get here."

"Good. I'm looking forward to it. I'll see you next week."

"See you."

* * *

"You did *what?*" June demands, her hands on her hips and her green eyes shooting daggers at Apollo. We're at Luna's place for dinner, all six of us, just two days after my talk with Apollo outside my house.

And from the look on her face, I'd say she's not even remotely happy.

"I called the custom company that Apollo recommended for my garage," I repeat. "They start tomorrow."

"Tomorrow," she echoes. "Do you have floor plans? Have you worked with an architect? Do you have permits and all the million other things that are required for this kind of project?"

"They're a luxury company," Apollo points out. "The point of hiring them is that they handle all those things."

"You're literally *always* on my shit list," June says, pointing at Apollo, "but now, you're right at the top."

"That's not new," Apollo shoots back. "I live in that spot with you, remember?"

"You just gave away my business," she says.

"No." I hold up my hands to stop them from bickering. "He didn't. Think about it, June. You have plenty of work with Luna's bed and breakfast, and you said yourself that no one would be able to get a project started for me until spring. Well, I can't wait that long. This is a solution. I chose a design they've used before, and they're making some adjustments for me. Ten garage bays is a lot, but they're making it work."

"I—" she begins but then stops. "*Ten* bays?"

Kristen Proby

"Yeah. I need to store my cars, and Zeke and I will be working on the custom stuff there, as well."

"That's a big garage," Luna adds as she pulls a pan out of the oven. "What about your house?"

"It can wait," I reply simply and watch as Luna reaches up high to pull down a serving platter. Just a tiny strip of skin shows from beneath her sweater, but it makes my mouth water. "The garage can't."

She glances my way and grins. I haven't been alone with her since the other day in this kitchen, and my hands itch to touch her.

"The garlic bread is almost done," she says. "Sarah, do you mind grabbing a breadbasket from that cabinet?"

"Sure," Sarah answers and immediately jumps up to help.

"How are you settling in?" Tanner asks her, just as I hear June whisper to Apollo that their discussion isn't over.

Apollo rolls his eyes.

"It's been a good few days," Sarah says as she helps Luna transfer hot bread into the basket. "I got a job at the diner. Gordy was excited to see me and hired me on the spot."

"Which we knew he would," June adds.

"And I've enjoyed being here with Luna. Although I know I can't impose forever, it's nice to know that even after all this time, my friends are here for me."

"You do *not* have to rush out of here," Luna says with a frown. "I hardly know you're here, you're so quiet. You don't have to worry about going anywhere else."

74

"A girl needs her own place," June says. "I get it. But Luna's right. You don't have to rush it."

"I might have an idea," I announce, getting everyone's attention. "There's an apartment above the garage that I just bought. It's small, and it needs a *lot* of work before anyone can move in, but if you want it, I'll rent it out to you cheap."

Sarah blinks, and then a slow smile spreads over her pretty face.

"Really?"

"Sure. It's just sitting there. It'll be loud during the day because of the garage noise, though. There's nothing I can do about that."

"I don't care about the noise. And I'll be working at the diner anyway," she replies, getting excited. But then her expression falls.

"What's wrong?" I ask her.

"I just—" She bites her lip and glances around nervously, her gaze landing on Tanner. She looks embarrassed.

"Excuse us," I say and gesture for Sarah to follow me outside. "What's wrong?"

She blows out a huff of breath and turns to me. "I appreciate the offer, Wolfe, but I can't afford to pay you a deposit and first and last month's rent. I just can't."

"Okay."

She shakes her head. "I'm not going to accept a gift that big."

"The money doesn't matter to me, Sarah."

"It matters to *me*," she says as she rounds on me, her

eyes hot with temper. "I can and will make my own way. I have a hell of a work ethic, and I will pay you for that apartment. I won't live there rent-free."

"Okay," I say again. "You can pay me whatever you think is fair. As I said, it's not a big place. And I don't give a shit about the deposit. You're not going to tear the place apart."

"No, I'm not," she concedes. "You said it needs some work?"

"Yeah, the floors need new carpet or hardwood, and it needs paint. Stuff like that."

"I can do it," she says and reaches out to grasp onto my arm. "I'll paint and clean it all up. I can tear out the old carpet if you'll have the new stuff put in."

"I definitely don't expect you to lay flooring," I agree. "Does this mean we have a deal? It'll be a couple of weeks before you can move in."

"Oh my God," she says with a bright smile and launches herself into my arms for a hug. "We have a deal! I can get started right away. Just tell me what color you want things painted."

"No way," I reply as she pulls away. "You can paint it whatever the hell you want. I don't have a preference."

"I'll make it so pretty," Sarah promises me just as the door opens, and Luna pokes her head out.

"Dinner's on."

"We're coming. I have an apartment," Sarah announces and starts to fill Luna in on the details as she walks back into the house behind her.

I join them, and Tanner crosses to me.

"That was nice of you."

"I have the space," I say with a shrug as the girls start talking about ideas for Sarah's new apartment. "Someone should use it."

"Still nice," Tanner says and watches Sarah.

"You should probably have a conversation with her," I suggest.

"Eventually," he agrees and takes a sip of his drink. "But for now, I'll let her do some healing."

"You're a patient man," Apollo says.

"Unlike me," I agree.

"There's no rush," Tanner says. "She's not going anywhere, and neither am I. I've waited all these years. A few months more won't matter."

"Patient," Apollo says again. "And smart. Come on, I'm hungry."

We join the girls, load up our plates, and then take all the food and drinks out to a picnic table in the gazebo so we can watch the sunset.

The sky is orange and pink as the sun starts to sink into the water.

"You know," I say after taking a bite of warm, crusty bread, "I've been around the world and have seen a *lot* of sunsets, but nothing compares to this. Absolutely *nothing*."

"Agreed," Sarah says and clinks her glass to mine. "I lived in Malibu, and while it's pretty down there, it's not like this."

"It's special here," Apollo says, seeming to think it over as we all watch the water. "Look!"

"We see it," Luna murmurs with a soft voice as two whales breach the surface and spout water into the air. "It's a mom and baby. They have been hanging out here for a couple of months."

"Special," I repeat, watching the whales and eating dinner with my friends as the sun slips away. When we've devoured the food, and the sun is gone, we all carry the dirty dishes into the house and help clean everything up.

No one leaves before Luna's kitchen shines.

"Six people in this space is a bit tight," Luna says with a laugh. "But I appreciate the help."

"If you cook and host, you don't clean up alone," June says. "Also, this was fun. We should do it more often. Maybe next time we don't invite Apollo. Hermes can come, though."

"Thanks," Tanner says dryly.

"Hey, I get to come, too," Apollo says with a frown. "You can just ignore me if you don't like it."

"I will," June says.

"Good."

"Good."

"Well, isn't it fun to listen to these two bicker?" I ask, my voice full of fake enthusiasm.

Luna sidles up next to me and slips her hand into mine. I feel like I just won the lottery.

"I think they secretly have a thing for each other," she says.

"Wrong," Apollo argues.

"Ew," June adds at the same time.

"Isn't it cute?" Sarah laughs.

"Whatever," June says and yawns. "I have to go home. I have an early start tomorrow."

That starts the big exit from the party, with Apollo and Tanner following June.

Sarah also says her goodnights and retires to her room.

"Thanks for dinner," I say to Luna as she shuts the door behind Tanner. "It was delicious and fun. You're an excellent hostess."

"I hope so. I'm going to be hosting guests all the time when the B&B is up and running, so this is good practice. I should do something once a week for all of you. Maybe I should even invite some other people from town. You know, those who don't care about hurting my feelings if it sucks."

I close the gap between us and cup her cheek in my hand.

"You're going to kill it, sweetheart. Nothing about this will suck."

"I hope you're right." Her eyes drop to my lips. "You feel this, right? This intense pull between us? It can't just be me."

"It's not only you," I confirm and move in even closer. "I feel it. I felt it the minute I looked down from that stage and saw you in the audience on the day of the race."

"I was surprised you noticed me," she admits and swallows hard. "And when you winked, I thought for sure you were aiming for someone behind me."

"No. Definitely not."

"Okay. Well, that's good. I would be embarrassed otherwise."

I let the pad of my thumb brush over her lower lip. "No need to be embarrassed."

I cover her mouth with mine, gently tasting the sweetness of her lips, partly from the lemon cake she served for dessert, but mostly just from the taste of *Luna*.

"Missed this," I whisper near her lips as I pin her to the door and press my body against hers. She's curvy and soft, and her breast fits perfectly in the palm of my hand. Her hands dive into my hair, and I'm lost to her, kissing her as if my damn life depends on it.

Because in this moment, it feels like it does.

Suddenly, we hear the shower turn on, and I remember that we're not alone.

I kiss her cheek, her temple, and then rest my forehead against hers.

"Sorry," she whispers. "I got caught up."

"You're not the only one," I reply and tip her chin up so she can look at me. "Let me take you out tomorrow evening."

"Like, on a date?"

"Yes, on a date. Away from here, where we can talk and do whatever it is that people do on dates."

"I'm down for that," she says with a smile. "I'll even wear something pretty."

"You always look amazing." I kiss her once more. "But I can't wait to see you. Sleep well tonight."

"You, too. By the way, how have the headaches been?"

Bad enough to piss me off.

But I don't want to worry her.

"Not too bad," I say instead. "I'm okay."

"Good."

She steps away from the door so I can open it and walk outside.

"I'll pick you up at six tomorrow night."

"I'll be ready," she replies and waves at me before closing the door.

Yeah, she's something special. I've known her for most of my life, but this...this is entirely different. I'm already addicted to her. The way she smells, the way she smiles, and definitely the way she feels against me.

I'm not used to going slow when it comes to things in my life, but I'm not going to fuck this up with Luna. We'll go at the pace that's comfortable for her and not a bit faster.

If that means hot, stolen kisses and holding her hand for a while, I can live with that.

I hope I don't have to live with it for long, but I can if necessary.

Because I have a feeling that Luna is the long haul, and I'm not willing to risk that. I won't lose anything else that means something to me.

Not again.

Chapter Six

Luna

"What's that smell?" I ask as I hold my hand over my nose and gaze around the old apartment above Wolfe's new garage.

"We might not want to know," June says, but Sarah's all smiles as she saunters around the small space, taking in every inch. "Taking the old carpet out right away will probably help with the stench. I don't even want to think about what these stains are. Mr. Barranger was a bit of a slob."

"Wolfe said I could choose the flooring *and* the paint colors. Should I do more carpet or hardwood? Laminate? I don't know. I built a house with Anthony about six years ago, but I didn't have a say in any of the choices."

"Not in *anything*?" I ask, surprised. "But you've always had a great eye for these kinds of things. You're an artist."

Sarah always loved to paint when we were kids. My parents bought her a paint set for her sixteenth birthday with canvases and brushes, and the pictures Sarah painted were beautiful. I still have one hanging in my bedroom.

"I'm not an *artist*," she says as she rubs a hand along the kitchen countertop and then frowns at the dust on her palm. "I definitely need to scrub in here."

"The canvas in my living room says differently," June says, and I nod in agreement.

"Either way," Sarah says, "I didn't have much say in most things. But *now*, I get to choose everything for this place. I know it's not a ten-thousand-square-foot mansion in Malibu, but it's *mine*, and I have a say in it."

"Okay. Well then, boss, what do you want?" I ask her. "Hardwood or carpet?"

"I don't want carpet," she decides. "I'd like hardwood or vinyl, and I can throw down rugs to make it warmer. And...look."

We follow her down a tiny hallway where the two bedrooms and bathroom are.

"This second bedroom is small, but I'm going to make it into a studio."

"It's perfect for that," I agree. "Are we sure no one died in that bathtub?" I say as I peek into the bathroom.

"It's rust," June says with a sigh. "You'll need a new tub. It's an easy swap, though. I'll let Wolfe know."

"I don't want to be difficult," Sarah says with a frown. "He's already giving me a deal, and—"

"Whether it's you or someone else living here, he has to replace the tub," June insists. "Don't worry about it."

"I'm going to make a list of all of the colors I want to

paint the walls." Sarah grins and then dances a little jig right in the tiny bathroom.

"There's a lot of building and renovating happening in our little group," I say as we walk to the stairway that leads down to the car. "It feels like we all have something in the works. We're going to work you to death, June."

"This is an easy job," June insists. "I can do that bathroom swap in an hour. Honest."

"Well, I'm coming tomorrow to tear out the carpet," Sarah says. "And I'm going to buy paint this afternoon so I can start on that, too."

"I can help," I offer, but Sarah's already shaking her head.

"I've got this. It'll be therapeutic to put some sweat into it, you know? But if I need help, I'll call you."

"Do that," June says. "And I'll call Wolfe about the bathroom and flooring. You'll have to pick stuff out for that, too."

"I'm going to kick ass at painting those walls," Sarah says as we all climb into my car. "I'll be moved in in no time."

"Are you trying to run away from me?" I demand, eyeing her in the rearview mirror.

"No. Of course, not. But I've *never* lived on my own, you know? I went from my parents' to Anthony's to your place. I'm excited to have my own little spot that I can make mine."

"I'm happy for you," I reply with a smile. "And you know I was just teasing. Okay, girls, shall we go to Gordy's for lunch?"

"Hell, yes," June says. "As long as Sarah doesn't mind eating where she works."

"I love it there," Sarah says. "Let's go."

Gordy's is up the bay a bit and not nearly as busy as I expected it to be when I pull into the parking lot.

It's an old-fashioned diner with the drive-up slots still active. If you don't want to go inside, you can park by a big, lit menu with a speaker, and a waitress will deliver your food on a tray that sits on your window.

We thought it was the best thing ever when we were kids.

Now, I prefer to sit inside at one of the old-fashioned red booths.

"Are you going to have to run food out to cars?" I ask Sarah as we walk in.

"Yeah, but I told Gordy that I won't wear roller skates. I'd break my neck on those things. He said that was fine."

We're chuckling when a waitress named Sunny comes to seat us.

"Oh, I haven't seen the three of you together in more years than I can count," she says as tears fill her eyes. "I knew that Sarah was back, of course, but seeing you together...well, it's just as it should be. Come on, I'll seat you in your regular booth."

"Thanks, Sunny," I reply as we follow her to the booth we always sat in, back in the far corner by the old jukebox.

"Do you all want your usuals?"

We share glances and then nod at the sweet woman

who's been waitressing at Gordy's for as long as I can remember.

"You got it," she says with a wink and hurries away.

"I think she knows what every single person in Huckleberry Bay orders."

"And some of the tourists, just by looking at them," Sarah agrees with a laugh. "She's the sweetest. What are you guys up to after this?"

"I have to get back to work," June says. "The crew will be at Luna's barn tomorrow morning to start in, and I want to make sure everything is ready to go. We should probably climb up to the attic space and make sure there's nothing up there."

"Nothing's up there," I confirm. "If there were, it would have fallen down years ago."

"Still, we should check," she says and sips the cherry cola that Sunny just dropped off. "The crew will work around the car for a day or two until Wolfe moves it."

"I think he's just waiting for confirmation on the sale of the garage," I reply. "I can't imagine Mr. Barranger forbidding Wolfe from storing the car in there, though."

"Mr. Barranger left," June says, surprising us. "He moved up to Portland to live with his son and grandkids. So, I can pretty much guarantee that it won't be a problem."

"Good."

"What about you, Luna?"

We pause as Sunny delivers our burgers and fries, and when she's established that we have everything we need, she hurries off again, and I pop a french fry into my mouth.

"I have to start taking notes from Rose's diary because I have questions. Oh, and I need to get ready for a date."

I smile in satisfaction when they both pause in their eating and stare at me.

"I hope it's with Wolfe," Sarah says.

"Of *course*, it's with Wolfe." I laugh and take a big bite of my cheeseburger.

"After the lip-locking I witnessed, it's not with anyone else," June says. "Is it weird, though?"

"In what way?"

"You've known him since you were kids. You used to play around the neighborhood together."

"Yeah, we did. But he's been gone for a long time, and I don't really know him at all anymore. Not as an adult. I only know how he was back then. And, of course, I knew his parents because they were our neighbors. But he's been gone longer than Sarah was and had a whole crazy career in Europe. Though, now that you mention it, I guess I need to start asking him some questions."

"Hard to do that when his tongue is down your throat," June says, and I toss a fry at her.

She just eats it.

"I was gone for a long time, but I'm pretty much the same as when I left," Sarah says, and June and I share a look.

"I call bullshit on that," June says. "Respectfully, of course."

"I mean, I was in a crappy marriage, but I'm still the same old Sarah."

"No way," I reply, agreeing with June. "Too much has happened to say that you're the same now as you were at nineteen. None of us is exactly the same. And trust me, we have questions for you, too, but we're giving you a chance to catch your breath."

"I appreciate that," she says softly. "And I don't think I should bare my soul to you guys over burgers at Gordy's."

"No, it needs to be over wine." I offer her a wink.

"Okay, back to your date," Sarah says. "Where are you going?"

"I don't know. He said something about dinner, but I don't know where. I'm letting him figure it all out."

"Nice," June says with a nod. "It's so *nice* when you don't have to be the one to do the choosing."

"Right?" I pop another fry into my mouth. "Men always complain that we never know what to eat, but at the end of the day, we just want them to *choose*."

"It's not our fault if they choose crappy places," Sarah adds. "We're so levelheaded. Why is it so hard?"

"Exactly."

When the food is gone, and we've said our goodbyes to Sunny, we walk back out to my car so I can drive us back to the lighthouse. About a quarter of a mile away from the restaurant, my car just...dies.

Right in front of Lighthouse Pizza.

"What in the hell?" I ask as the car coasts to a stop. I try to start it again, but nothing happens.

"It's dead," June says helpfully.

"Crap." I hit the heel of my hand on the steering wheel and then look at my friends. "We'll have to roll it out of the street."

"Like, *push* it?" Sarah asks, sounding mildly horrified.

"Yep. June, you and Sarah take the back, and I'll steer and push at the same time."

"I feel like we're kind of badass," Sarah says as she and June jump out and assume their positions at the back of the car. "We're ready!"

I have the driver's door open, and with it in neutral, I help them push while steering the car toward the pizza place's parking lot.

Just as I'm about to turn off the main road, a Porsche Cayenne pulls up beside us and the driver's side window lowers.

Wolfe.

"Hi there. Um, what are you doing?" he asks with a sexy grin.

"Oh, you know," I reply and blow some hair out of my eyes, "Getting our cardio in, that's all."

"It's dead," June says. "Don't stop pushing. We're on a roll!"

We get my car situated as good as it's going to get in the closest level parking spot, and I put it in park and engage the parking brake.

When I climb out, Wolfe's right there.

"You okay?" he asks, all business as he takes my shoulders in his hands.

"Yeah, it just died as I was driving it. I have no idea why."

"Hmm." He pulls the hood release and walks around, propping the hood on the stick-thing before bending over and perusing the engine.

"Okay, that's kind of hot," June whispers, and Sarah grins.

"You said it," Sarah says.

"Why does his butt look so good in those jeans?" I ask and make them both laugh.

"What's going on back there?" Wolfe asks.

"Nothing. Can you fix it?"

"Of course," he says and stands, whipping another of those handkerchiefs out of his pocket to wipe off the engine grease. "But not without a brand-new alternator and my tools."

"Damn."

"Don't worry, I'll take you home before I dig into this."

"I'll just run inside and let someone know that I have to leave it here for a little while."

I jog into the restaurant and give the owner of the pizzeria a heads-up.

"No problem," they say with a smile. "Thanks for letting me know."

I see everyone waiting for me in Wolfe's Porsche when I walk back outside.

"Ready," I say as I sit in the passenger seat and fasten my belt. "Nice car, by the way. I bet you don't have trouble with the alternator in this."

"Thanks," he says as he pulls out onto the road. "And so far, no problems with it. My stuff arrived today."

"All of it?" I ask.

"Yeah. And thank God Barranger said I can move some stuff into the garage because I definitely wouldn't have enough room at my parents' place."

"I'm not using some of the storage space in the lighthouse," I offer. "If you need a place for boxes and stuff..."

"Thanks. I might take you up on that."

He turns onto Lighthouse Way, drives past his house, and then pulls to a stop by mine.

"Thanks," the three of us say in unison as we climb out of his car.

"No problem. I should have your Mazda done in about an hour."

I blink at him. "An *hour*?"

"Sure, it's just the alternator." He winks at me. "Trust me. This is what I do."

"Oh, I trust you, I'm just surprised, that's all. That's pretty fast. Let me know what I owe you."

He just grins and drops back into his Porsche, then drives away.

"I totally get it," June says as we watch him disappear around the bend. "Wolfe got hot while he was gone."

"Yeah. I can't argue that."

Once inside the house, I make myself some tea and grab the old diary, sitting in my favorite comfortable chair by the windows as I open the weathered box that holds the old book.

I wonder if I should wear gloves or something to

protect it. When we were kids, Sarah, June, and I didn't even consider that just the oils from our hands might damage it. Not to mention, we shouldn't have left it up in the lighthouse for all those years.

But we didn't know any better.

"You're safer now," I say softly and open the book to the last pages.

March 22, 1873

He's been gone for so long. Much longer than the few months he promised when he left nearly a year ago. My heart can't bear the thought of him somehow being lost at sea, but I also don't know what the alternative could be. Lucas Winchester has begun courting me. He's a good man, kind and quick to laugh, and I know that I could have a good life with him here at the lighthouse. My father would like to turn the keeping of the light over to Lucas if I'll marry and settle here with him.

But, oh, how I long for the man I truly love. Could I learn to love Lucas given time? I believe so. But not with the passion I feel for the one I lost. It's so deep that my heart aches with it. He is the great love of my life, and I fear that I've lost him forever.

My sweet DP.

I frown and look out the window where the ocean glimmers in the sunshine.

DP? I don't remember finding that before. Obviously, Rose married Lucas. I know that he was my great-great-grandfather.

But who was DP? And did he ever come home, or was he truly lost at sea?

I try to turn the page, but it's stuck.

"I don't want to rip it," I murmur softly and wiggle my thumbnail between the two pages. Luckily, they're made of thick paper, and after some considerable work, I'm able to pry them apart.

April 1, 1873

The storms have raged for more than a week, and it feels like a mirror to the storm in my soul.

That's it. That's where it ends.

I turn the page over. In small writing at the bottom of the page, I read, *New barn. Loft.*

"Loft."

I frown, and then my heart races.

"The attic!"

I race through the house, out the front door, and to the barn.

"June!" My heart's in my throat as I hurry inside and see my friend prying some boards off the inside of the far wall. "It's in the attic."

"What is?" she demands. "What's going on?"

"I have to go up there," I reply and cross to the ladder that leads to the platform above.

"Be careful on that ladder," June advises. "I think it's original to the building."

"Great," I mutter and start up, carefully stepping on each rung. When I can see the floor, I cringe. "There's lots of mouse poop up here."

"Hope and pray that only mice have made a home up there," she says from below.

"You're not helping," I reply and step all the way up onto the platform. "You know, I'm not excited about heights."

"Too late now. What are you looking for?"

"Another diary. Hey, June?"

"Yeah?"

"There's no door up here." We're both quiet for a second. "So, every time we've heard a slamming door—"

"Don't say it," June says, her voice strained. "Just don't."

"Okay, Rose," I whisper as I gingerly feel my way across the platform, careful not to step through any rotten boards. "What do you want me to find? What did you hide up here?"

I see some old shelving units standing against the walls. Obviously, they used to store stuff up here.

There are also some old cylinders that look as if they were used to store things and keep them out of the elements.

I'll have Apollo and Wolfe come and get those down later.

But in the far corner, under the window that surprisingly still has its glass, is a trunk.

"You've got to be kidding me," I say aloud.

"What did you find? I'd come up, but I don't think it's safe."

"There's a bunch of stuff up here," I call down. "Including an old trunk. And I'll bet you anything it's Rose's."

It's padlocked shut and rusted, so I can't open it, which might be the worst kind of torture there is.

"I need the guys," I say as I take one last look around before walking back to the ladder. "Hopefully, this holds long enough for them to haul this stuff out of here."

I carefully climb down the ladder and sigh in relief when I make it to the floor.

"There's quite a lot up there," I say, shaking my head. "How, I'm not sure."

"Your dad probably just assumed, like you did, that it was empty."

"I suppose so," I agree. "I'll text the guys to come and help, and then I have to get ready for tonight. But this means I have a *really* fun project for tomorrow."

"Wear gloves when you dig around in there," June advises. "There could be spiders and stuff."

"Oh my God, now I don't want to."

"You can do it," she says and smiles cheerfully. "You're a badass."

* * *

"I still can't believe you fixed my car so fast," I say as Wolfe and I leave the little seafood restaurant on the waterfront. He brought me north of Huckleberry Bay to Pacific City for dinner.

It was nice to get out of town with him for a couple of hours. Away from where everyone knows us both so well, and to a place where no one knows us at all, and we could chat without any interruptions.

"It wasn't a big deal," he says and opens the car door for me. "Mind if I take you somewhere...fun?"

"I don't mind at all."

He grins and closes the door. When he's settled in the driver's seat, he sets off on Highway 101 south, back toward home.

About a mile before the turnoff for Lighthouse Way, Wolfe pulls onto a little dirt road that leads to the cliffs.

I can see the lighthouse down the coast, and the view of the water is gorgeous from up here.

"It's private here," he says as he turns off the ignition and faces me.

"Did you bring girls up here when you were a teenager?"

His lips twitch into an amused smile. "I'm going to plead the fifth on that one. It's a good spot to watch the sunset."

We're not in the Porsche tonight. Wolfe surprised me by pulling up in a little red Ferrari convertible.

It still smells new.

He pushes a button, and the top of the car folds back, leaving us sitting in the open air, watching the sun set on the Pacific Ocean.

"I don't think it gets much better than this," I breathe. "Did you miss it? Home?"

"I didn't think so," he admits and glances over at me. "I was too caught up in my job, in living in Europe, and the life I'd built there. A few months ago, I would have scoffed at the idea of being homesick. But now—"

He shakes his head and looks back out at the ocean.

"Now?"

"Is it possible to be homesick after you've already returned?"

I grin and shrug. "I don't see why not. You missed it. You just didn't realize it at the time. When I went away to college, I couldn't wait to get back home. I didn't understand why anyone would want to live away from the ocean."

"I hear you," he says. "Maybe that's one of the things that I loved about Monaco. I was still on the water."

He reaches over and takes my hand, pulling it to his lips.

"So, this is a small car," I notice, glancing around. "Can you put that seat back farther?"

"I think so." He reaches down to his left, and the seat moves, stopping about six inches back. "What did you have in mind?"

"Well, it seems like a waste to come out to make out point and not make out." I squeal as Wolfe pulls me onto his lap. I move up to straddle him, fitting snuggly between his hard abs and the steering wheel.

"You can't see the sunset facing this way," he whispers, making me smile.

97

"It's okay. I've seen a lot of those." I brush my fingers through his thick, brown hair before leaning over and covering his mouth with mine. The kiss starts slow but quickly escalates, turning into molten lust.

"Fucking hell," he mutters as he shifts and pushes my hair back over my shoulder.

He's warm and hard and smells like pure sin as I begin grinding my core against him. I can feel his hard length straining against his jeans, pressing against my white cropped pants.

He kisses my neck as his hand pushes under my blouse. I bite my lip, still tasting him there. I lose myself so quickly with this man and without hesitation. I instinctively trust him, and I *want* him with everything in me.

I grind down on him, and he mutters a curse before finding my mouth once more, his fingers flicking over my sensitive nipple through my bra.

"I've never wanted anyone the way I want you," he growls. "That's not a line, Luna. God, I fucking crave you."

"Same," is all I can say before I frame his face with my hands and kiss him again, needing his mouth on mine. His lips skillfully move against mine, tasting and savoring, and our bodies move in a dance as old as time. "Too many clothes."

"Shit, babe," is all he says before I hear a loud *whoop* and surface to see flashing lights behind us.

"Uh, Wolfe?"

"Fuck." He helps me untangle myself and moves me

over to the passenger seat just as Sheriff Daniels saunters over to the driver's side window.

His old eyes light with humor when he sees who we are.

"I should have known it was Wolfe Conrad," he says with a grin. "Hello, Luna."

"Hi." I smile, but I know my face is bright red with embarrassment.

"Can I send you a case of Jack Daniels and call it a day?" Wolfe asks.

"You always were a smartass," Sheriff says, but his tone is jovial as he takes in the Ferrari. "This is a honey of a car you've got here. I guess it would be a waste not to bring a pretty girl to this spot in it. Not that she doesn't have a great spot of her own, just down the road a ways."

I cringe and then resign myself to being permanently embarrassed.

This news will spread through Huckleberry Bay like wildfire.

"You might want to take this little party down there," he advises and then starts to back up. "Happy to have you home, Wolfe. Stay out of trouble."

The sheriff winks at me, and then he's back in his cruiser and pulling away.

I let out a breath as Wolfe laughs beside me. "You should see your face."

"I can honestly say that was a first for me."

I look over at him and narrow my eyes. "But it wasn't for you."

"Everyone should get caught at make out point at

least once in their lives," he says as he starts the car. "It builds character."

"Right. That's why my face is bright red."

He laughs and drives me down the highway to our turnoff and then to my house.

"Would you like to come in?" I ask.

"Yeah." He reaches for my hand again and then kisses my knuckles as he looks over at me. "I would like that."

I grin and move to open the door, but he stops me, so I wait for him to cross to my side of the car and open it for me.

"You're a gentleman."

He just smiles as I lead him to the door, but as soon as we walk inside, I know that any thoughts of sexy time tonight are completely blown.

"Sarah?"

My friend is curled up in the corner of the couch, crying her eyes out.

I turn back to Wolfe and offer him an apologetic smile. "I think I have to handle this."

"Another raincheck," he says and tips up my chin so he can kiss me softly. "Call me later and let me know that everything's okay?"

"Bet on it. Thanks for tonight."

"You're welcome."

He kisses me once more, and then he's gone. I turn back to Sarah.

"Honey, what's wrong?"

"I'm so sorry," she says and wipes at her tears. "You shouldn't have told him to go."

"I'm not going to ignore you like this and drag him off to the bedroom so I can have sex," I say dryly and reach for a box of tissues. "Talk to me. What happened? Did Anthony call?"

"No. I won't hear from him." She blows her nose. "I tried to talk to Scott tonight. I went to his house and caught him just as he was getting home from work."

Oh, boy. I know what's coming.

"I take it he wasn't excited to see you."

"Not only that, he threw me out. Said he's not interested in seeing me ever again and told me to mind my own fucking business. His words."

That starts a whole new flood of tears.

"I knew he'd be mad," she says and reaches for another tissue. "But I wasn't prepared for just *how* mad. He has a right to be. But, man, it hurts."

"I know." I rub big circles on her back. "The rest of us accepted you right away despite the hurt we carry because we're your friends, and that's what friends do. But he's your little brother. There are bound to be some abandonment issues there."

"God, maybe I shouldn't have come back."

"I think coming back was the right thing. There's just a mess that you need to clean up. But it'll be worth it when you're done."

She blows out a breath and dabs at her eyes. "Yeah. Yeah, it will. But he might not ever want to talk to me."

"He'll come around. Just keep trying."

SEPTEMBER 2, 2010

DEAR DIARY,

SOMETIMES, LIVING WITH A ROOMMATE SUCKS. EVEN WHEN THAT ROOMMATE IS JUNE. I LOVE HER TO DEATH, BUT I MIGHT MURDER HER IN HER SLEEP IF SHE DOESN'T STOP USING ALL THE CREAMER AND LEAVING THE EMPTY BOTTLE IN THE FRIDGE, ONLY FOR ME TO NOT HAVE ANY FOR MY COFFEE.

WHAT KIND OF MONSTER DOES THAT?

YOU THINK YOU KNOW SOMEONE UNTIL YOU LIVE WITH THEM. IT'S A WHOLE NEW EXPERIENCE.

I'M GOING TO START HIDING CREAMER SOMEWHERE.

LOVE,

LUNA

Chapter Seven

Wolfe

"Will it hold all three of us?" Tanner asks as he, Apollo, and I stand below the platform in Luna's barn and stare up at it.

"I hope so," Apollo says grimly, his hands on his hips. "I'll go up first and test it out. It's my ancestral home. If it kills one of us, it should be me."

"Not gonna disagree," I say as Apollo starts up. "I don't have much faith in that ladder."

"How did we get talked into this?" Tanner asks me as we watch Apollo climb.

"Luna asked. I said yes. That pretty much covers it."

He smirks as Apollo reaches the top and walks around a bit.

"It's stable up here," he calls down. "Surprisingly. There are some round cylinders, some odds and ends, and a trunk. The trunk is going to be a bitch. It's old and looks heavy."

"How did they get it *up* there?" I ask, looking around. "I don't see a pulley system."

"How should I know?" Apollo calls down. "It's up here now. I think we'll start with the small stuff. We'll do a chain. Tanner, come stand at the top of the ladder, I'll pass to you, you hand to Wolfe."

"Can do." Tanner climbs up, and it only takes us about ten minutes to get a good pile of stuff down. Some of it is light enough for Tanner to toss down to me. Other things are heavier, but we manage without any problems.

"Now, the damn trunk," Apollo says, looking down at us. "It's not *too* heavy, but it's fucking awkward. And it's wood, so I'm worried that the bottom might be rotted out."

"Drag it over to the edge and we'll figure it out. We might have to cut the lock and take stuff out of it, then lower the empty trunk."

"Good idea," Tanner says with a nod, and we wait for Apollo to drag the trunk to the edge of the platform. "Let me test it."

Apollo reaches out and lifts the end of the trunk, peering under it to see what the bottom looks like.

"I think it'll hold. Tanner, if you take that end, I'll start down with it."

Between the three of us, we muscle it to the ground without dropping it and destroying the trunk *or* killing ourselves.

"Nothing else up there?" I ask Apollo as I catch my breath.

"Nothing but mouse shit and dust. Probably a spider or two."

"Well, those can stay up there," I reply. "Let's haul this to the house. Luna's excited to dig in."

We manage the transfer it all in two trips, with Luna excitedly doing a happy dance and shaking her sexy ass as she points to where she wants us to set everything down.

"I want the trunk in the living room. I hope there aren't any spiders."

"Nothing fell off and bit us," I reply as Apollo and I place it where she points. "Keep your shoes on so you can step on any that crawl out."

"Great, thanks." She scrunches her nose and then looks excited again. "This is so fun. I wish I'd known that all of this was up there way before today."

"I'm glad you thought to look before any demo started." Tanner looks at his watch. "I have to go open the gallery," he says, stepping back. "And I can't wear dirty jeans and a stained shirt to do it, so I'd better run home. Good luck."

"Thanks for coming to help," Luna says with a smile.

After Tanner leaves, it's just the three of us in Luna's small living room.

"I'm nervous," she admits and swallows hard. "But I *need* to know what's in this trunk."

"I brought the bolt cutters," Apollo says and makes quick work of the old, rusted padlock. "There you go."

Luna dives at the trunk, opens the lid, and sits back on her heels, staring.

"What is it?"

"So much," she says and looks up at me in surprise. "There are clothes in here, dried flowers, jewelry. And...*look*."

She lovingly pulls out an old, leather-bound book. "Another diary. I *knew* it!"

"I love that you're interested in all of this stuff," Apollo says and kisses his sister on the head. "I have to go to work myself. Have fun. I can't wait to hear about what all you find."

"I'll make a list of everything so I don't forget anything. You know how I love a good spreadsheet."

Apollo nods at me, and then he's gone.

"There are some newspapers in here from the turn of the twentieth century," she says in awe. "And none of this is ruined. There's no mold. It's crazy."

"I thought the same about the car," I reply. "How it all stayed safe in that damp barn, I'll never know."

She looks over at me and then grins. "This is *awesome*."

"I know you want to read that diary, so I'll get out of your hair. I have to get to the house so the crew can start on the foundation of the new garage."

"Oh, that's right. Good luck. And thanks for doing this."

"Anytime. If you need anything else, just call me." I kiss her lips, then wink at her and set off for my place.

The crew is already there. When I approach, the foreman, John, walks over to greet me.

"We'll have the foundation poured tomorrow," he

says. "We're digging and getting things started now. Thankfully, the ground is quite level already."

"Here's hoping it goes smoothly," I reply.

* * *

"Am I hallucinating?" Zeke says two weeks later as he places the last tool on the wall. "Are we finally done?"

I glance around the garage that I purchased less than a month ago and let out a long breath. "I think that's it. My friend, we are ready for business."

"Holy shit," he says with a big grin and eyes the old Ford waiting in bay two. "We get to start on that honey."

"Finally," I agree.

Zeke's been here for just over a week. It's been the busiest few weeks of my life, and that's saying quite a bit.

But the apartment is ready for Sarah, thanks to all her hard work and some help from June, and Zeke and I are ready to get started fixing cars.

"You know," Zeke says as he plays with a socket wrench, "I still haven't met this Luna. You've talked about her, but I haven't met her."

"I haven't seen her since before you got here," I reply and drag my hand down my face.

"What? Why not?"

I just stare at him. "Been a little busy, man."

"You're an idiot. You have to *make* time. This is done, and we won't be able to get started on anything until tomorrow. Go see her."

I'm already walking out the door. "See you tomorrow!"

I can't just show up on her doorstep out of the blue, so I swing by the grocery store and then the floral shop. I also stop by my place to take a quick shower and check in with John, who clearly has everything under control.

I drive to Luna's, a picnic basket in the car, and park close to the gazebo, where I unpack and make it look nice before knocking on her door.

When Luna answers, she looks surprised to see me.

"Uh, hi," she says and tucks her hair behind her ear. "Are you okay?"

"Of course. I have a surprise. I hope you're hungry."

I hold my hand out for hers. After a brief hesitation that I don't like—*at all*—she takes it, and I lead her out to the gazebo.

"You made a picnic," she says with a smile.

"And these flowers are for you," I add, pointing to the yellow bouquet.

We sit side by side at the picnic table, and I pull out the sandwiches and salads that I picked up, along with some lemonade. I save the cheesecake for dessert.

"This is really nice," Luna says and smiles at me. "Thank you."

"I've missed you," I reply, drinking her in. "It's been a crazy couple of weeks."

"Tell me everything."

"You don't want the sordid details."

She nods. "I absolutely do. Give them to me."

I take a bite of my pastrami sandwich. "Well, as you

know, we moved the car out of the barn and took it to the garage. Zeke got to town, and he's been settling into his new place as we got the garage ready for business. Equipment was delivered every day."

I sip my lemonade and watch the way her jaw moves as she chews.

God, she's fucking sexy.

"What else?" she asks.

"The new garage at my place is starting to come along. The foundation's down, and the walls are going up. The roof trusses should come in the next couple of days."

"It's moving so fast. There's improvement every day."

"I know. It's impressive that they brought the whole crew down from Washington to do this. But it's exactly what I was hoping for. Anyway, I've also been handling some of the apartment stuff for Sarah, arranging for flooring and new bathroom fixtures. June's been a huge help there, even though I know she's been busy on your project."

I glance back at the barn, which already looks so different from how it did just two weeks ago.

"Talk about change," I mutter.

"It startles me every time I look out the window," Luna says with a soft smile.

"I bet. Anyway, with all the stuff happening, by the time I get home late into the evening, my head is pounding, so I crash and get up the next morning to start all over again."

"I'm sorry," Luna says softly and reaches over to take

my hand. "But I have to admit that I'm glad to hear you've been so busy. I thought maybe I hadn't heard from you because you just decided you weren't interested anymore."

I frown at her and then reach out and brush my fingers down her cheek.

"You thought I *ghosted* you?" I'm more than a moron. I'm fucking stupid. "Shit, Luna, I'm sorry. It wasn't that at all. I'm damn horrible about texting. I hate that. And things have just been overwhelming."

"I get it," she replies with a nod. "In the future, maybe you could just shoot off one of those texts you hate so much just as a compromise."

"I'm a selfish dick." I shake my head. "I'm *so* sorry. I should have brought more than flowers and sandwiches."

She raises an eyebrow. "Like what?"

"I don't know. Diamonds?"

She laughs and then shakes her head. "It's okay. No need for that. I've been busy, too, with all of Rose's things and doing some research. I've learned a lot about her, but I have more questions that I have to go to the library and into the county records for."

"Like what?" I ask, relieved that she forgave me so quickly. She will *never* have to worry again whether I'm interested in her. Jesus, how could I be so stupid?

"Like who she was in love with before she married her husband."

"She doesn't say?"

"She only gives initials. It sounds like it was a bit of a

110

scandal. I haven't had any luck yet, but there has to be information somewhere."

"You'll find it," I reply with confidence.

"On top of that, I've been helping Sarah shop for furniture. She arrived here with *nothing*, Wolfe. She invested all those years in that marriage, and because Anthony coerced her into a prenup, she has nothing more than what fits in two suitcases."

"She needs an attorney." I clean up the remnants of our food as I talk. "She was young, and I'll bet she didn't have an attorney look at it back then. I'd bet a million dollars a good lawyer could get her a settlement at least."

"She says no," Luna replies. "But I think she's resisting it because she doesn't think she can afford it. She found some really beautiful things at second-hand and thrift shops, though. And June and I got her a new bed as a gift. I didn't feel right about her sleeping on an old mattress."

"If I'd known, I would have just furnished the place for her."

"I don't think she wanted that," Luna says quickly. "She *wants* to do most of this on her own. You did a lot with the vinyl flooring and the new bathroom. She loved painting and cleaning the place. She's beside herself to move in."

"Tanner was going to help her with the furniture today," I reply. "Then she'll finish up tomorrow."

"June and I will help, too."

"Zeke and I can help, as well. We're right downstairs."

"Any extra hands will help." She smiles and then leans over to kiss my shoulder. "Thanks for all of it, Wolfe. I know this isn't ideal for you, and you must be struggling with it, but we all appreciate you. And *I'm* especially glad you're here."

I sigh and kiss the top of her head.

"I'm glad I'm here, too. If the fucking headaches would stop, I'd be even happier."

"Are they getting bad again? I thought they'd slowed down."

"It's random." I shrug. "And when they decide to pop up, they just suck."

She stills. "If they stop, you'll leave and go back to racing."

Not long ago, I would have immediately agreed. But now, after everything that's happened, I'm not so sure.

"That's not going to happen," I reply and link my fingers with hers. "I will never be given the green light to drive professionally again. I had a traumatic brain injury, which means that career is done—even if the headaches stop."

"I didn't mean that to sound selfish."

"No, it's okay. I like knowing that you enjoy having me here."

I tip her chin up and kiss her, and the ache I've felt for her over the past two weeks starts to ease just a little.

"I missed you, too," she says at last. "And from now on, if I don't hear from you, I'll call you myself."

"Anytime, sweetheart. Day or night. I'm at your disposal."

"Oh, I like that."

I laugh and pull out the cheesecake. "Now, we have to discuss something serious."

She opens the container and takes a bite of the dessert and says, "What?"

"Well, with Sarah moving out tomorrow and everyone settled in where they're supposed to be, I'd like to spend time with you tomorrow evening. Just you and me."

"I'd like that," she says. "I'd like that very much."

"Me, too."

"In fact, you can help me look through some of the stuff from the barn attic," she adds. "And we can talk about, you know, our feelings."

"Sure. We can do that." I run my tongue over my teeth. "But then I plan to fuck you until you can't remember your name."

She chokes on the cheesecake, reaches for her lemonade, sips, then laughs.

"Well, okay, then. We can do that, too."

"Good. Because while I was fine waiting for a little while, I'm dying to be inside you."

I kiss her temple.

"So much for not interested," she says with a smirk. "Why do women overthink everything?"

"Because I was stupid and didn't reach out to you. Two weeks is a long damn time. I really do apologize. It won't happen again."

"No. It won't. Because I'll come and find you if I have

to. Not in a scary stalker kind of way. But you know what I mean."

"You are the best part of my life right now, Luna Winchester. You can bet that I won't be far away at any given time—also not in a stalker way."

Those sweet lips hold their soft smile as she peers up at me with those stunning whiskey-brown eyes.

"I'm really glad you came over here today."

"Is it because of the cheesecake?"

"That and because I always feel better when I talk with you."

With those sweet words, something in me settles into place.

Even sex doesn't feel quite as intimate.

"Me, too." I kiss her forehead and then her nose. "Me, too."

And with her hands on either side of my face, I kiss her lips again, softly. So softly, it makes my skin hum.

And I know, down to my bones, that I've found my home.

Chapter Eight

Luna

Today went better—and faster—than expected. I don't know why I thought that moving Sarah into her new apartment would take all day, given that she doesn't have much to speak of in terms of furniture. And it's just a little apartment. It's adorable, and I can't wait to see what she does with it.

So, with Sarah getting settled in her brand-new digs, I have a couple of hours to myself before Wolfe comes over for dinner.

With my diary in hand, I walk out to the gazebo to enjoy one of the last days of summer while I jot down some thoughts. There isn't much wind to speak of, and it's a picture-perfect day on the cliffs.

I need to take advantage of days like this because the wet season will be here before I know it.

I take a deep breath and grin as a bald eagle soars overhead, looking for his lunch.

Opening my journal, I turn to the first clean page and start writing.

SARAH'S HOME! HURTING SOMETHING FIERCE, BUT SHE'S HOME. WE MOVED HER INTO HER NEW APART-MENT TODAY, AND SHE WAS LIKE A KID ON CHRISTMAS MORNING. SHE ACTUALLY KICKED US ALL OUT SO SHE COULD NEST FOR THE REST OF THE DAY.

WOLFE'S ALSO BACK IN TOWN, AND IF ALL GOES AS I THINK IT WILL, HE'LL BE IN MY BED VERY SOON. HE'S ALSO HURTING AFTER LOSING HIS CAREER IN A FREAK ACCIDENT, BUT HE'S DOING SOME NESTING OF HIS OWN WITH A NEW BUSINESS AND RENOVATIONS TO HIS PROP-ERTY RIGHT NEXT TO MINE. IT'S SO GOOD TO HAVE HIM HERE! I DIDN'T REALIZE HOW MUCH I'D MISSED HIM UNTIL I SAW HIM AGAIN. HE'S NOT THE BOY I ONCE KNEW, BUT THE MAN HE'S BECOME IS DEFINITELY SOME-THING TO WRITE ABOUT.

I feel someone sit beside me, but I know that no one's there. It must be Rose.

"It's fascinating to me that you can just wander around the property at will," I say aloud, but I don't look up from my book. "You're not tied to any one spot." I continue writing.

. . .

I FOUND A WHOLE BUNCH OF ROSE'S THINGS IN THE BARN LOFT. JUST IN TIME, TOO, BECAUSE I WAS ABOUT TO START THE DEMO SO THAT I CAN RENOVATE IT IN ORDER TO OPEN THE B&B.

A whoosh of air swirls around me, pushing my hair across my face, and I look up to brush it aside. Something tells me to stand and look down at the rocks that lead to the sand below. It's a bit treacherous, but with patience and care, a person can maneuver their way down to the beach from here.

I stand and look down, shocked to see a man halfway between here and the sand. With one glance, I can tell that the tide is coming in, but he's just standing there, looking down.

"Hey!" I yell down. "Get up here! Hey!"

But he doesn't move. I can't tell if he's ignoring me or if he can't hear me. When I squint and concentrate harder, I realize that it's *Wolfe*.

"Wolfe!" I yell and start to ease my way down to him. I've always hated climbing down from up here. The rocks are slippery, and my parents drilled it into us that it's too dangerous.

They weren't wrong.

"Wolfe!" I call again. "Damn it, what are you doing?"

When I finally reach him, sprays of water are almost hitting him now because the tide is coming in so fast.

"Hey," I say and touch his arm. He recoils. "Oh, God. Head?"

He nods slowly.

"Okay. Take my hand. I need you to focus, Wolfe. The tide's coming in. Fast. I'll get you up. Just follow me."

"Got it," he says, his voice rough with pain. I slowly start the ascent. My heart's pounding, not just with the effort of climbing the rocks but also with fear. My God, what if I hadn't seen him?

What if Rose hadn't alerted me?

"We're almost there," I assure him as calmly as I can, even though my stomach roils with nerves.

At least going up is easier than climbing down.

Finally, when we reach the top, I lead Wolfe to the gazebo so I can grab my journal on the way to the house.

"I'll just go home," he says roughly.

"No way. You're coming inside with me."

He doesn't argue, and with his hand still firmly in my grasp, I lead him into the house, through the living space, and to my bedroom, where he slowly lowers himself onto the bed.

"I'll be back with some ice," I whisper and hurry out to the kitchen.

So, this is what it feels like to have an adrenaline rush during an emergency.

My hands shake as I grab a gel ice pack from the freezer, then wrap it in a tea towel and hurry back to the bedroom.

"Thanks," Wolfe whispers, gratefully taking the ice pack from me and pressing it to his forehead.

I lower the blinds on the window as quietly as possible, and when I turn back to him, I can see by his breathing that he's fallen asleep.

God, he must be exhausted. What happened down there? I know without a doubt that he's not careless enough to go for a walk down on the beach when he has a headache.

It must have come on fast and taken him by surprise.

I ease down onto the bed and lie facing him, watching his face in the dim light. His breathing is even, but every once in a while, his brow furrows as if he's in pain, even in sleep.

I feel so helpless. I wish I could do more for him than offer a dark room and an ice pack. I know there are medication options for migraines. Is he just too stubborn to take any? Or maybe it doesn't work for him.

I have so many questions.

But I also finally—*really*—get it. There's no way he could drive a car at two hundred miles per hour with the risk of a headache like this coming on at any given moment.

I want to lean over and kiss his forehead, but I remember how he reacted to my touch that day in his house and even down on the cliffs just a few moments ago.

It hurts him.

Instead, I just blow him a kiss and then tiptoe out of the room, silently closing the door behind me.

I'll let him sleep it off.

Relieved that Wolfe is safe, I take my journal to my

favorite chair by the windows, but I don't open it again to write.

Instead, I watch the spray of water through the window. It may take roughly six hours for the tide to change, but it sure can sneak up on you.

I'm just relieved that I saw Wolfe down there and could get to him and was able to get both of us up before he got seriously hurt.

"Thanks, Rose," I whisper. "I owe you one."

I smell roses for just a moment as if she's saying, *"You're welcome."*

The adrenaline is wearing off. I lean my head back on the chair, still looking outside as I take a long, deep breath. I like knowing that Wolfe's in the house with me. I hate that he's hurting, but I really like having him here. The past two weeks sucked. I was fine the first couple of days that I didn't hear from him. I knew he was busy. But then a few days turned into a week with no word, and then that turned into two.

And although I didn't say anything to anyone, not even June because she would have hunted the man down and punched him in the nose, I was so sad. I'd decided that Wolfe had changed his mind and wasn't interested in me.

I know better than to assume I know what's going on in someone's head.

I should have called him. Or sought him out.

But now I know better. And I understand what it's like to be so consumed by what's going on in my life that I forget to communicate with people I care about.

"I'm an overthinker," I murmur and then let my heavy eyelids close.

* * *

Thirty minutes later, I wake and walk into the kitchen to make some tea and get dinner started. Before I found Wolfe on the cliffs, I'd planned to grill some steaks, but I think I'll switch things up and make a hearty chicken soup with homemade bread.

I've just pulled the chicken out of the fridge when I see Wolfe walk into the room.

"Hey," I whisper, not able to judge how he feels.

"You're a miracle," he says simply and walks right to me. He takes the chicken out of my hands and sets it aside, then wraps his arms around me and hugs me close.

"I take it you're feeling better?" I ask as I lean my head on his chest, enjoying the way he holds me. "You didn't sleep very long."

"Better," he confirms. "It wasn't as bad as it could have been. I could use some water."

"Of course." I turn and pull a glass out of the cabinet, then fill it with filtered water from the fridge. "You scared me out there."

"Scared me, too," he says and gulps down the water.

I turn away to wash the chicken, but before I can, Wolfe's arms encircle my waist from behind, and he buries his face in my neck.

"Thank you," he whispers and then kisses me, just below my ear. "Thank you so much."

I cover his hands with mine and tilt my head, giving him better access. "It's okay."

He kisses the top of my shoulder and then my neck again, and it sends tingles down my arms.

"I couldn't hear you," he whispers. "I couldn't hear anything at all. And I couldn't see. Fucking head. But you were there as if I'd conjured you from my imagination."

"I think Rose warned me that you were in trouble." I'm having a hard time forming words while his mouth does such delicious things to my skin. "Holy hell, that feels good."

"You taste good," he whispers. "You always taste so fucking good."

His hands move up under my shirt and skim across my stomach, then up over my ribs. I turn in his arms so I can boost myself up onto my tiptoes and kiss him.

I've wanted him for *weeks*. And, finally, here he is, with no interruptions. All mine.

He boosts me up, but not onto the kitchen counter this time. No, he just carries me back to my bedroom, his hands planted on the globes of my butt before gently and oh so tenderly, laying me on the bed.

I reach out for him, but he takes my hand. With eyes the same color as the raging sea outside on mine, he kisses my palm and then pins it to the mattress over my head as he leans over to brush his nose against mine.

"We're in no hurry, sugar," he whispers and kisses me, long and deep. "I'm going to savor every moment of this. Every." He kisses my nose. "Single." Kisses my chin. "Moment."

I groan and writhe beneath him, unable to lie still. My body has come alive, humming in anticipation as he drags that amazing mouth back to my neck.

"God, that's my spot." I moan.

"Your spot?" He smiles down at me. "What does that mean?"

"The spot that makes me nuts. You know, the *spot*."

"Ah, that spot." He kisses me there again, slower this time, and butterflies explode in my belly. "But have you ever considered that you might have more than just one?"

"No, that's the one that does the trick."

He clucks his tongue as he slowly unbuttons my shirt and parts it, revealing my simple white bra and breasts that I always thought were just a little too big.

"Why stop at one?" He unfastens the front clasp of my bra, and his eyes darken as he lowers his head and tugs one tight nipple between his teeth.

"Oh," I breathe as my hips shimmy. His hands roam down to my waist, his fingers dipping under the waistline of my pants. Again, I reach for him.

"This is all about you," he says as he kisses my hand once more.

"Well, *I* want to touch you."

He flashes me a sexy, cocky smile and dips his head to kiss my stomach as he unfastens my pants. I lift my hips helpfully as he drags them down my legs before tossing them away.

"I'm practically naked," I say, hissing when his fingers gently rub either side of my core at the tops of my inner thighs. "And you're completely dressed."

"Want me naked?"

"Hell, yes."

"Then lie back like a good girl and let me have a little fun. Then, I'll reward you."

My eyes blink open in surprise as I stare at him. "Like a *good girl*?"

"That's what I said." He's completely unconcerned as he dips his head and drags his tongue along the sensitive place where his fingers just were. *So close* to my core that I groan in anticipation. "I think we might have just found spot number two."

He's not wrong.

I moan again when Wolfe mirrors that move on the other side. When he *finally* parts my lips and drags his tongue up and down, I arch my back and come apart at the seams.

"And number three," he murmurs before going back for more, pushing me higher and higher until it feels as if I might burst right out of my skin from the pleasure.

"Get." I lick my dry lips. "Naked. Please."

He presses wet kisses to the insides of my thighs and then boosts himself up to whip his shirt over his head before tossing it aside.

"Good God." I push up onto my elbows and watch in fascination as his rock-hard abs move beneath his smooth skin as he works his pants over his hips, and his erection springs free. "Good God."

"You said that already." But his smile is satisfied when he covers me once again and takes my mouth with his, but not in a frenzied way.

He's good to his word, continuing to take things slow and steady as if he's not killing me softly with his hands and mouth.

"Oh, my God, Wolfe, I need you."

He pauses in his exploration of a breast to look up at me. "Say it again."

"Need you."

"No, my name."

I take his face in my hands and smile softly. "I need you, Wolfe."

He fuses his lips to mine, the first signs of urgency finally breaking through as he nudges my legs aside and settles himself between them. I feel his dick, hard and heavy, against me as I lift my legs to wrap around his hips.

Yes, yes, yes.

Finally!

But rather than push inside, he stops and stares down at me.

"Shit."

"What? If you stop now, I swear to God, Wolfe—"

"I don't have a fucking condom, Luna."

I blink and then shake my head. "I'm on the pill."

He sighs. "I swear to you, I'm fine. We can stop and have this conversation if you want, but I assure you, I'm healthy."

Without another word, I reach between us and take him firmly in my grasp, leading him to me.

I gasp as he pushes—so damn slowly—inside of me.

When he's seated as far as he can go, he shoves his fingers into my hair and sighs.

"Jesus, sweetheart, it's as if you were made for me."

I grin and tug his lower lip between my teeth, then kiss him. "Might have been."

And with that, he starts to move. Long, easy strokes, taking his time in leading me to that glorious peak of warm sensation.

With a growl, he picks up the pace as if he can't help himself. As if the finish line is *so close* that he can't help but race just a little faster.

Every muscle in my body tightens as I'm thrown over the cliff into oblivion. I hear Wolfe groan as he pushes in one last time and stills as he follows me right over the ledge.

"Christ, you'll kill me," he whispers as he tries to catch his breath.

"You found at least six spots," I inform him, still panting myself. "Maybe six and a half."

"Come on, there were at least nine, sweetheart."

"Nine?" I frown at him as he rolls to the side, taking his weight off me. "No way. I would have remembered nine."

"It's okay. I'll find them all again. Just give me about ten minutes to recover, and I'll remind you."

I chuckle and brush his brown hair off his forehead. "I don't know about you, but I'll need some food before I can do anything else. I'm starving."

"Now that you mention it," he says as he kisses my hand, "I could eat."

"Can I ask a question before I go cook you a meal?"

"You can ask me anything, anytime, babe."

"Do you eat gluten? Because I'm in a serious relationship with bread, and this could be a deal-breaker."

His sober eyes fill with humor as he leans over and kisses me, long and soft. "If you cook it, I'll eat it. Even gluten."

"Okay, then." I brush my nose over his. "This might work out after all."

I roll away, then tug on some fresh underwear and a clean pair of yoga pants and a T-shirt as Wolfe watches, then run off to the bathroom.

"I'm making chicken soup with homemade bread. Does that work?" I call out.

"Hell, yes, that works. How can I help?"

I step out after cleaning myself up and grin at him. He's so sexy with tousled dark hair and that satisfied grin on his impossibly handosme face.

"You can keep me company in the kitchen."

"That, I can do."

I leave the bedroom as Wolfe climbs out of bed and pulls on his clothes. I've just started washing the chicken as he joins me.

"I would normally roast a whole chicken for this, but all I have is chicken breasts. It'll be faster this way."

"I can chop stuff or knead or stir. Just give me direction, and I'm your man."

"Okay, I'll take you up on that."

Over the next hour, we enjoy being in the kitchen. He's messier than I prefer, but we have fun cooking together. And when the bread's in the oven, and the soup is simmering on the stove, Wolfe sits in a chair and tugs me onto his lap.

"While that finishes up, I have another question," I say and lay my head on his shoulder.

"Shoot."

"What happened out there today?"

He sighs and kisses my head, breathing me in. "I went for a walk after we finished up at Sarah's. It's good exercise for my leg, and it was a nice day. I always climb down the rocks to the beach."

"My parents would have killed you for that when you were a kid."

"Mm." His hand drifts up and down my arm. "I've done it dozens of times since the accident. But today, the headache hit when I was on my way back up and at the base of the cliff."

"Out of the blue?" I guess.

"Always. They come on hard and fast, and I can never anticipate them. I was just trying to get to the top so I could get home and fall into bed. But I couldn't see."

I take his hand and link my fingers with his.

"That's the worst part. It's like I'm suddenly in a black tunnel. I know the water was loud around me, but I couldn't really hear it."

"I yelled and yelled for you."

"I'm sorry." He kisses my forehead. "I didn't know you were there until you touched me, and even that about pushed me out of my skin. I wouldn't wish that kind of pain on my worst enemy. Thank God you came for me. I was stuck there on the rocks."

"Do me a favor?"

"I know what you're going to say."

His voice is hard, and I sigh.

"I know it sucks, but *please* don't do that without at least letting me know you're going. I'm not going to treat you like a child and demand that you don't go or say that you can't go alone, but just let me or *someone* know. Please?"

"Okay. I can do that."

"Thank you. You've become important to me, Wolfe. I don't know what I'd do if something happened to you."

"Hey, nothing's going to happen." He holds me close, and we're quiet for a long moment until the timer on the oven goes off.

"Let's eat," I suggest and kiss his cheek before climbing off his lap.

"It smells good," he says as he follows me to the kitchen. "But, you know, we might have to work the bread off later."

"With cardio?"

That cocky smile of his spreads over his face again. "The *best* cardio there is, sweetheart."

NOVEMBER 2, 2015

DEAR DIARY,

WHY ARE SMALL TOWNS SO...AWFUL? FULL OF GOSSIP AND ALWAYS KEEPING AN EYE ON WHAT EVERYONE IS UP TO. HELL, SARAH'S BEEN GONE FOR MORE THAN EIGHT YEARS AND PEOPLE STILL TALK ABOUT HER. IT MAKES ME WANT TO PULL MY DAMN HAIR OUT.

IF YOU DON'T KNOW WHAT JUST ABOUT EVERYONE IN TOWN IS DOING, JUST STAND IN ONE PLACE FOR FIVE MINUTES AND YOU'LL HEAR ALL THE GOSSIP IN NO TIME!

PEOPLE NEED TO MIND THEIR OWN DAMN BUSINESS. LIKE, WHO FREAKING CARES WHO WOLFE CONRAD IS SEEING NOW? ALL OF HB IS SO INTERESTED IN WATCHING HIS RACES, NOT TO SUPPORT HIM AND SEE HIM SUCCEED BUT JUST TO SEE WHO HE HAS ON HIS ARM AT THE END OF THE RACE.

IT'S DISGUSTING.

LOVE,

LUNA

Chapter Nine

Wolfe

"Walls are up, and we're ready to start the roof," John says as Luna and I join him in the driveway. The walls of the new building tower over the existing house.

The garage is going to be fucking huge.

I can't wait.

"Good timing. It's supposed to rain next week."

"That's my thought exactly," John agrees. "But we have a problem."

I raise a brow and sip my coffee. "And that is?"

"They made the roof trusses already. We just have to crane them in. However, this space to the left of the house isn't wide enough to get back to where we need to be." John points to the left of the carport attached to the house. "We either need to take down some trees or the carport."

"Carport," I immediately reply. "No contest. I don't want to lose the trees."

"That's what I would do, as well," John says with a nod. "Especially since there's nothing in the carport, and you plan to demolish the house next year anyway."

"Exactly." I narrow my eyes as I let my gaze skim the house. "You don't think taking the carport down will cause a domino effect and make the rest fall, too, do you?"

"It shouldn't," he says. "It's a lean-to, not a load-bearing structure. It should come right down without an issue. In fact, I have the backhoe ready now. You're welcome to watch while I take it down."

"Let's do it," I confirm.

John hurries away and climbs into the backhoe himself, starting the engine.

"What are we watching?" June asks as she joins Luna and me in the driveway.

"He's going to take down the carport," Luna tells her. "What are *you* up to?"

"I was on my way to your place to get started on my workday and saw the two of you out here. Thought I'd stop to see what you're looking at."

June bites her lip and narrows her eyes, and I turn to watch John raise the bucket on the backhoe and then bring it down on the flimsy roof of the carport.

It crumbles without an issue.

And then, right there before my very eyes, the entire exterior wall of the house comes down with it.

"Thought that might happen," June says cheerfully. "But no one asked for my opinion. Gotta go."

She waves and saunters back to her truck, headed up to the lighthouse as I stare in disbelief.

"Oops," Luna says. "Is that the kitchen sink?"

"Yep," I confirm and sip my coffee. I'm not even mad.

"Shit. I'm sorry, Wolfe," John says as he hurries over, his face grim. "That shouldn't have happened."

"Well, it's not the best timing, but as you said, it was going to come down anyway. I was just hoping it could wait until next year."

"It's not habitable," John says and props his hands on his hips.

"Looks like you're staying with me," Luna says brightly and squeezes my hand. "We can go in and gather your clothes and things."

I frown down at her, and John clears his throat.

"Uh, I'll let you two sort this out," he says and walks away.

"I can get a rental," I say immediately, but Luna shakes her head.

"Why?" She looks back at the house again. "You'll want to be close by while your garage is built. I'm a hundred yards up the road. Also, you've spent the past three nights in *my* bed. You only come down here for clothes."

"I don't want to assume—"

"I offered." She smiles up at me. "Don't overthink it, Wolfe. That's my job."

I laugh and kiss her forehead. It's true, I've quickly become addicted to being with Luna, and now that we have a physical relationship, I have no interest in being anywhere but with her at night.

"Okay, but if you get sick of me, you can throw me out anytime."

"So noted." She laughs and finishes her coffee, tossing it into the nearby trash. "I think I have to go soothe June's rumpled feathers."

"She didn't seem mad. She laughed."

"That was sarcasm—the kind with annoyance under it." She shrugs a shoulder. "She's still sore about the garage, which is silly because she doesn't have time for it. It's pride, I think."

"I'm pretty sure if she doesn't want to sleep ever again, she could work here a few hours a week."

"I'm positive that she doesn't want that. She's just stubborn." Luna boosts up onto her toes and plants a kiss right on me, in front of the crew and everyone.

I wrap my arms around her and give it right back.

"I have to drive up the coast a bit to look at some lighting choices today," I inform her. "Ride with me?"

"Sure, sounds like fun. And maybe I'll take a look around for some lighting for the B&B while I'm there."

"Two birds, one stone. I'll pick you up in about an hour."

"Perfect. Do you want me to help you gather your stuff before I go talk to June?"

"No, I don't have much. I'll grab some stuff and won't be far behind you."

"Okay. See you soon."

She blows me a kiss and then sets off, moving up the slight hill to her place. I can't help but watch as her ass sways back and forth as she walks. Luna is curvy in all the right places.

And she's all *mine*.

I walk into the house and sigh when I look to the left and notice I can see right through the kitchen to the trees beyond. I'm not sentimental about anything in the house, so it won't hurt my feelings if they tear it down as it stands and haul it all away.

But the timing couldn't be worse.

With a resigned shrug, I get to work shoving my clothes into suitcases, then gather my toiletries and take a quick walk-through to make sure I haven't forgotten anything.

I grab the family portrait taken when I was in the first grade off the wall and take it with me.

The rest of the family photos are already in my storage unit.

After I load my SUV, I drive it up to Luna's and then jog back down to drive the Ferrari up, as well.

"Hey, John," I call out before I leave the house.

"Yeah?" he says as he walks over to me.

"I don't need anything else from inside. Go ahead and take it all down. You'll have better access to the garage."

He sighs. "I'm sorry, Wolfe."

"Don't sweat it. Go ahead and have it cleared away. I'll have my phone if you need anything."

"I'll see to it," he says and walks away, calling out to his crew. "Change of plans!"

I drive away with one final look at the house I grew up in.

* * *

"That was productive," Luna says as we drive down the coast toward home. "It was so nice that they had the lighting samples all ready to go for you."

"No guesswork," I agree. "Because I'm no interior decorator."

"I think it's fun," she says with a grin. "And that would be why we were there for an extra hour while I picked out some stuff for the B&B. Thanks for being patient."

"You fed me," I reply with a shrug. "It was an even trade."

After spending a significant amount of time in the lighting store, Luna took me out for lunch. I started to object because I prefer to buy the meals, but she just laughed at me and took the check out of my fingers.

I don't think I've ever had a woman do that before.

And while it's not something that will become a habit, it was kind of...refreshing.

"Did you talk with June?" I ask her.

"Yeah, she's fine. She said she didn't want to laugh so hard she peed her pants in front of you, so she excused herself."

"June doesn't have much of a filter."

"She has *no* filter," Luna says. "Despite what she claims. And it's one of the things I love about her. You never have to wonder where you stand with her. And although she's blunt, June would rather gnaw her arm off than hurt anyone's feelings. It's rare to find someone who says it like she sees it *and* is mindful of her words."

"She doesn't seem to give a shit when it comes to your brother."

I glance over in time to see Luna cringe.

"No, you're right. She's not exactly careful when it comes to Apollo."

"What's the story there?"

"Honestly, I'm not sure. It's just sort of always been the case. Even when we were kids, no one could make Juniper mad the way Apollo could. They're just like water and oil."

"It's sexual tension," I say and feel Luna staring at me, so I look over at her. "It is. Trust me. I'm a guy, and I see how they look at each other when they think the other doesn't notice."

"No, it's just a weird, mutual dislike. Trust *me*. I've known them both all my life."

"I don't think so."

Before we can argue the point further, a little Audi R8 passes me on a double line and cuts in front of me just before a dump truck hits him head-on.

"What in the hell?" Luna gasps.

"Fucker," I mutter. This stretch of highway along the coast is twisty, with a cliff drop-off on the right. There's ample shoulder space but no room to be an asshole.

My Ferrari handles the curves like a dream, and I

ease off the gas to put some space between the Audi and us.

Driving is what I do. I'm in complete control.

But I have Luna with me, and the asshole in front of us apparently thinks it's fun to fuck with the luxury car.

"Why is he doing that?" Luna asks, gripping onto the door as the car ahead swerves back and forth, then cuts over to the left lane into oncoming traffic before slowing down so he's right next to me. "He's flipping you off! Does he want to race?"

"Probably," I say grimly, not looking over. "He's going to kill himself."

"There's no room for this," Luna says. "And these are blind corners."

The Audi honks and then zips up again, cutting me off before slamming on his brakes.

I brake as well and clench my jaw.

"This fucker is dangerous."

"I'm taking down his license plate," Luna says, tapping on her phone. "And then I'm calling the sheriff."

The asshole ahead speeds up and then slows down, trying to antagonize me. Suddenly, the sky opens up, and rain comes down *hard*. I'm right back in track mode, concentrating on the road and the car in front of me, aware of all the obstacles around my car.

"Shit," I mutter and flip on the wipers. The rain is sporadic. I can hardly see for half a mile, and then it stops altogether before starting again.

"This is *crazy*," Luna mutters and presses her phone to her ear. "Yes, this is Luna Winchester. I'm on Highway

101 about five miles north of town. There's an Audi R8, Oregon license plate number 991 GJR. He's driving dangerously, and I'm afraid he's going to kill us or someone else. Yes. Yes, we're behind him. Great, thank you."

"I could pull over," I say as I shift down. "But that doesn't seem safe, either."

"He's going to hurt someone," Luna says. "Oh, God, Wolfe, he's—"

"I see."

He swerves onto the shoulder and almost goes over the cliff, then overcorrects into oncoming traffic.

"He has to be wasted," I mutter. "No one drives like that when they're sober."

Red lights rush up behind me, and I ease onto the shoulder, getting out of the way. Luna sighs in relief, and then, to our utter horror, the Audi sails right over the side of the road onto the cliffs below.

"Oh my God," she whispers. "Oh my God!"

"Stay here." I get out of the car and run over to where the sheriff's car is parked by the edge. Sheriff Daniels hurries out of the cruiser, his radio in hand.

"I need an ambulance and backup," he snaps out, then turns to me.

"He was fucking with us on the road," I immediately begin. "In oncoming traffic, then close to the edge. He would brake then pull up next to me. Flashing his lights, flipping me off. He had to be intoxicated."

"Do you know who he is?"

"No. I've never seen him before. I think he was just a

young guy with a fast car who wanted to fuck with the Ferrari. That's the feeling I got anyway."

"He was crazy," Luna says, surprising me.

"I told you to stay in the car."

"No way." She peers over the side and swallows hard. "There's no way he survived that."

"I have crews coming to try to save him," the sheriff says grimly. "I'm afraid it will be a recovery, though. I'll need to take your statements, but my priority is putting out cones and keeping people clear of here."

"I can help," I offer right away and turn back to Luna. "Please, get back in the car. Or, at the very least, go stand over there. I'm going to help the sheriff until his people get here."

"Okay," she whispers, and with wide, haunted eyes, carefully walks back to the car, opens the door, and sits in the passenger seat.

I join the sheriff at the trunk of his cruiser, and between the two of us, we set out cones and flares to alert traffic.

Before long, a wrecker, more cruisers, and an ambulance arrive.

I move out of the way and get in the car with Luna, and we watch quietly as the scene unfolds before us. It takes an hour for the rescue team to get down to the car. I can't hear what they're saying, but I can see by the grim look on Sheriff Daniels's face that the news isn't good.

"This is the weirdest day," I mutter and reach for Luna's hand. She clings to me and wipes a tear from her cheek.

"We watched a person die," she says with a sniff. "What was the point of all of that, Wolfe?"

"I don't know." I kiss the back of her hand, and the sheriff finally crosses over to us.

"We're going to be here for a while," he says when I roll down the window. "Why don't you folks go on home? I'll get a quick statement from you and you can get out of here."

"Do you know who he was?" Luna asks him.

"Yeah, we were able to ID him. He's a kid from Newport. On his way home from college for a few days."

I swear under my breath, and wish that the whole damn mess never happened.

Once we've given our statement, he nods, taps the car once, and then walks away. I pull away from the scene, careful to drive slowly around the crew.

We're quiet on the short drive back to the lighthouse. When I park, Luna hurries out of the car without waiting for me to open her door.

But she doesn't walk into the house. She sets off for the gazebo instead.

It's still drizzling, but the structure is covered. Luna's hugging her arms around herself when I walk up behind her.

"Talk to me," I urge and wrap my arms around her from behind.

She pulls away.

"That scared the hell out of me," she finally says and turns her tear-filled eyes to me. "But you were so solid. So *sure* of yourself."

141

"I was sure of my car and my ability to drive, but I'm not typically in a situation like that, sweetheart. In a race, I can anticipate what the other driver might do because we all have the same goal."

I swallow and drag my hand down my face. "This wasn't the same thing. Not even close. And I'm sorry you were there for it."

"I'm sorry that *I* fell apart," she says, frustration in her voice. "I'm always the calm one. I voice of reason. And I lost my shit. I don't know what I would have done if I'd been the one driving."

"Whoa." I shake my head at her. "Are you kidding me right now? You did *not* lose your shit. You called the cops. You took down the license. It's okay to be freaked out by something like that. Hell, it freaked me the fuck out, too."

"You were so calm," she says again.

"I was terrified, Luna. Jesus, I had you with me. What if he'd pushed us over the side? What if we'd rear-ended him, and you were hurt?"

Just the thought of it, the mere possibility of it, has me breaking out in a sweat.

The rain starts to pound down around us again, hitting the metal roof of the gazebo. It's deafening, and we simply stand there, breathing hard and staring at each other.

"This day has been full of what the fucks," I say at last.

"You can't see it through the rain, but it's a full moon tonight," she replies softly and steps to me, reaching for my hand. "What if you'd had a headache in the middle of all of that?"

I lick my lips and tip her face up so I can look into her eyes.

"I would have immediately pulled over," I reply easily. "Your safety is something I won't ever fuck around with, Luna. I would have safely gotten us to the side of the road, and you would have driven us home."

"Okay."

"I can't have you afraid of being in a car with me."

"I'm not *afraid*. It's a concern. Not when things are mellow, but in today's situation, the stress could have caused a migraine. And then what?"

"Like I said," I repeat and step closer to her. "I would pull over. I'm not stubborn enough to think that I can just deal with it and get you home. I won't risk you. Not ever."

"I know."

"Do you?"

"I do. I was just so scared, and I had a horrible vision of you being overcome by pain while dodging that asshole and the rain. It was a bad moment."

"It could happen," I reply honestly. "I won't lie and say that it's not something to worry about. I have been driving before when one came on."

Her eyes widen. "What?"

"I pulled over and waited it out. Luckily, that one only lasted half an hour. I'm smart, and driving is second nature to me."

"Okay." She sighs and closes her eyes. "Okay."

"I'm proud of you."

Her eyes snap back open at that. "What? Why?"

"Because you may think that you lost your shit, but you were rock-solid. Upset, sure, but you didn't scream, and you didn't grab onto me or distract me. You did everything exactly right."

"It didn't feel like it."

"Trust me. You were awesome, and I'm proud of you."

"Now that it's all over, can I admit that it was kind of sexy to see you so in control of that car?"

I lift an eyebrow, relieved that the worst of the storm has passed.

"Is that right?"

"Yeah, you have these stupidly hot muscles in your arms that flex in just the right way when you grip onto the wheel or shift gears. And you set your jaw and look all fierce and...alpha."

She smiles, and I can see that she's trying to lighten the mood.

"So, what you're saying is, we should drive fast more often, but maybe in far less intense circumstances?"

"It wouldn't make me sad. But for tonight, I'm just relieved that we're both okay. And my heart hurts for that guy's family. He made a *really* bad life choice."

"It was a waste," I agree.

She steps into my arms and holds on tightly.

"Can we just stand here for a while like this?" she asks against my chest.

"For as long as you'd like."

Chapter Ten

Luna

"Is royalty coming over?" Wolfe asks as I fuss with a stack of napkins.

"I *like* to play hostess," I remind him. "And I want everything to look pretty and inviting. If you think this is fancy, just wait until the B&B is up and running."

"You don't break out these fancy little forks for me." He picks one up and eyes it.

"It's for appetizers," I inform him. "And if you'd like to use little forks, which look hilarious in your big hands, by the way, we'll use them later. I just have to open the wine, and then I think everything is ready."

"There's no need to be nervous." Before I can start fussing over a vase of flowers again, he takes my hand and pulls me against him. "Everything looks great. Everyone will have a great time."

I smile and take a deep breath. I haven't had a girls' night in a really long time. And today, not only are June and Sarah coming over, but all the sisters from Three Sisters Kitchen are, too.

"I've seen some pretty posh parties in my time," he says and tilts my chin up to meet my gaze with his.

"Of course, you have. You're a celebrity race car driver."

"That's right. And as such, I can assure you that this rates up there with some of the fanciest. Don't worry, sweetheart."

He brushes his lips across mine and then sinks into me, kissing me until I can't even remember why I was worried in the first place.

"For the love of God."

I pull back and look at the open front door—when did June open it?—and see all five women grinning at us.

Well, four are grinning. June looks pained.

"Every time I turn around, you two are wrestling around like a couple of teenagers," June complains.

"I think it's sweet," Cordelia says with a wink.

"Well, you have to go," June informs Wolfe. "This is girl time."

"I'm aware," Wolfe says with a good-natured smile as he loops his arm around my shoulders. "And I'm going. I'm hanging with Zeke, finally digging into the Ford. Just call if you need me."

"We won't need you," June says.

"Speak for yourself." I pin June with a glare and then offer Wolfe an apologetic grin. "Have fun with the car."

"I plan to. Have a good time, ladies."

He walks out the front door, and all of us watch him go.

"So, how do we order one of those?" Darla asks.

"He fell into my lap." I shrug and then clap with excitement and gesture for the ladies to follow me into the kitchen where Darla and Mira set platters on the counter. "I'm so glad you're all here. Okay, I don't think you all know Sarah."

"We met her at the diner," Mira replies with a wink.

"And I go into the restaurant for their breakfast," Sarah agrees. "We've met."

"Perfect."

"Can I ask a favor?" Cordelia asks. "I *really* want a tour of this place. The food will keep in the fridge and oven for a little while, if that's okay."

"Of course." I love showing off the property, so we stow away the food, and I lead everyone outside and over to the lighthouse entrance. "We'll start here. It's over a hundred steps to the top, but I'm game if you are."

"We are," Mira says with a grin. "I've often wondered why you don't offer tours. You'd make a killing with the tourists."

I unlock the door, lead them inside, and reply as we start up the steps.

"I *love* talking about the lighthouse, but I don't like the idea of people driving up here and just wandering around. This isn't a state or federal park, it's my home."

"That makes sense," Cordelia agrees. "And let's be honest, a lot of people don't respect boundaries."

"Exactly." I nod and stop halfway up so everyone can catch their breath, including me. "Let's rest for a second, and I'll fill you in on some history. If you're interested."

"Tell us *everything*," Mira says with an excited grin.

"You know, I'm not sure that I even know the history of the lighthouse," Sarah says thoughtfully. "It's just always been here, and we hung out up here when we were kids."

"Same," June says. "I don't know all of it, anyway."

"Then let me change that." I clear my throat and glance out the narrow window that looks out at the sea. "The tower and the light were built in 1870, making it the oldest standing lighthouse in Oregon. The original lightkeeper was Reginald Masterson, my three-times great-grandfather."

I turn to June and Sarah.

"Rose's dad."

"Ah, makes sense," Sarah says with a nod.

"It's amazing that it's been in your family from the very beginning," Darla says.

"I agree," I reply. "So far, we've been lucky enough to keep it in the family. Most lighthouses are now automated, but some, like this one, are still maintained by the lightkeeper. That's been me for the last several years."

I lead them to the very top, and we all watch for a few moments as the lens spins in a circle.

"How far out at sea can the light be seen?" Darla asks.

"On a clear night, as far out as about twenty-seven

nautical miles offshore before it's out of sight due to the Earth's curve."

"So cool," Cordelia murmurs. "The glass on these lenses is just amazing."

"It's a Fresnel lens, which are designed to keep the light in a narrow beam," I say and then laugh. "I sound like a big nerd."

"The kind I want to hang out with," Sarah says, and the others nod. "This is awesome. When was the house built onto the tower?"

"They built the first cabin the same year, 1870, but it was just a tiny building. Once the light was going, they constructed the existing house in pretty much the same footprint that exists now. Of course, we've all updated it here and there, but it's pretty much the same silhouette, although my father added about a thousand square feet to it when we were kids. Then, after the original structure, they added the other outbuildings over the course of a few years, including the barn that is currently under renovation for the new bed and breakfast."

"We want to see that, too," Mira says. "We're totally nosy."

"That doesn't bother me at all."

I lead them back down and outside, then gesture to the ocean.

"About three miles due west of here is a big shipwreck."

"Now you're just pulling our legs," Darla says as she shields her eyes from the sun and stares out at the ocean.

"No, ma'am. It's the truth. In 1912, the J Blue sank just three miles from port. Remnants still wash up from time to time."

"Does anything...you know, *creepy* happen up here?" Mira asks.

"Boy, does it," June says with a snicker.

We laugh, and I lead everyone out to the barn.

So much has already changed out here. New walls. New floor. There are even studs up where the rooms will be.

Not to mention a second story.

"It's way bigger than I thought it would be," Cordelia says.

"We're adding on to the original structure, and creating a lot of extra square footage," June says. "Essentially, the new building is being built *around* the old one."

I tell them about the guest suites, the gourmet kitchen and dining room, and the vast library I have planned.

"I'm going to come stay here once a year," Cordelia decides. "What a treat, Luna."

"Thanks. I think it's going to be something really special. And speaking of that, I can't wait to see what you brought for us to try today."

"Yes, let's go eat," Mira says as we leave the barn and walk back to the house. "Now, it won't hurt our feelings if you don't like everything or even *anything* that we brought, but I wanted to give you a nice variety of things to try. There is breakfast food here, along with some snacks and other fun treats."

Over the next half hour, I fall completely head over

heels in love with every single thing these amazing women brought over. Omelets and French toast with fresh clotted cream. Caprese salad. Muffins and cookies. Sandwiches and wraps.

Every single morsel is absolutely divine.

"How are we supposed to choose?" Sarah asks. "I mean, I know it's Luna's decision, but it's all to die for. I don't know how you'll narrow it down."

"Well, you don't have to," Darla suggests. "We could put together weekly menus so every day is different. Heck, you could even do a monthly rotation. And we can work in seasonal meals, as well. I think we just wanted to make sure that we're headed in the right direction with this."

"It's amazing," I confirm. "If you guys make all the meals, I won't need that gourmet kitchen."

"Well, that's something to talk about, as well," Cordelia says and shares a smile with her sisters. "We have a business proposition for you."

I raise an eyebrow and sip my wine. "I can't wait to hear it."

"So, we were thinking," Mira says, scooting to the edge of her seat in excitement, "because you're building a state-of-the-art kitchen, what if we, Three Sisters Kitchen, run that piece of the business? We'll work the kitchen, offering the meals and snacks all made on-site with the farm-to-table strategy we use in our restaurant now. It would be an extension of us, offered through your B&B."

"Honestly, I planned to do a lot of the cooking

myself, supplementing with treats from you," I reply, thinking it over and not hating the new idea at all.

"So much goes into a business like this," Cordelia says, fiddling with the pendant hanging from her neck. "The kitchen is just one piece. You also have the inn side, tours of the lighthouse, housekeeping, the grounds. I could go on and on. If 90 percent of the kitchen duties are taken off your plate, it frees up your time for everything else. We would have a chef here in the morning from six until noon, seven days a week."

"Can you spare a chef?"

"We'll hire to fit the need," Cordelia says. "Listen, I don't want you to feel like we're trying to take this over because that's certainly not our intention. We are just *so* excited and want to be a part of it. The restaurant business has been in our family for generations, just like the lighthouse has been in yours. This is what we know."

"Well, that makes sense." I glance over at Sarah and June, who have remained quiet, listening. "What do you think?"

"They're right in that you can't do it all yourself," June says. "You'd hire employees anyway."

"True."

"But also," Sarah adds, "I would like clarification on one thing. Are you asking to go into business with her, meaning you'll *own* the kitchen? Or are you asking Luna to hire you as an independent contractor?"

"Honestly, we'll take whatever we can get," Darla says and turns to me. "If you want a partner, even if it's a small percentage that only covers the kitchen, we'll buy in and run that piece. If you simply want to contract with us, we're happy to do that, too."

"If we were to be owners," Cordelia continues, "we would pay for the kitchen renovation."

I gawk at her. "Cordelia, that's one of the most expensive pieces of the project."

"Trust me, we're aware," Mira says with a smile. "And while breakfast and a snack are included in the room rate, we would offer lunch—whether in the dining room or a to-go sack—as an add-on sale."

"I absolutely *love* that you're excited about the bed and breakfast," I say slowly, thinking it over, feeling more than a tiny bit overwhelmed. "But we don't know each other very well. Not yet, anyway. Why do you want to help me like this?"

"Because it's going to be a success," Darla says flatly. "We can *feel* it. Investing in our community, in a fellow kick-ass businesswoman, is something we want to do."

"And I want to feed your guests," Mira says. "I'll take the breakfast shift here, five days a week."

"Wow." I need to take another sip of my wine, and when I do, I suddenly smell roses. And then one of the bedroom doors slams shut.

"What in the hell?" Darla asks.

"That's Rose," I inform them. "And you should know now while you can still change your minds, that she hangs out here often. Not just in the house but also in the barn, at the top of the lighthouse, and even at the gazebo."

"A free-range ghost," Cordelia says with a delighted laugh.

"She's pretty harmless," June says. "I hardly even know she's around."

"Has she shown herself to you?" I ask June in surprise.

"Mostly, she just moves stuff around," she replies. "She has a sense of humor."

"Well, that'll bring adventure to our lives," Cordelia adds. "And I can't speak for my sisters, but it doesn't scare me away."

"Me, neither," Mira adds.

"Nope," Darla agrees.

"I'm going to take a couple of days to think about it," I say. "I don't want to make any rash decisions."

"There's no rush," Darla assures me. "And don't worry, we'll talk you into it with our southern charm."

She adds just a little more twang to her voice, making me laugh.

"It's a very tempting offer. And I am grateful for it."

* * *

"I think you should do it," Sarah says after the sisters leave, and it's just the three of us sipping the last of our wine and nibbling on the lemon bars that Mira made. "It takes a lot off your plate as they said."

"But don't let them bully you into it if you want to do it all yourself," June adds. "I know you've had a vision in your mind for a long time for this, and you need to do what's right for you."

"Agreed," Sarah says with a nod.

"I love the Three Sisters Restaurant," I say slowly. "Like, *love*. The style, the smells, the menu, it's all fantastic. And I like them a lot, too."

"You'd want a really good contract drawn up," June reminds me. "You can't do something like this with a handshake."

"Of course." I nod and take a deep breath. "Let's be honest, Mira is a hell of a lot better as a chef than I am."

"You can still hire her as a contractor," Sarah points out. "I don't think either one is a bad idea. It's just up to you to decide how you want to run your business."

"She's right," June says.

"Thanks. I was hoping you guys would have a firm opinion one way or the other. This doesn't help me."

"At least you know we don't hate one of the options," June says.

"Yeah. I'll sleep on it. June, I didn't realize how far along you'd gotten out there already."

"I have a good crew," she says with a smile. "It might not be the fancy one that Wolfe has working down the hill, but we get the job done."

"You have *got* to get over that," I tell her.

"I'm not upset."

Sarah and I both roll our eyes.

"I'm not." June pouts for a second. "It's just—"

"Nothing," I interrupt. "It's nothing, June. It's his house, his property, and he's not obligated to check with you on it. You're so busy with the inn and other jobs you have all over town, him doing that actually took something off your plate."

"You have to sleep sometime," Sarah says softly. "You can't do everything, even though you want to."

June shrugs a shoulder. "Yeah, well, I *am* busy."

"Exactly."

"I started painting again," Sarah announces with a satisfied grin.

"What? That's awesome."

"I got my studio set up in the extra bedroom, and I was up all night last night, painting with some pretty watercolors I picked up. It feels so damn good, you guys."

"I'm *so* glad," I say and reach out to take her hand. "You look like a huge weight has been lifted compared to the day you got here."

"Are you kidding? I'm safe. For the first time in more than a decade, I feel totally safe. It's the best feeling, and I have you guys to thank for that."

"You have *yourself* to thank," June says.

"For some of it," she concedes. "But, honestly, if he hadn't thrown me out, I don't know if I would have left—even with the affairs. Because I was afraid. I hadn't talked to you in so long, I didn't know if I should come here. But I'm so glad I did. The apartment is perfect for me, I love working at the diner, and I finally feel...*secure.*"

"Because you are," I reply. "And I want to see what you've painted."

"I need a little more practice," she says with a smile.

"But, trust me, you'll get to see. I'm hoping that maybe I can paint some pieces for your guest rooms in the B&B."

"Oh, my God. I would love that, Sarah. It'll have a piece of all three of us in it, just as it should. Because even though I might own it, you two put so much soul into this property over the years, you're a part of it. And having you be part of it in a tangible way just makes me so emotional."

"Oh, Lord, she's going to leak," June says to Sarah. "Good going."

"I can't help it." I laugh and wipe away a tear. "It's happening, finally, and I'm so damn excited. I think I should get a website built, and maybe even start taking reservations for late next summer."

June narrows her eyes. "Are you giving me a *deadline*, Winchester?"

"Uh, yeah. I have to be able to pay you, you know. And I need customers for that."

"I think that's a good idea," Sarah says. "I could probably draw up some artist renderings of what it'll all look like until you have actual photos to add to the site. I bet you'll get reservations."

"I think you're right. Let's get started on that next week."

"I'm down," Sarah says and taps something into her phone. "This is fun."

"Maybe you should start lighthouse tours in the early summer before the B&B is open for business," June muses. "I loved it when you told us the history of the light. You should have a big sign made with the story on it, and I can set it up by the entrance to the lighthouse."

"That's a good idea," I reply. "And I could set the tours up as by appointment only so I don't have a bunch of people roaming around the property."

"You can run that through your website," Sarah adds.

"See?" I ask and sit back in satisfaction. "It's all coming together."

APRIL 15, 2020

DEAR DIARY,

WE HAVE THE BEST NEW RESTAURANT IN TOWN! IT'S CALLED THREE SISTERS KITCHEN, AND THE SWEETEST WOMEN OWN IT. THEY MOVED HERE FROM SOUTH CAROLINA, I THINK, AND I AM OBSESSED WITH THE FRESH FOOD THEY OFFER. IT'S A FARM-TO-TABLE RESTAURANT, AND WE'RE SO LUCKY TO HAVE IT HERE IN HB! GETTING NEW THINGS IN TOWN IS RARE, AND I'M THRILLED.

I'VE BEEN PONDERING THE IDEA OF OPENING MY OWN BUSINESS. I'D LOVE TO CONVERT THE OLD BARN INTO A BED AND BREAKFAST. I THINK IT WOULD BE SO FUN! I'M GOING TO START ASKING AROUND ABOUT HOW TO GET STARTED ON IT. I HAVE A BUSINESS DEGREE TO PUT TO USE.

LOVE,
LUNA

Chapter Eleven

Wolfe

"Start her up," Zeke says as he leans over the engine of Luna's classic Ford. I press the button on the floor, and the engine roars to life. Zeke's head pops up, and he's grinning from ear to ear. "We did it."

"It's so sexy," I mutter, running my hand over the leather bench seat.

"I can't believe it was in a barn all those years and not inside of a garage," he says as he wipes his hands on a rag. "It was in such good condition."

"I think the ghost was looking out for it," I reply and turn the car off, then look up when Zeke barks out a laugh. "What?"

"Sure. A *ghost* made sure that it didn't mold or rust or fall apart."

"Do you have a different explanation, Einstein?"

"Luck?"

I raise an eyebrow and step out of the car, carefully

closing the door. "I don't buy that it was luck. I'm just grateful that it *was* in such good shape, or it would have taken much longer than a month to rebuild it."

"It just needed a little TLC," he agrees. "A little paint, some new tires, and elbow grease. I wouldn't believe it if I didn't see it myself."

We both turn when there's a light knock on the door and Sarah pokes her head in the garage with a tentative smile.

"Hi. Sorry to interrupt."

"You're not interrupting," I assure her. "Come on in."

"I wanted to stop down and give you something." She bites her lip and steps inside, a large, brown package in her hand. "I made you a thank-you gift. It's really for both of you. To show my appreciation for letting me live upstairs."

"You pay rent," I remind her. "You don't have to give us gifts."

"It's just a little something." She awkwardly passes it over. I hold it up, tear off the paper, and then Zeke and I stare at it in awe. "It won't hurt my feelings if you don't like it or if you don't want to display it in here. I just thought it was something fun."

I look from the painting in my hands to Sarah and back again.

"Are you kidding? This is so great, Sarah."

"It's the garage," Zeke says, stepping closer. "But made to look like it would have in the 1950s."

Watercolor paints depict Wolfe Automotive with our

logo over the big garage bay and several old-fashioned cars parked outside.

Luna's Ford is on the lift inside.

"I have just the spot for it."

Zeke nods. "With you there. I'll grab the hammer and nail."

Immediately, we get to work hanging the art on the wall behind our counter where customers come when they drop off their automobiles, and again to pay and take them home.

"Everyone will see it here." I nod in satisfaction as Zeke levels it out. "Did you paint it on this canvas with this particular place in mind? Because it fits perfectly."

"Actually, I did," Sarah says with a proud smile. "It was just a blank wall, and it needed a little pizzazz but still in a very masculine way."

"You did that," Zeke says. "That's kick-ass, Sarah. Thank you."

"You're welcome," she says, clearly relieved that we both like the painting. "I have to admit, it looks really nice. I'm glad you like it."

My phone rings, and I frown at John's name on the screen. "Hey, John."

"Hey, I was wondering if you had some time? I could use you here at your place."

"Sure, I'm on my way."

"Great."

I hang up and let out a gusty breath. "Something's wrong at the new garage. I need to swing over there. Why don't we take the Ford to Luna? Show it off?"

"It's done?" Sarah asks. "It's so pretty."

"All finished," I confirm.

"Yeah, let's do it," Zeke says.

"I'm coming, too," Sarah says, looking as excited as we are that the car is finished. "I can't wait to see the look on Luna's face when she sees it."

Zeke and Sarah ride in the Ford, and I follow behind them, stewing.

What's wrong now? I swear, it's been one thing after another with the new garage. After they tore down the house and hauled the debris away, they found a busted water main that had to be fixed. Then, because of all the water, we had other issues.

I just can't take any more bad news about this thing.

I pull into the driveway and frown. All the trucks are gone. The dumpster that's been a permanent fixture for more than a month? Gone, too. The only one here is John, who's walking out from the garage's side door.

"What's wrong?" I ask when I approach him.

He smiles, shakes his head, and looks back at my building.

"Not a damn thing. We're done."

I blink at him and then look at the new garage. "What?"

"Done." He passes me a box. "Your keys, garage door openers, and everything else you might need is in there. Of course, everything is passcoded and state-of-the-art, so you don't actually *need* the keys or the openers, but just in case, here they are. I keyed in all the codes you gave

163

me. There are instructions in here on how to change them, should you ever need to."

He goes on to tell me about the security system, the heating and cooling units, air purifiers, and everything else I'll need to know, but I can't stop staring at the building.

From the outside, it looks like a rustic barn. Someone who's never seen it before might believe it's been here for decades.

Which is exactly what I wanted.

"Why don't I stop talking, and you go on inside? I'll give you a minute."

I hear Zeke and Sarah pull in behind me, but I don't look back as I head to the door, push it open, and walk in.

Of course, I've been in here many times since the project started, but it has a completely different vibe now. It's quiet and clean. There's absolutely no dust—though, given the air filtration system I had built in, there shouldn't be.

Dust can kill a car.

The floor gleams. Two of the bays have lifts, and there's a big fan in the twenty-foot ceiling.

Benches and tools line the back wall. Hoses for air, oil, and fuel. There's ample storage for parts and tires.

It's as state-of-the-art as it gets and will be perfect for housing my personal cars, as well as any luxury custom jobs that come in.

I'll recommend to Luna that we store the Ford here.

I walk to the staircase on the far wall that leads up to a small loft-style apartment. Windows open to the forest behind the building, and there's even a great balcony where I can put a grill and some furniture.

The space is open, the kitchen, living, and dining spaces spilling into each other. The bedroom and bathroom are the only rooms with doors.

It's everything I could need. Hell, it's better than that.

I asked for a luxury garage with a living space, and that's exactly what I got.

I walk back outside and find John and Zeke chatting.

"Where's Sarah?" I ask.

"She walked up to see Luna," Zeke says and then gestures to the garage. "Well?"

"It's fucking amazing." I shake John's hand. "And I'm grateful that you were able to get it all done so fast, even with the stumbling blocks we had to deal with to get here."

"This is what we do," John replies. "And I'll be honest. I'm jealous of this one. Ten garage spaces? I mean, it just doesn't get much better than that. Not in a personal garage."

"You did a great job. If you ever need a testimonial, I'll be happy to give you one."

"Are you kidding?" John asks with a laugh. "From Wolfe Conrad? Of *course*, we want one. That would be great. Well, I'm driving up to Seattle today, so I'll pass it over to you. Enjoy."

He waves, hurries to his truck, and then drives away.

"This is surreal," I mutter when I turn back to the garage.

"It's fucking badass," Zeke says. "We're going to do some incredible work in there."

"Hell, yes, we are." I meet his fist with mine when he offers me a fist-bump.

"Are you moving in there?" he asks.

"Not if I can help it." I gesture to the Ford. "Let's go show Luna her shiny ride."

We climb into the classic car, and Zeke drives us up to the lighthouse. Sarah and Luna are at the gazebo, laughing.

At times, like now, when Luna's smiling and carefree, she just takes my breath away.

There's no denying it, I'm completely in love with her. Living with her over the past month has only cemented for me that she's everything I didn't know I was missing.

When the girls hear the engine, they look our way and hurry over to us.

"You've got to be kidding me," Luna breathes as she runs her hand along the hood. "Look at this *color*. It's so perfectly red."

"Zeke and I did a lot of research. That's the original paint color for this specific car. The leather, the instruments, everything is exactly how it looked when new."

"It's so cool," Sarah gushes. "I got to ride in it. It's not cushy, I'll say that, but the novelty of riding in it totally makes up for the lack of comfort."

"Yeah, they weren't made the way cars are now, with better suspension and such. But I don't think your customers will complain."

Luna shakes her head and then hurries around me so she can sit in the passenger seat.

"It's not so bad," she says with a smile. "Everything in this thing is so different. I'll have to learn how to drive it."

"There will be a slight learning curve," Zeke says. "But you'll catch on. It's not hard."

"What do I owe you for this?" she asks.

"Nothing."

She frowns and shakes her head. "No way. I know it wasn't free to get it looking like this. I can pay for it."

"Honestly, it was so much fun to do," Zeke says. "That was payment enough."

"You can't run a business if you give your services away for free," Sarah reminds us.

"No, but we can do favors for our friends," Zeke says before I can. "And this was absolutely a pleasure. Now, how am I going to get home?"

"Oh, me, too," Sarah says.

"Take the Porsche," I say and toss Zeke the fob.

"Thanks." He winks at Luna and turns to Sarah. "Shall we?"

"You bet. I'll call you later, Luna."

The two of them walk down the road leading to my place.

"Do you think something might happen there?" I ask Luna.

"No," she says, still stroking the inside of the car. "She's always had a thing for Tanner. How she ended up marrying that other piece of shit and moving away, I'll never be able to figure out."

"I haven't seen Tanner around lately," I reply.

"I think he's trying to give her space to heal," she says as I sit in the driver's seat and start the car. "Are we going for a ride?"

"I want to show you something."

I take off down the road. It's only a short ride before I turn into the new garage's driveway.

"We can park it in here."

I tap my phone screen, and the bay on the far right opens. I drive inside.

"Holy crap, is it *done*?"

"Yep, John just left. He handed it over to me. This is the first car that I'm parking inside."

"This is *amazing*," she says as she gets out of the car and looks around, trying to take it all in at once. "It's so shiny and new, Wolfe. I absolutely love it."

"I do, too. Come upstairs."

I take her hand and lead her up to the apartment, and she continues to smile.

"You already had it furnished?"

"I worked with a decorator. She did it," I reply. "I honestly didn't really care about the color scheme. I told her I just wanted it to be comfortable."

"It's like butter," she says and drags her hand over the marble countertop. "This kitchen is what dreams are made of. And look at this view!"

She wanders to the balcony and pulls open the French doors.

"Oh, Wolfe, you can have your coffee out here or a beer after a long day. You can even hear the ocean."

I walk up behind her, wrap my arms around her, and hug her tightly.

"It's a great spot," I agree as she turns in my arms and looks up at me with suddenly worried eyes. "What is it?"

"Are you moving in here?" she asks.

"Do you want me to?"

She frowns and looks at my chest. "It's a beautiful apartment. You spent a billion dollars on it, and the plan was always for you to live up here while you built another house."

"It wasn't *quite* a billion dollars, and yes, that *was* the plan."

"It'll be very comfortable for you," she says and looks around again. "I haven't seen the bathroom, but I bet it's beautiful."

"It even has a steam shower," I inform her.

She doesn't smile.

"Awesome."

I lead her back inside, close the French doors, and take her hand so I can sit on the couch with her.

"We need to talk about this, sweetheart. Yeah, in the beginning, the plan was to live up here until I built something else. But I think quite a lot has changed in the past month."

"You lost so much," she murmurs. "And you were so angry in the beginning. And you *should* be hurt. Is all of this really enough for you?"

I sigh, and look around the loft, and then back to Luna. "It hasn't been easy. And there are moments that I'm still really pissed off that I lost something that I love

169

so much. And I *do* love to drive, Luna. But I'm not giving up cars altogether. With this place and the garage in town, I'll be working with automobiles every day for the foreseeable future. Having that, while also having *you* and my friends is pretty great."

Hope springs in those gorgeous brown eyes. "Yeah, it is great. And I'm so relieved that you're healing, Wolfe. That despite the headaches, you're moving forward with your life and setting up roots here in this community. And I love having you with me at the lighthouse, don't get me wrong. But this place is spectacular and brand-new. It would be a waste to let it just sit here."

"Are you saying you want to move up here? Your house is bigger, but if you want to, we can live here."

She frowns. "I'm confused."

"There's nothing confusing about this. I want to be wherever *you* are, Luna. So, if we're at your amazing lighthouse, that's great. If we're in this smaller but newer apartment, that works for me, too. As long as I'm with you, I'm home."

"Well." She swallows hard and pushes her hands through her hair. "That was swoony."

"It's the truth. So, the question is, do *you* want me to move out?"

"I'd rather be with you, too," she says. "I just thought you might not *want* to live at my place. It's older. And, yeah, it's pretty and historical, but it's not fancy."

"Have I complained?"

"Not even once," she confirms.

"Having money doesn't mean I need fancy."

She raises a brow and looks around at my posh new garage, and I have to laugh.

"Okay, point taken. But this involves *cars*—and, yes, that means fancy. Hell, our properties together are big enough that we could build a new house just about anywhere. Or we can stay in your house. The beauty of this whole situation is...we have loads of options."

"I guess I hadn't thought of it like that." She lets out a long breath as if she's immensely relieved.

"Have you been worrying about this?"

I tug her to me and cuddle her close.

"Kind of. Yeah, okay, I have been. Because I knew they were getting close to finishing this, and I *like* having you around."

"Yeah?" I grin and lean over to kiss her cheek. "Is it my sparkling personality that you enjoy?"

"Sometimes, you're grumpy," she says and tilts her head so I have easier access to her neck.

Her *spot*.

"Me? Never." I skim my knuckles over her collarbone, down to her breast, and find that her nipple is already puckered through her shirt. "I'm just a whole ray of fucking sunshine."

She giggles and then moans when I latch my teeth onto her neck and give a little tug.

She sighs and leans into me, and I immediately stand and pull her into my arms, carrying her to the new bedroom.

"Ooh, we can try out the new mattress?"

"There's no time like the present," I agree and lay her

171

down. I hover over her and then kiss her fucking senseless.

I love how she holds onto me as if I'm a lifeline when her body is burning up.

I love the sounds she makes as my mouth travels over her soft-as-hell skin.

And I fucking *love* the way she looks at me, her eyes bright with lust as I push my hand down her pants and find her hot, wet, and ready for me.

"You take my breath away," I whisper to her.

She closes her eyes and arches her back, pushing into my hand, urging me to touch her harder, faster.

But I just kiss her jaw and slowly work her up until she's moaning and gasping my name.

"That's right," I whisper against her ear. "Go over, baby. Just *feel* what I'm doing to you, and go over."

She tightens and cries out, her hips pulsing as she falls over that glorious edge and into absolute ecstasy.

When she surfaces, she pushes on my shoulder and urges me onto my back.

"My turn," she says and shoves my shirt up my torso, then makes fast work of my jeans, nudging them down my hips.

She takes me in her hand, and just when I think I'm going to lose my fucking mind, Luna smiles sweetly and licks around the head of my dick in satisfaction.

"Mm," she says before sinking over me, pulling me all the way into her mouth.

I'm pretty sure my head is about to explode.

Chapter Twelve

Luna

Few things are as exciting as watching Wolfe become aroused and feeling him harden in my mouth.

It's damn powerful.

His hands sink into my hair and fist, not pulling hard but tugging with just the right force to make my already pulsing core tighten in anticipation.

I've never been this aggressive when it comes to sex. This *confident*. But with Wolfe, I'm not afraid to be assertive and tell him what I want.

Take what I want.

Just as his hips move, and Wolfe groans long and deep with satisfaction, a loud pounding sounds on the door downstairs.

"Motherfucking Jesus Christ," he growls in frustration.

"I don't think those words go together," I mutter as I

look up at him. We pause, staring at each other, his dick still firmly in my grasp.

"Be quiet, and they'll go away," he whispers.

I bite my lip, and Wolfe's eyes narrow.

"You're the sexiest woman I've ever met in my life, Luna Winchester."

I grin, but the pounding on the door starts up again, and I shrug in apology. "They're not leaving."

He rolls to the side of the bed and stands to pull his jeans up over his hips, tucking himself away, his mouth set in a grim line. I can't help but grin as I put my clothes to rights and follow him.

"Unless someone is bleeding or dead," he grumbles as we pad down the steps, "they can just fuck right off."

Wolfe flings open the door to find June, a scowl on her pretty face, and her fist raised to pound again.

"Took you long enough," she says and then takes in our appearances. "Ew. Why? *Why* am I always privy to your pervy ways?"

"What do you want, June?" Wolfe asks and leans on the doorframe, not inviting her inside. "And make it good because you interrupted something *damn* good."

"I don't even care," she says and raises her chin, then looks at me over his shoulder. "Would you *please* get up here and calm your ghost down?"

"What?"

"Rose will *not* shut up."

"She's talking to you?"

"She's slamming things. Moving things. Pounding on the walls. She's just being super needy, and I don't have time for this, Luna. Not to mention, it's freaking my people out. One walked out and said they wouldn't come back while Rose is around. I can't say I blame him."

"Well, that's weird. She never does stuff like that."

"I told everyone to take their breaks. Sent them into town for pizza and then came to get you. This is the weirdest request I've ever made, but will you *please* come and calm down your ghost?"

Wolfe raises a brow at me, and I can only shrug.

"Yeah, I'll come check it out. Let's go."

We snag our shoes, and the three of us walk up the road to my property.

It's a pretty fall day with the leaves turning yellow and orange on the trees and the heavy scent of the ocean in the air. It rained all last week, so having a couple of days of sunshine is a welcome break from the gloomy weather.

"I wonder what has Rose all stirred up," I muse aloud as we come around the bend and see the lighthouse, my home, and the barn. And just as we start to walk across the grass that leads to the soon-to-be B&B, the roof caves in on the front right-side corner of the building.

We stop in our tracks, stunned. I can't believe what I'm seeing.

"What in the actual fuck?" Wolfe says as I immediately reach for June's hand.

"You know for sure that everyone's out of there?" I demand.

"Yeah." She swallows hard, her green eyes wide and gaze stuck on the barn. "Yeah, they all left. Holy shit."

"Stay here," Wolfe instructs before jogging over. From the big doorway, he peers inside.

"I was working right in that exact spot," June says, shaking her head in disbelief as she pulls her cap off and pushes her hand through her red hair. "My God, Luna, I thought Rose was just being a drama queen, trying to get attention. But she *saved* me. She freaking saved my crew."

"I figured it had to be something. I've never known Rose to freak out like that," I say, feeling my stomach roil at the possibility of what could have happened in there. "She slams a door here and there, sure, but nothing like you explained."

"Now we know that when Rose has a meltdown, we should listen."

A light breeze blows over us, and I suddenly smell roses in the air.

"Thanks, Rose," I whisper. "How far back do you think this will put us?" I ask June.

Her mouth opens and closes, and I feel like a big jerk.

"Don't answer that." I lean my head on her shoulder. "I'm sorry, that was an asshole thing to say. The important thing is that everyone is okay. There hasn't been an inn here for over a hundred years. A few extra weeks or even months won't matter. Just ignore me."

"You're not an asshole," she whispers and rests her cheek on the top of my head. "I think this is the first time in my life that I've been happy about a ghost."

"Me, too."

Wolfe is shaking his head and rubbing his fingertips against his forehead as he walks back to us.

"It's definitely not safe in there," he says and huffs out a breath. "Looks like a ceiling beam gave out."

"We haven't replaced them yet," June says. "I didn't think the old ones were so rotten they'd give way. They were just...*old*. Shit, I'm sorry, Luna. I'll cover the cost of this."

"Hey, this isn't your fault," I insist. "I'm just so relieved that you're safe. We'll figure the rest out."

"Look," Wolfe says, pointing to the upper window of the barn on the left, where the roof is still intact.

"I see her," I whisper.

A woman looks down at us through the window. She looks *sad*. She's in an old-fashioned dress and has her dark hair pulled back from her face.

"Whoa," June breathes. "We've never *seen* her before."

"Not like that. Um, June? Is there even a floor right there?"

"Nope."

"So, she's a floating ghost," Wolfe says with a nod. "Good to know."

"I think they can go wherever they want," I say.

"How do you know?" June demands.

All I can do is shrug, and then Rose drifts away, leaving the window empty.

"I need liquor," June decides. "And food. But first, alcohol. I think I'll go meet the others at Lighthouse Pizza. Do you guys want to join us?"

"I could eat," Wolfe says, surprising me. I thought for sure he'd decline and take me back to the garage to finish what we started earlier.

But June's upset, and he knows she needs us.

And if that doesn't make a girl fall in love, I don't know what would.

"I'll call Sarah," I announce and reach for my phone. "Let's get the whole gang there and blow off some steam."

"Thanks," June says with a sigh. "Thank you."

"You never have to thank me when pizza is involved," I reply.

With June settled in at home, happily drunk and ready to go to sleep, I'm in my living room, kneeling next to Rose's trunk. Wolfe's still out with Apollo, Tanner, and Zeke. Sarah and I took June home, and then Sarah wanted to go back to her apartment to paint, so I headed to the lighthouse alone.

It was the perfect time for me to come and spend some time with Rose. She's been on my mind so much since the barn caved in this afternoon.

She saved my best friend's life.

Is it possible to thank someone who's been dead for more than eighty years?

Since we found all of Rose's belongings in the barn loft, I've read through a good bit of the diary, but I haven't had the chance to really examine everything in the trunk.

Honestly, I've been nervous.

"I don't want to hurt anything in here," I say and sit back on my heels. "At a hundred years old, this stuff has to be fragile."

I brush my fingers over the bouquet of dried flowers, relieved when they don't crumble.

I *very* carefully move them onto the sheet pan I lined with parchment paper and carry them into the kitchen.

They'll be safer on the counter where I can't accidentally sit on or drop them.

That would be my luck.

The trunk is a treasure trove. I find a dress—a beautiful red gown with black gloves and black shoes that Rose must have worn to a formal event. There is even a gorgeous hairpin made of rhinestones and black feathers.

"I'll definitely save this for later. Maybe I can wear it to something someday."

I systematically take every piece out of the trunk, lay it all on the floor, and then take a deep breath and look around at everything.

There's a photo album that I can't wait to dig into. There is a large envelope full of papers that look official. Maybe the deed to the land and lighthouse is in there. That would be awesome. We have a more recent deed, but the original one from the 1860s when the land was purchased has been lost over time.

There's a jewelry box that has some really beautiful pieces inside, at least from the quick look I take, not wanting to get too stuck on any one thing and not make my way through the whole trunk.

"I can take some of the pieces to Mr. Hart to see if anything is real or if it's costume jewelry."

Hart Jewelers has been a staple in Huckleberry Bay for many years.

There are newspapers that announce the end of World War I.

And, in the very bottom of the massive trunk, I find a loose photo.

"Well, isn't he handsome?" I murmur and flip it over, hopeful that someone wrote the man's name on the back.

D.P. 1870.

I blink and then quickly flip it back around, crawling over to hold the photo under the light of my lamp so I can see it even better.

"So, *you're* DP," I mutter. "You were a hottie, sir. I see what Rose saw in you for sure."

The young man, likely in his mid-twenties, is dressed in a suit and posing for the photo.

"I wish it was just a *little* clearer," I whisper. "Of course, cameras were a bit different than they are now."

Okay, that's an understatement.

I set the photo aside, excited to show it to June and Sarah later, and just as I'm about to carefully pack everything back inside the trunk since I have nowhere else to put this stuff, there's a knock on the front door.

"Come on in," I call out and smile when Apollo opens the door, then pauses when he sees the mess.

"Is this a bad time?"

"No, I was just looking through Rose's things. You

should go through this stuff with me, you know. She's your ancestor, too."

"I'd rather eat glass," he says cheerfully. "I'm glad you're fascinated by this stuff because I have zero interest."

"But it's so *interesting*."

"Like I said, I'm glad you think so."

"I found some clothes and jewelry. If it's worth a lot of money, I'll totally share it with you."

He just blinks at me, and I shrug.

"Sorry, that's not why you're here. Why *are* you here? And where are the other guys?"

"Tanner and Wolfe were still playing pool when I left. None of us drank much...well, except for June. But it was fun to let off some steam. Wolfe's good at the darts, but Tanner's kicking his ass at pool, and Wolfe's too stubborn to call it a night."

"I'm glad they're having fun." I grin and gently lay the dress back inside the trunk, then close the lid. I keep the photo album out so I can look through it with a cup of tea later. "What's on your mind?"

"Maybe I just wanted to come hang out with my sister for a while."

I grin and reach over to ruffle my brother's hair. "That's nice. It's a lie, but it's nice."

Apollo smirks, and then his expression sobers. I feel the first pang of concern.

"Talk to me."

"I don't want you to freak out."

"I can't promise that."

He blows out a breath and rubs his hands together as if he's suddenly nervous.

"Jesus, Apollo, what did you do? Rob a bank?"

"No." He smiles softly and then shrugs one shoulder. "I've had some medical stuff going on, and I didn't think I should keep it from you anymore."

"What do you mean, *medical stuff*?"

"I was having...symptoms. And before you ask what kind, it's the kind your sister doesn't want to know about. Anyway, I saw my primary doctor, and now they've referred me to a urologist. They might have used the C-word as a possibility."

"The C-word. As in...*cancer*?"

"It's highly unlikely, Luna."

"Cancer." I shake my head and pace the living room. My heart is pounding, and I suddenly feel as if I might throw up. "Hell, no. No way. You're *thirty-five*, Apollo."

"I've not been given a diagnosis," he insists. "It's just something to rule out. I have to get an ultrasound and talk with the specialist."

"Apollo, *Dad* had testicular cancer."

"I know," he says softly. "But he's fine now. He did great."

"Obviously, we remember this differently," I reply and prop my hands on my hips. "I remember Dad being so damn sick from chemo and radiation."

"But he's fine *now*," he stresses. "Even if that's what's going on here, which I think is unlikely, it's very early, and there's every reason to believe that I'll be fine."

"Why?" I shake my head and feel the tears coming. He doesn't want me to freak out? Of course, I'm going to freak the hell out. "This isn't fair. Why does shit like this happen to good people? To the *best* people. You wouldn't hurt a fly."

"I might hurt a *fly*."

"You're kind and sweet, and you're *mine*. If something happens to you, I'll be so mad at you, Apollo Winchester."

"Nothing's happening," he assures me and crosses over to pull me into his arms, hugging me close.

"What if they have to take out your...you know, your balls? And the future woman you love only wants a man who can give her children."

I feel him smile against my head.

"Now you're taking this a bit too far, Luna."

"It could happen," I insist and feel fear take up residence in my throat, almost choking me. "What if you can't have babies?"

"Maybe I don't want kids."

I jerk back and stare up at him in horror. "You don't want to make me an aunt? What did I ever do to you?"

He laughs and tugs on my hair. "I'm not scared, Luna. No one has given me a reason to worry or be afraid, but I didn't want to start going to specialists and stuff without giving you the heads-up."

"Yeah, that's a good call because you wouldn't have to worry about being able to have children if I found out you were keeping something like this from me. I'd just kill you."

"Have you always been so violent, or is that something new that's come to light as you got old?"

"Hey, who are you calling old? You're *way* older than me."

"Three years is not *way* older."

"It is when you're on this side of the three years," I reply with a grin, trying not to show him how fucking terrified I am.

I remember what Dad went through all too well, and I don't want that for my brother.

I wouldn't wish that on anyone.

"Do me a favor, okay?"

I frown at him. "Sure. What's that?"

"Let's keep this between us for now. I know you'll want to talk to Wolfe and the other two amigos, but until I've seen the doctor later this week and I know what I'm dealing with, let's just keep it between us."

"Yeah, of course."

He wants me to keep *this* a secret? How am I supposed to properly freak the hell out if I can't confide in June and Sarah? In Wolfe.

Am I just supposed to stew over this news for a whole week? By *myself*?

"You look...too calm," he decides.

"I'm perfectly calm."

I tap my right foot, and Apollo notices and smiles. "That's your tell when you're lying. You know that, right?"

"Okay, I'm freaking out. But that doesn't help you." I

blink furiously as the tears want to spill over. "You're my brother, and I actually *like* you. I know that's rare, okay? Sure, June likes her sibs. Cullen and Lauren are awesome. But more often than not people can't stand their family, and I love you so much, and what if you die?"

"I think I liked it better when you were pretending to be calm."

I can't help but laugh as I brush the tears aside.

"I'm not going to die. Well, I will someday, but not from this. Not anytime soon. You're stuck with me for a very long time."

"Good, because no one else annoys me the way you do."

He just laughs and plops down in my chair, dragging his hand down his face.

"Have you called Mom and Dad?" I ask him.

"Nah." He shakes his head at my stony stare. "There's no need to worry them when there's *nothing* to worry about right now. If it turns out to be something, of course, I'll call them. If it's nothing, like I know it will be, there's no need to sound a false alarm."

"You're probably right," I reply. "They'd get on the first flight home."

"There's no need for that either," he says. "We'll see them at Christmas."

I nod as the door opens. Wolfe walks in and then stops, looking between the two of us.

"Did I interrupt?"

"Nope," Apollo replies. "I was just about to leave

anyway. It was fun hanging out tonight. We need to do it more often."

"I'm in," Wolfe says, but his eyes don't leave mine as Apollo hugs me and kisses my forehead.

"I'll call you on Friday," Apollo says and then leaves, closing the door behind him.

"Everything okay?" Wolfe asks.

"Sure."

No. No, it won't be okay until a doctor tells my brother that he doesn't have cancer. Why did I promise that I wouldn't tell Wolfe?

That was not my smartest move.

"Did you guys have fun?" I ask, pasting a bright smile on my face.

"Yeah." He narrows his eyes on me again, and I almost break.

I'm *so* not good at secrets.

"Yeah, we had fun. What did you do this evening?"

"Me?" I look around the living room, trying to remember. "Oh, I just looked through Rose's trunk. There's some cool stuff in there. I think this is the guy she was in love with when she was younger."

I show him the photo. He glances at it, but I can tell his heart's not in it.

He wants to know what's going on with me.

And I'm not allowed to tell him.

FEBRUARY 12, 2003

DEAR DIARY,

LIFE FUCKING SUCKS SOMETIMES. I HATE WATCHING MY DAD STRUGGLE SO MUCH WITH BEING SICK FROM CHEMO. HE JUST LOOKS HORRIBLE, AND I KNOW HE FEELS WORSE, EVEN THOUGH HE TRIES TO SMILE AND PRETEND LIKE HE'S FINE.

HE'S NOT OKAY.

NOT TODAY, ANYWAY.

BUT HE WILL BE. BECAUSE THERE'S NO WAY I'M GOING TO THINK ABOUT THE WHAT-IFS OF WHAT COULD HAPPEN IF THE CHEMO DOESN'T WORK.

IT HAS TO WORK.

LOVE,

LUNA

Chapter Thirteen

Wolfe

I wish she would talk to me. For three days, since I walked in on a conversation between Luna and her brother, she has been acting...differently.

She's moody. Irritable. When I simply asked her this morning if she'd like me to empty the dishwasher, she snapped and bit my head off.

And then quickly apologized.

I have a full day of work at the garage with Zeke today, but I won't leave this house until I figure out what's going on with my girl.

"Hey," I say as I walk into the living room where she's curled in a chair, looking through that old photo album. She glances up and wipes a tear off her cheek. "Okay, that's it. I need you to talk to me, sweetheart. You haven't been yourself, and no matter how much you tell me that it's nothing, I know it's *something*."

She sniffles and reaches for a tissue, then blows her nose and sighs.

"I'm fine."

I want to lose my shit. Instead, I simply pick Luna up right out of that chair, sit down, and settle her on my lap.

"Baby, you're not fine." I wipe a tear off her smooth cheek. "And I can't express to you how much I hate seeing you cry. Do I have to beat someone up? Did you read something sad in Rose's diary? What is going on with you? Maybe you want me to move out?"

"No," she says quickly and buries her face in the crook of my neck. "No, I don't want you to go. I know I've been testy and overemotional, and I'm sorry. It has absolutely nothing at all to do with you. You're wonderful."

I feel my lips tip up with relief. For a brief moment this morning, I had convinced myself that she had changed her mind about *us*.

It was a bad moment.

"Tell me what's on your mind." It's not a request, nor is it a plea. Still, she shakes her head.

"I can't."

"Why?"

"Because." She sniffs, and then her shoulders shake as the dam bursts, and she starts sobbing against me.

Her absolute devastation breaks my heart into a million pieces.

"Shh, it's okay," I soothe, rubbing my hand up and down her back. I kiss her head and murmur to her. I don't know what else to do as she clings to me and cries it out.

"I'm sorry," she whispers when it seems the worst of it is over.

I pass her a handful of tissues and kiss her forehead.

"There's no need to be sorry."

"I w-w-want to tell you," she says as she wipes at her face. "But I promised my brother that I wouldn't say anything to *anyone*."

"So, it's about Apollo?"

She nods and lets out a little cry of despair.

"Okay. I get it, Luna. It's perfectly fine with me that you need to keep your brother's secret, but it kills me that it's torn you up like this."

"I don't mean to take it out on you." She finally takes a long, deep breath. "I know I've been short and bitchy the past few days, and I hate myself for it."

"Stop beating yourself up, babe." I take a clean tissue and swipe under her gorgeous brown eyes that are now rimmed in red from so many tears. "I'm a big boy, and I can deal. I'm just not good with secrets."

"I'm not either!" She shakes her head. "I *hate* them. I mean, I'm not talking about the small ones that you keep between your girlfriends and stuff like that. But these *big* secrets? I can't handle it. But Apollo asked me not to say anything to anyone, and I agreed. Why did I agree to that?"

"Because you love your brother."

"Yeah." She sniffs, and the tears threaten again. "I really do."

"Hey, no more tears." I pull her in for a quick kiss. "It's okay, Luna. Everything's going to work out and be just fine."

"I don't think I realized until you said that how much I needed to hear it."

"In the future, if you have something that you can't tell me, just say so. I won't try to drag it out of you. But we all need *this*. Someone to assure us that it'll work out."

"Yeah. Yeah, we do." She tips her head to the side, studying me. "Who does that for you?"

Before the accident? I would have said that I didn't need it.

But now... "You."

A smile spreads across her face, and she leans in to kiss me. "I don't think I've ever said those words to you."

"You've shown me," I reply, enjoying her. "You take care of me when the headaches hit. You supported me through the garage build. You're *here*. You don't always have to say the words."

"You're good for me," she whispers and tips her forehead against mine.

"And you're everything good about my life," I reply, meaning every word. "Do you feel any better?"

"A lot better," she confirms. "And the second I'm able, I'll tell you everything."

"That's all I can ask."

* * *

"I need caffeine," I say to Zeke several hours later. "I'm going to walk down to The Grind and grab a coffee. You want anything?"

"Yeah, the usual. And if they have any of those chicken salad sandwiches, snag a couple."

"Be back in a few," I reply with a nod and walk out

the door. The Grind has the best coffee in town, and it's just around the corner from my garage on Main Street and across from the bookstore. The outside seating is spectacular with a deck and a view of the Pacific.

It's a hotspot in Huckleberry Bay, but it's not too busy today when I walk inside. About half of the tables are taken, some with laptops, others with new books from across the street.

And up at the counter stands Apollo Winchester.

"Well, hey there," he says when he sees me. We shake hands. "How's it going at the garage today?"

"We're muddling through," I reply and turn to Daisy to order. "Zeke wants his usual, and I'll have mine, too. Oh, and three chicken salad sandwiches."

"You got it, handsome," Daisy says with a wink. She's the owner of The Grind and flirts with everyone, male or female, young and old. The customers adore her. "I'll throw in some cookies, too. Ava, grab some Oregon Trail cookies, will you, hon?"

Daisy and her crew get to work on our orders, and Apollo and I chat about nothing particularly important until I finally just say, "I'm confused."

Apollo blinks at me. "About what?"

I rub my hand over my mouth and then take my order when my name is called. Apollo walks with me to a nearby table where we sit across from each other.

Luna's brother is a tall man, lean and well-built from years of working construction and now as an electrician. He has the same dark hair and eyes as his sister, but their personalities are very different.

Where Luna is organized and sweet, Apollo is goofy and tends to live minute by minute. They couldn't be more different. But the bond between them has always been strong.

"What's up?" he asks.

"I want to ask you the same question," I say. "Your sister has been a wreck for the last few days and won't tell me why. I get that it's none of my business, she just says that she's worried about you. But you seem...*fine*. You're acting completely normal, so I'm a little thrown off balance."

Apollo sighs and takes a sip of his latte. "I'm sorry she's been upset. Listen, I have some medical stuff happening, and I thought I should tell her about it. I actually find out tomorrow how serious it all is. So, for now, yeah, I'm fine. Like I told her, there has been no reason *not* to be fine."

"Except that the people who love you worry," I reply simply. "If the tables were turned—"

"I get it," he interrupts. "And I apologize. Like I said, I'll know far more tomorrow. I expect it to be good news."

"I'll be hoping for that, too. She kept your secret, by the way. Wouldn't say a word about what was bothering her."

"She's probably bursting at the seams," he mutters. "My sister is great at a lot of things, but keeping secrets isn't one of them. It's *not* a secret, though, really. I just asked her to keep it between us until I know more."

"It's killing her, but she's as good as her word," I

reply. "And I'll be hoping for the best. If you need anything, let us know."

"Thanks. And I just have to say, thank you for being so good for her."

Luna's words from this morning echo in my mind.

You're good for me.

"I know I came on a little strong when you first started things with her," he continues, "but she's my sister. And you're—"

"I get it," I assure him. "I totally get it. I'm not going anywhere. Not now or ever. I've set down roots here, and I'm happy in Huckleberry Bay. I'm happy at the lighthouse."

"Good," he says. "You did a damn fine job on that old car from the barn, by the way."

"It was sincerely our pleasure. I'm just glad we got it out of there before the roof caved in. As it is, it barely missed June."

Apollo stops cold and narrows his eyes at me. "What?"

"You know that June was there. That's why we all went out the other night."

"I knew she was *there,* but I didn't know she was inside the fucking building."

"She wasn't inside," I reply, shaking my head. "Because Rose warned her—if you believe that sort of thing. And I hate to admit it, but I'm starting to. She was safely outside, but she'd been working in that corner all morning."

Apollo frowns down at the table.

"What's going on between you two, man?"

"Nothing," he says and raps his knuckles on the table-top. "There's nothing there."

I simply raise my eyebrows, but he doesn't say anything else about it.

"I'd better get back to work," he says, no longer his happy-go-lucky self.

He's not upset by his personal worries, but the idea that June might have been hurt seems to have hit a nerve.

Interesting.

"I'd better get these sandwiches back to Zeke before he sends out a search party."

"I'll be in touch," Apollo says as we walk out of the café and go our separate ways. When I get back to the garage, Zeke is getting his ass handed to him by an eighty-year-old woman.

"I *know* what you people do to old ladies like me," she says, wagging her finger in front of Zeke's face. "You take us to the cleaners, that's what!"

"No, ma'am," Zeke says, shaking his head. "Forty dollars isn't a bad price for an oil change, and I threw in the new filter for free."

"Well, hello, Mrs. Snow," I say with a wide smile. June's grandmother is maybe the brightest character in our town. With her colorful wardrobe, pink hair teased into an old-fashioned beehive, and bright red glasses on her face, she looks like she belongs in a cartoon.

But she's real, and right now, she's mad at Zeke.

"How are you?" I ask her, catching her attention.

"Well, now, aren't you a handsome one, Wolfe Conrad?"

"What am I, chopped liver?" Zeke asks.

"You'd be more attractive if you weren't trying to pull one over on me, *Zeke*. If that is, in fact, your real name."

"That's his real name," I assure her. "I don't think forty dollars is too expensive for a good oil change, Mrs. Snow."

"Are you kidding me?" She stares at me as if I've lost my mind. "Why, back in 1965, I paid all of three dollars and fifty cents. And right here at this very garage."

"You weren't even alive in 1965."

She narrows her eyes at me. "I had my own children by then, thank you very much. Now, what are you going to do about this Zeke guy price-gouging me?"

"Well, we're far out of the sixties, Mrs. Snow. But how about this? I'll mark it on your account in the computer that for every five oil changes you pay for, you get the next one free."

She purses her lips, thinking it over, and then nods. "I suppose that's as good as I'm going to get. I'm telling you, this is the fleecing of America. We have to drive cars, and those cars need oil."

"You should write to your congressman," Zeke says.

"Don't you get smart with me, young man." She glares at Zeke, then takes her keys and wanders out to her car, a brand-new Buick, and drives away.

"Well, she's a delight," Zeke says, his voice heavy with sarcasm.

"She's not so bad," I reply and pass him his coffee and sandwiches.

"Do you think she'll be mad when she finds out that we give that same deal to all our customers?"

I grin, shrug, and drink my coffee. "Who's gonna tell her?"

* * *

"I'm going to blindfold you," I announce and watch as Luna's eyebrows climb into her hairline in surprise.

"I didn't realize you were into that sort of thing. But, okay, if you insist."

"Not like that, smartass, although that might be something to play with later. I'm going to blindfold you as I lead you outside. I have something for you."

"Is it a new car?"

I blink. "Uh, no. I didn't realize you were in the market for one. I'll happily buy you any car you want. You know that's my thing."

"No, sorry." She shakes her head and laughs. "That was a bad joke. My vehicle is just fine."

"Well, it runs, anyway."

"Not all of us need a fancy ride, Mr. Conrad."

"I disagree. But stop changing the subject and come here."

She complies and smiles as I tie the black silk fabric over her eyes. "Can you see?"

"Nope."

"No peeking."

"I'm not, but you'd better hold my hand, or I'll fall on my face."

"I've got you, babe." I take her hand in mine and guide her out the front door, down the steps of the porch, and over to the gazebo. It's a fantastic sunset tonight, and I brought home some of her favorite things to help cheer her up.

Once I have her seated at the picnic table, I take off the blindfold and grin as she looks around, her eyes going wide.

"Holy crap, there must be a hundred candles lit," she says and then launches herself into my arms. "This is so romantic."

"I thought you could use a pick-me-up." I kiss her, drag my hands down her sides, and then gesture to the table. "Dinner isn't fancy, it's pizza."

"Pizza." She sighs and sits, eyeing the box as she might a lover. "I *love* pizza, and I try not to eat it often. This makes twice in one week."

"That's okay. I brought fruit, as well."

She glances around, frowning. "Where?"

I hold up a wine bottle. "Grapes."

Luna giggles as I pour her a glass, and then she taps hers to mine.

"This is so nice," she says as I open the box of pizza. "And you brought me more yellow roses."

"They remind me of you." I offer her a slice and then plate mine before securing the box lid. "They're happy. Cheerful."

"I haven't felt happy *or* cheerful this week."

"I know. I thought maybe this would help."

"It does." She chews and looks around at all the candles. "Wait, these are the flameless kind."

"I didn't want to burn anything down. After the barn incident, I wasn't taking any chances."

She smiles, then nods in agreement. "Good call on that one. I thought I'd put candles like these in all the guest rooms of the B&B to offer the romantic candlelight but also to avoid any fire hazards."

"You can keep these for it," I offer.

"But they're expensive, and this is a *lot*."

I just sip my wine, watching her. "Trust me, it's fine. You'll put them to good use, and I'll know where I can borrow some from time to time."

She smiles. "Thanks. Thank you for all of this."

I take her hand in mine, and we watch as the sun slips into the water to the west. Birds dip and dive in the wind, and we can hear the waves crashing on the rocks below.

"It's a special spot," I say, breaking the silence. "I lived on the water in Monaco, and it was beautiful."

"I can only imagine."

"No, I'll take you there one day. It's something I want to share with you. It's beautiful in its own way, but this... it's just so dramatic. Moody. And when I'm up here, a calmness just settles into my chest. It wasn't always that way. I couldn't wait to leave when I graduated. To see the world. I loved going at top speed and didn't plan to ever slow down.

"If the accident hadn't happened, I likely wouldn't have. I would have left as planned and gone back to my life. I don't think I would have even given Huckleberry Bay a glance in the rearview mirror on my way out of town."

Luna squeezes my hand, letting me talk.

"I *loved* my life, Luna. The money, the cars. And, yeah, the women—please don't take that the wrong way."

"I'm not," she says, and I can see by the calmness in her eyes that she means it.

"I had no intention of slowing down. But now, with so much changing in my life over the past six months or so, I can't imagine going back to that. It was exhausting, and there was so much pressure in every area of my life. To drive faster, better, cleaner. To make more money. To win. Always, to win."

"And you did. A lot," she reminds me.

"Did you watch?" I ask, surprised.

"Sometimes. If I knew it would be televised here, I'd watch. You were so...*sure.* Calm and confident. And maybe a little arrogant. You're still those things."

"If you're not, you don't win. It's part of the sport."

"I see that. But you're not an ass with it, you know? You're kind. You know you're good, but you don't shove it in anyone's face. Hell, you could buy and sell this whole town, but you're respectful and nice."

"Having a lot of money doesn't make someone better than anyone else," I reply. "It's convenient. Trust me, I've been poor, and I've been wealthy, and I don't plan to go back to poor. But being well-off has its own host of issues. It's just money."

"That's exactly something a wealthy person would say."

"But it's true." I look down at her and feel the punch in the chest that hits me whenever I look at her. I'd spend every last dime to keep her safe and happy. "People enrich a life. Relationships are what make a person rich. Money? Like I said, it's convenient, but it doesn't buy what you have here. The tradition, the passion, and the happiness that this property brings you."

I gesture around us.

"It took generations of hard work to build this. And, well, I think it was an act of God to make the cliffs and the ocean. I've never been particularly religious, but I don't think this is random."

"I don't either," she agrees.

"This got really serious," I say at last and kiss Luna's forehead. "Maybe we should clean this up and go inside."

"Let's take the pizza and wine in," she suggests, standing. "We can clean up the rest later."

She reaches for the black tie and waggles her eyebrows.

"You don't have to ask me twice."

Chapter Fourteen

Luna

"It's your fault." I crook my finger at Wolfe as he closes the front door behind him and sets the pizza and wine on the kitchen counter. "You're the one who brought up the whole blindfold thing."

"I had no idea it would get this kind of response." He slowly walks toward me as if he's stalking his prey. And trust me when I say I'm perfectly *delighted* to be this man's target.

Bring. It. On.

As he slowly walks toward me, I move backward in the direction of my bedroom, keeping just out of his reach.

And when he extends his hand, I turn and run for the door, excitement and *fun* coursing through me.

Before I reach the bed, Wolfe picks me up from behind and lays me down on the mattress, then quickly covers me so he has me trapped under his long, lean body.

202

"You think you can run away from me?" he asks as he drags his nose up the side of my neck. He's teasing me, and I absolutely *love* it.

"I like playing with you," I breathe and arch my neck when he grips my skin in his teeth. "It's fun."

"Hmm." He takes the tie out of my hand, but he doesn't place it over my eyes. "I'm not going to blindfold you because I want to see your eyes when I do to you what I have planned."

I feel those eyes widen.

"But I do want to tie your hands to the headboard. Is that okay?"

"Hell, yes, it's okay."

He snickers and then has to rest his forehead on my shoulder as he laughs. "Why didn't I know that you have a kinky side?"

"You never asked. And besides, I didn't know either. It's not *that* kinky."

His eyes narrow on me now. "And what would you consider *more* kinky?"

"Oh, you know, whips and toys and people watching. That sort of thing."

He finishes tying my hands above me. It's not so tight that I can't move, but I can't pull them away.

And then he plants his lips just under my ear and whispers, "No one's ever going to watch us, sweetheart. No one. I'm way too possessive of you, in every way, to *ever* share you like that."

"Good." I have to swallow hard. "Same goes."

"But if you want to play with other stuff, we can

explore those things. Together. But for today, bondage it is."

I grin in anticipation and bite my lower lip as Wolfe works my jeans down my legs and then does the same with my panties.

But before he tosses them onto the floor, he *smells them*. Then throws them over his shoulder.

"You liked that."

I don't say anything as he pushes my shirt up under my chin and unfastens my bra. I'm lying mostly bare before him, and he eats me alive with his gaze.

Wolfe Conrad wants me. That's not something I ever have to wonder about.

"You undo me," he says softly, dragging his hands down my torso to my hips. "You're gorgeous, in *every* way. Even when you're biting my head off over the dishwasher."

"Sorry." I cringe, but he just shakes his head and chuckles.

"No. Even when you're frustrated or sad or worried, you're so damn beautiful, Luna. I can't take my eyes off you, and when you're like this?"

He clicks his tongue and shakes his head, taking me in from head to toe.

"You take my fucking breath away."

He kisses me then, hard and long, his hand on my throat as his mouth makes love to mine. Instinctively, I move my arms to touch him, but all I manage is to pull against the restraints.

He grins down at me. "You're stuck."

"I want to touch you."

"Give me just a little time," he says and presses gentle kisses to my cheek, my neck, my chest. "But if it's too much, at any point, just say so, and you'll be free. I promise."

His gaze latches to mine with that vow, and I nod in agreement.

Hell, I'd do *anything* for this man.

"Just enjoy," he suggests as he nibbles around my navel, sending fresh goose bumps over my body. "Because I'm sure as hell enjoying *you*."

I let my eyes slide closed, and for what feels like *forever*, Wolfe takes his time, kissing and licking, touching and tasting his way over my body. It's as if he has all the time in the world, and I'm his only focus.

Feeling like I'm the center of his universe is like a drug.

He licks the inside of my thigh, and I sigh.

He kisses behind my knee, and I moan.

And when he brushes his fingers up and then pushes them into my core, he growls in satisfaction. I can't help but arch my back and move my hips.

"Goddamn, you're always ready for me," he mutters. I open my eyes and find him stripping off his clothes as if he can't get out of them fast enough. Finally free of anything separating us, he plants his hands on my ass and lifts me to meet his mouth. And then he freaking *feasts* on me.

I don't just fall over the edge into bliss. I fucking *explode*. There's no sweet buildup; there's only fire.

I feel Wolfe tug on the restraints.

"Touch me," he says with a rough voice. I open my eyes again to find him covering my body with his, his eyes hot with lust and need, and his jaw clenched as he positions himself between my legs and slides right inside of me. "Ah, damn."

"Yes." I loop my arms around his neck, pulling him closer. "God, I love feeling your weight on me. I love feeling *you* on me. Inside me."

He's everywhere, and yet it's as though he's not close enough.

I grab his ass, bringing him closer, and with his eyes on mine, he sets a delicious pace that has us both gasping for air. When I can't hold back any longer and contract around him, he follows me into oblivion.

Later, after we've had more pizza and wine and are curled up by the fireplace, Wolfe kisses my head.

"You're everything I didn't know I was missing," he whispers.

"I'm glad you found me," I reply and smile when he simply kisses me once more. And in that exact moment, I know without a shadow of a doubt that I'm irrevocably in love with this man.

* * *

"You were a little vague in your text when you invited us over here," June says as she leads me into Sarah's apartment. The enticing smell of tacos immediately hits, and I grin.

"Did you *cook?*"

"I'm good at it," Sarah confirms with a smile. She's wearing a white apron covered in little red cherries, her blond hair is up in a haphazard ponytail, and her cheeks are flushed from the heat of the stove. "Come in, you guys. I made tacos and homemade pico and guacamole to go with the chips. I also have copious amounts of tequila."

"This is my kind of party," I say as I set my purse on a table by the door and cross to the countertop that separates the kitchen from the living room. "What's the occasion?"

"Divorce." Sarah smiles brightly as she reaches for a manila envelope and holds it high. "The papers arrived this afternoon. All I have to do is sign them, and then I'm free. I can get on with my life."

"Wow." June stares at the envelope and then at Sarah. "Should you have an attorney look those over? Anthony might be trying to pull something over on you."

"I already did," Sarah assures her. "There wasn't much to surprise me with since I signed the prenup all those years ago. I get squat. But you know what? I don't want anything from him. I'm doing just fine on my own."

"Honey, you're doing better than *fine*," I remind her and reach for a chip. "You're kicking ass."

"Thanks. I think so, too. And I have my two best friends here with me to celebrate."

"We're having a divorce party," June says with a grin. "I like it."

"Meow."

We look down at a cat, who just came walking

around the corner. It's a *big* tabby with bi-colored eyes and half of an ear on one side. Its whiskers are crinkled in spots, making it look as if it went four rounds with the champ.

"Oh, that's Petunia," Sarah says brightly. "I rescued her from the shelter the other day. Wolfe didn't have a problem with it, and she just *needs* me, you know? And I need her, too."

"She's..." June tips her head to the side. "A cat."

"Hello, darling." I crouch next to her and reach out to pet her. Petunia immediately butts my hand with her head and starts purring in cat ecstasy. "She looks a little rough around the edges. Like she's seen a *lot* of life. But it's clear she just wants love."

"She's me," Sarah says quietly and pours the taco meat into a bowl. "And now, she has a safe place to live, also like me."

"Sarah," June says and hurries around the counter to loop an arm around our friend's shoulders. "We've got your back."

"Even Petunia's?"

"I'm not really a cat person," June begins but then softens when Petunia ribbons her way between June's legs before coming back to me. "Okay, yeah, even Petunia."

"She's just the sweetest thing," Sarah says. "She sleeps with me and just wants to cuddle all the time."

"She's practically drooling while I pet her," I agree with a laugh. "She's cute, Sarah."

I give the cat one last scratch and then go wash my

hands at the kitchen sink so I can eat some of the delicious-smelling tacos. When our plates are loaded up, the three of us settle around the coffee table on the floor of the living room with chips and salsa before us.

"Oh, tequila!" Sarah exclaims and jumps up to retrieve the bottle, shot glasses, and some limes and salt from the kitchen. "I don't have any margarita mix."

"Don't need it," June says with her mouth full of chips as Sarah pours the first round.

"To being free of a man who didn't love me," she says, holding her glass in the air. "And to endless possibilities."

"Hear, hear," I agree before licking the salt off my hand. I shoot the alcohol and reach for a wedge of lime. "Oh man, that burns."

"You two and your training wheels," June says, shaking her head. She didn't use the salt or the lime.

"Sarah, can we ask some questions? Now that you've been here for a couple of months and the divorce is pretty much final and everything?"

"You guys can always ask questions," Sarah says. "And I'll answer if I can."

"What was it about him that made you just *leave*?" I ask her. "Just quit your job, uproot from your town and your friends, and follow him."

"Anthony was charming," she murmurs. "And in the beginning, he was *so* nice to me. Attentive and generous and affectionate. He was older and seemed to know just about everything. I was dazzled by him. Completely and totally in love. He charmed me so quickly that I didn't even look back when we left because I figured I'd be able to come back to see you guys all the time."

She frowns and stares at the bottle of tequila.

"But?" June asks.

"Listen, it was great in the beginning. And then, over time, he became more controlling and more...intense. He didn't want me to go to college, he wanted me to take care of the home. He didn't even want me to have a job because he was wealthy enough that I didn't need to."

"But what if you *wanted* to?" I ask, but she shakes her head.

"I learned over those first couple of years that it wasn't about what I wanted but had everything to do with what *Anthony* did. I felt like I couldn't complain because I was living in a gorgeous house with views of the water, and we traveled all over the world. I carried designer bags and wore expensive shoes. I drove a fancy car. I had everything a girl could want."

"Except love and friends," June adds.

"Yeah. I didn't know it at the time, but Anthony started having affairs shortly after our third anniversary. He's not a pedophile, but he really likes young women. That eighteen to twenty-one range is his favorite, and I truly believe it's because young women are easier to manipulate and control."

"And let's not forget," I add as I pour us another round of shots, "your parents were the *worst*. So, it's not like you had a stable family life here in Huckleberry Bay to come back to."

"You're right about that," she agrees. "When I found

out that my parents moved to Tulsa, I didn't give even one shit. I hadn't seen them since way before I left town with Anthony. I did feel guilty about you guys and Scott, but again, I thought I'd be able to come visit. And I totally planned to send money home to Scott to help him out."

"But Asshole Anthony wouldn't allow it," June guesses.

"Not only would he not allow it," Sarah adds, "but he got *irate* if I even suggested it. Why didn't I just appreciate what he gave me? Why wasn't he good enough for me? He hit me with one hell of a guilt trip, let me tell you."

"Was he physical?" I ask her. "I know June asked you before, but you never really answered her."

"He only hit me once," she says and meets my gaze without flinching now. "The day he kicked me out. I was *so* pissed. He flung the new girl in my face, said he wanted to marry her and that he had no use for me. There were a lot of hurtful words, but that wasn't new. When I told him that I'd contest the prenup, he backhanded me. And when I wouldn't back down, he beat the shit out of me."

"Jesus, Sarah. You didn't have any bruises when you got here," June says.

"No. I didn't want to come here like that. So, I spent a month at a shithole hotel while the bruises faded, and I came to terms with it all. It took a chunk of the money I'd squirreled away, but that was okay."

"Why didn't you press charges?" I demand.

"Why?" she asks. "So he could harass *me* more? So I

could feel worse? I knew the bruises would heal and that getting away from him was what I needed. And he gave me a way out. But I really hated that he sent me out virtually penniless with only what I could fit in my suitcases. I did take the jewelry, and I still have that in case I need to sell it for more money."

"You should have gotten a good attorney," June mutters. "That asshole got off scot-free."

"He won't be happy," Sarah says. "Because he *can't* be happy. He's always looking for the next best thing, whether that's with women or in business. I'm surprised he hasn't lost more money than he has because he's just so bad at it all. I *will* be happy. Hell, I'm happier now than I have been for the past decade in this little apartment with my sweet cat and my best friends. I came out ahead in the long run."

"I'm so glad you sent me holiday cards all those years," I tell her.

"He found out once and went into a week-long rage. He didn't know that I had the post office box. But I didn't care, I did it anyway. I needed some kind of link to you."

"I'm sorry I never replied," June says with a cringe. "I should have. I've just been so *mad* at you for so long. Because I'm a stubborn ass."

"I understand," Sarah says. "I was mad at me, too. Scott's *so* angry. I don't know if that relationship will ever heal, but I'll keep trying."

"He'll come around," I reply with more confidence than I feel. "He just needs some time."

"I have lots of that. I don't plan on going anywhere."

Sarah takes a bite of her taco. "So, yay for a divorce party!"

"Yay!" we echo and clink our shot glasses before drinking.

"I can't believe how fast this year is going. June, your grandma must be getting ready for her Halloween party," I say to her.

"Does she still do those?" Sarah asks.

"Every year, without fail," June confirms and scoops up some guacamole. "And, yeah, we're less than two weeks away, so she's already started with the decorations. I'm not allowed to help. She has a whole team of people who do it."

"What's the theme this year?" I ask her.

"Grimm's Fairy Tales," June says with a grin. "It'll be fun to see what she does with it. We're all going, of course."

"Even me?" Sarah asks.

"Of course, even you," I reply. "It's gotten even better over the years. You'll love it. Annabelle has made it spookier and goes way over the top. It's awesome."

"I can't wait," Sarah says. "How about you, Luna? How's it going?"

I shrug a shoulder and eat another chip. "It's going. I really needed this night with you guys to unwind a bit because it's been...crazy the last few weeks."

"How so?" June asks.

"Well, we all know about the barn situation. I've been digging through Rose's stuff, which is really cool, but it

213

also leaves me with more questions, and I don't want to have to dig for answers. I just want to *know*."

"Patience, my friend," Sarah says with a wink.

"And then with Apollo's health scare on top of everything, it's just been a lot."

"Wait, what?" June asks. "What the fuck are you talking about?"

"I wasn't supposed to tell anyone, but he got the results back, and he's fine, so now I can talk about it. He had a scare last week. You guys remember when my dad went through cancer when we were teenagers?"

"Yeah," Sara says with a frown.

"Well, there was concern that Apollo might have had the same thing, but it turned out to be benign. He's fine. Still, I was a wreck for a few days."

June's quiet, and then, without a word, she stands, marches to the door, grabs her purse, and just slams out of the apartment.

I stare at Sarah. "Was it something I said?"

"Oh, I don't know, Luna, it might have something to do with the fact that June's in love with your brother."

I scoff and shake my head. "Whatever. She does *not* love Apollo, Sarah. They can't stand each other. She hates him."

Sarah bites her lip and then says, "Does she, though?"

I look over at the door that June just marched through and frown.

"Well, shit."

OCTOBER 11, 2011

DEAR DIARY,

PUMPKIN SPICE LATTES ARE MY NEW OBSESSION. THE GRIND HAS THEM FOR THE FIRST TIME THIS YEAR, AND ALL I CAN SAY IS: I'M GOING TO BE BROKE SOON BECAUSE I CAN'T STOP BUYING THEM.

ALSO, I CAN NEVER TELL JUNE THIS BECAUSE IT WOULD FREAK HER OUT, BUT HER OLDER BROTHER CULLEN HAS GOTTEN HOT. HE'S ALSO A COP, SO MAYBE IT'S JUST THE MAN IN UNIFORM THING? I DON'T KNOW.

LOVE,
LUNA

Chapter Fifteen

Wolfe

I pull on the red fleece shirt and button it, still not entirely sure how Luna managed to talk me into this.

"She had your dick in her hands and was driving you out of your mind," I remind myself in the mirror. "You would have done *anything* for her in that moment."

I'm furry.

I sat still for two hours this afternoon while a makeup artist glued fur around my face and on my hands. She painted on a black nose and whiskers.

I pop the fangs into my mouth and smile.

"Thith ith ridiculouth."

"You look *amazing*," Luna says from behind me. I turn and grin when I take in her costume.

She's in a simple and modest black and white dress, but the red cape falls over her shoulders, and she's arranged the hood over her head. I can still see her dark hair and her gorgeous face.

"No, that'th you," I reply and let the teeth fall out of my mouth. "You're beautiful."

"And *you're* the big, bad wolf," she replies and crosses to me, leaning in to kiss me. "The fur tickles my lips."

But her hand cups my package, and I lift a brow.

"What a big *dick* you have."

"All the better to fuck you with." I grin and go in for another kiss. If I'd known before that this would be my life after racing, I would have beelined it home.

It's a good thing I didn't know.

"We don't have time for this," she murmurs against my lips. "But later, I'll wear the cape and nothing else."

"Fuck the party. Let's skip to the good stuff."

Luna laughs and steps out of my grasp. "Hell, no. We're going. It's a Huckleberry Bay tradition, and I'm dying to see what Annabelle has done with her house this year."

"Did I tell you that she yelled at Zeke at the garage?" I follow Luna down the hall to the kitchen, where she snags her basket to complete the look of her costume. "She was unhappy with our oil change prices."

"For someone with so much money, she sure is cheap," she says with a shake of her head. "But also, she's kind of awesome."

"How did she come into her money?" I ask as we walk out to the car.

"I have no idea," Luna replies. "As far as I know, no one knows. Not even June. She's just always been an eccentric, rich, older woman. Even when we were kids, she seemed old. But she's so colorful at the same time."

"An interesting woman indeed," I agree and drive down Lighthouse Way, then take a left to drive just a little farther out of town.

Annabelle Snow's house is an old Victorian that sits up at the top of a small mountain. She has a view of the ocean while being nestled up to the Oregon mountains.

It's the best of both worlds.

"It's all lit up," Luna says as we climb the winding road and can see bits and pieces through the trees. "She made it look like a *gingerbread* house! Like in Hansel and Gretel! Oh my gosh, this is just fabulous."

Luna's grinning like a kid going to their first Halloween party as I park the car, and we get out and walk the short distance to the porch, which is covered in lollipops, gumdrops, and chocolates.

"It's *real* candy," she says as she touches a sucker. "This had to take hours. Days."

"I'm glad I wasn't the one gluing the candy to the house," I agree and knock on the door.

A short person draped in black with a huge wart on their nose opens it.

"What's the password?"

Luna bounces with glee. "Pumpernickel! The password is pumpernickel."

"You may proceed," the warted woman says and steps back, gesturing with a long, bony finger for us to enter.

There's the typical smoke caused by dry ice and water that you'd expect at a Halloween party. The lights are dim, and I hear music, but also someone reciting what sounds like fairy tales over a loudspeaker.

What large teeth you have, Grandmother!

I smirk down at Luna.

"Look at you!" June exclaims as she hurries over, gazing at us with yellow eyes. Her cheekbones could cut glass, and she's leaning on a staff with a crystal ball. "Well, how perfect is this? Red Riding Hood and—"

"The big, bad Wolfe," I reply and wink.

"So appropriate," June says with a grin. "Come on. There's food and all kinds of fun things—games and trivia and prizes. Grandma isn't cheap when it comes to the prizes. I have my eye on the Yeti cooler. Also? Sarah's already here. She's over by the punch table. Go check her out, and I'll find you guys later."

"I could use some punch," I say as I lead Luna over to where a small group stands near the table. As the crowd parts, I hear Luna gasp beside me.

"Sarah?" Luna says as the woman turns around and grins.

Her blond hair is so long it trails not just to the floor but across the room.

"People are going to trip over your luscious hair," I say with a laugh.

"So far, so good," Sarah replies. "It's my first Halloween party in a *long* time. I wanted to make a statement."

"Statement made," Luna says.

"And you two look fantastic," Sarah says. "I love that Wolfe's a wolf. Very appropriate."

"See? Told you," Luna says to me and bumps me with her hip. "You look good with some fur and fangs."

"Did you see June?" Sarah asks. "She's Maleficent."

"We did," I say. "Everyone looks great."

"Hello, dearie." Sarah looks up into Tanner's eyes and blushes.

It's damn adorable.

"You're Rumpelstiltskin," Sarah says to Tanner.

"Yeah, but now I wish I'd dressed as the prince who saves Rapunzel instead."

"I don't think you could beat this costume," Sarah replies. "Besides, *this* Rapunzel doesn't need saving."

"No," Tanner agrees. "She certainly doesn't. Save a dance for me, yeah?"

"Sure."

Half the town has to be crammed into this house. It's a *big* house, but it's packed with people, laughing and talking, all dressed like something from a fairy tale.

There are even mice and a pumpkin hanging out with Cinderella.

"People take this very seriously," I observe as I pass Luna some punch.

"Absolutely," she agrees. "Also, I'm just saying that I don't think I can bob for apples. Not with this makeup."

"We'll skip that, then. I'm pretty good at trivia, you know."

Luna sips her punch. "I had no idea. Now, we have to give that a go. First, let's find Annabelle and gush over this party. She loves that."

We make our way through the crowd, keeping an eye out for Annabelle but also taking in all the fun costumes.

The three sisters who own Three Sisters Kitchen are

dressed as the three fairies from Sleeping Beauty. They have a fake fight with Maleficent that ends in laughter and high-fives.

I have to admit, it's pretty fun.

"There you are," Annabelle says, and I have to blink to take her in. This is the small, warted person who let us in the front door.

"I didn't even recognize you."

Her smile is wide and happy and shows off a toothless mouth. I don't know if that's the magic of makeup or if she really does wear dentures. "That's the best compliment you could have paid me, Wolfe. You two did *not* disappoint me with your costume choices. Are you having fun?"

"You've put on the best party I've ever been to," I inform her. "And I've been to parties literally all over the world. No one holds a candle to this."

"Well, you're a charmer as well as handsome, Wolfe Conrad. Now I won't feel so crabby about paying for my oil changes."

I laugh and lean over to kiss her cheek. "Next one's on me."

She's lit up like the Fourth of July as she walks away into the crowd to mingle with her other guests.

"Trivia time," June announces as she strolls by. "Come on, we're holding it in the library."

I wink at Luna as we follow June into a room that looks as if it were plucked out of Beauty and the Beast, with floor-to-ceiling bookshelves and the sliding ladder that goes with them.

Belle herself is standing behind a podium, holding cards.

"Hello, friends," Belle—aka Dotty Harmon, the owner of Books on the Bay—says with a wide smile. "I'm your trivia host this evening. Now, gather 'round, and we'll get started. The winner will receive this beautiful cooler to store all your porridge and gray stuff in."

She winks as everyone chuckles and then pulls a card.

"Okay, question number one...Which one of these is *not* one of the seven dwarves?"

* * *

"I can't believe you beat June at the trivia," Luna says beside me as we drive up Huckleberry Way. The sky opened while we were at the party, and rain falls almost sideways with the howling wind, battering my SUV. "You two were *so* competitive! I thought it was going to become a fistfight."

"She was a worthy opponent," I reply with a wink.

"She tossed the cooler back at you when you tried to give it to her."

"And that's why she's worthy. No one wants their adversary to give them charity. But don't worry, I'll buy her a better one, and we'll all be happy."

Luna sighs and leans her head back on the seat. "It was all so much fun."

"I'm glad you enjoyed it," I reply and reach over to squeeze her hand. "I don't think I've ever seen anything like it. You know, you could easily host parties like that—not Halloween, of course, because Annabelle definitely has the market covered on that one—but maybe a holiday party at the B&B."

"I know," she says with a giddy smile. "I already plan to decorate the inside and outside of the B&B and lighthouse with amazing lights and garlands for the holidays, and I want to host a holiday party for the town. I can't *wait* for next year."

As I drive up to the house, Luna sits up straight in her seat and gasps.

"What's wrong?"

"The light's out." She's out of the car before I even come to a complete stop and racing through the storm to the door of the lighthouse. By the time I get to her, she has unlocked the door and is climbing the steps, taking two at a time, leaving puddles of water behind her.

Except on the racetrack, I don't think I've ever seen someone move so fast.

"This has *never* happened," she explains as we reach the top, and she takes a minute to catch her breath. She flips on a light and starts digging around in the lens while writing notes on a pad and murmuring to herself. "These bulbs were designed to last *decades*. I believe the last time it was changed was in the 1950s."

"You're kidding."

"No, I'm not. They also don't make bulbs like this anymore. They're much smaller now but should last just as long. I have a changer installed that should have automatically switched from the burned-out bulb to the new one. I don't know why it failed."

She's bustling about, checking things, and I feel helpless.

"How do I help?"

"Hold your phone's flashlight over here so I can see better. Of *course*, this happened at night."

"Can it wait for morning?"

"You don't understand," she says quickly, "this is an operating lighthouse. It could be catastrophic for ships that use the light as a guide to navigate up and down the western coastline. As it is, I don't know how long it's been out. I have to fix it. Right now."

"Okay, we'll fix it."

She tugs her cape off and lets it fall to the floor out of her way. She's wearing gloves, likely because of the heat coming off the old bulb, and I stay quiet as she does her job.

Her hands are steady.

Her eyes are full of confidence and determination.

God, she's fucking *amazing*.

"Close your eyes, this will be bright," she warns me, and I follow the order just before the light illuminates again. "Thank God."

"Now what?" I ask her.

"Now, I make a couple of quick phone calls to the Coast Guard to let them know that it's been fixed, and then, first thing in the morning, I'll be calling the manu-facturer of this supposedly high-tech bulb changer to find out what in the hell happened."

She pulls out her phone and taps the screen.

"Hello, this is Luna Winchester."

I listen to her give the pertinent information to the person on the other end of the line, and when she hangs up, I simply pin her against the wall in the cramped space and kiss the fuck out of her.

The storm rages outside, hurling water against the windows. The building creeks and seems to move with the wind.

It's damn creepy on a stormy night like this, but I don't care.

All I can think about is getting my hands on her.

"As sexy as this is," she says when I move down to her neck. "I can't get over the fur all over you. We have to get that off, Wolfe."

I laugh and kiss her forehead, then back away and pick up her cape.

"Can't forget this." I wiggle my extra-bushy eyebrows at her.

"Definitely not. Whew, that was an adrenaline rush."

"So, that bulb hasn't been replaced in roughly *seventy* years?"

"No," she says, shaking her head. "We have replacement bulbs, of course, but according to the records, it's never been changed. We've changed the lenses more often. Dad will be fascinated when I tell him about it."

We walk down the steps, much slower than we climbed them.

"Does it always sound like this during storms?"

"Like it's haunted?" she asks and turns to smile up at me. "Yeah. It used to creep me out as a kid."

"It might creep me out a little now."

She laughs. "I know that anything or anyone who might still be here, like Rose, isn't going to hurt me. If anything, she looks out for me, so I'm not scared of the noises anymore. I love a good storm. It's my favorite. I used to hate it when I was a kid because it meant that I couldn't play up here or even outside with you. But now, I enjoy the sounds and the way the ocean looks."

After we hurry in the rain from the lighthouse door to the front door of the house and are safely inside where it's warm and dry, Luna flips a switch to start the gas fireplace.

"Let's get changed and comfortable," she suggests.

"I'm going to need you to help me out of this fur."

"Happy to. It's all water-soluble, so it shouldn't be hard."

Famous last words.

An hour later, fresh from the shower, I finally feel like myself again, and Luna is still snickering at the ordeal we just went through to get the fur and the glue off my skin.

"I'm going to need skin grafts to repair this," I say, examining the damage in the mirror.

"You'll be fine in a day or two," she says as she walks up behind me and kisses my shoulder. "Also, you looked hot as the wolf. Totally worth it."

"As long as you liked it, it's definitely worth it."

She grins, and I turn to her, intending to haul her off to bed.

"I'm hungry," she says, catching me off guard.

"Now?"

"Yep. I'm going to make some grilled cheese sandwiches. You want?"

"Sure." She takes my hand and pulls me through the house to the kitchen. "How can you be hungry at this hour? It's past midnight."

"I think the adrenaline of changing the lightbulb burned a lot of calories." She pulls bread, cheese, and butter out of the fridge and sets a pan on the stove to heat up. "It was *such* a rush, Wolfe."

"It's your version of what I feel like while racing a car."

She stops and points at me with a spatula. "Yes. Exactly. I hate that the light was out, and I hate even more that I don't know how *long* it was out, but holy cow...that was a rush. I just hope I don't have to do it again for as long as I'm the lightkeeper here. I mean, if I have to, I can. But I don't want to."

She bustles about the kitchen as efficiently as she did up in the lighthouse and whips up a couple of sandwiches that look like they belong in a restaurant.

"You're going to make your guests *very* happy with food like this," I inform her and take a bite of the gooey sandwich.

"Not often," she says with an excited smile. "Because I've decided to take Three Sisters up on their offer."

"What offer?"

She frowns and blinks at me. "I didn't tell you about them offering to buy into the B&B and run the kitchen part of the business?"

"No." I shake my head, surprised that I'm not at all irritated about being left out of some of Luna's big news.

This is *her* business. It's really not any of my concern how she decides to run it.

But I enjoy listening to her tell me about it.

She outlines what the sisters want to do, and I find myself nodding, liking the idea.

"So, it's still special for your guests, but one less thing on your plate."

"Exactly," she says as she sets our empty plates in the dishwasher. "At first, I wasn't sure because I've always thought that it would be all *mine*, you know? But it's not nearly as sexy or romantic as I imagined. It's a *lot* of work, and I don't want to overwhelm myself and take on too much, too fast. I think partnering with the food experts is a good idea, and it enables us to offer our guests so much more than just a quick breakfast and a basket of snacks."

"I agree." I take her hand in mine and nibble on her knuckles, then lead her to the living room, where the fireplace continues to burn. We sit on the couch together, snuggled up. "I think it's a smart move. They've done an excellent job with the existing restaurant, and I think that when all four of you put your heads together, you'll make something incredible."

"Yeah." She grins and leans her head on my shoulder. "I can't wait."

Chapter Sixteen

Luna

The storm has been unrelenting for three days. I haven't even left the bed yet to look outside, but I can still hear the rain falling on the roof and the heavy water overflowing the house's gutters to crash onto the earth below.

It's as though Mother Nature is making up for the relatively dry summer we had, all in the span of just a few days.

Before I can roll out of bed, Wolfe's arm snakes around my middle. He tugs me against him and starts to kiss the back of my neck. He's warm and firm, and given the way a certain body part presses against my backside, I'd say he's in the mood for a bit of morning fun.

Which suits me just fine.

His lips cruise along my shoulder, and then he turns me onto my back and smiles down at me as he gently brushes a lock of hair off my cheek.

"Good morning, gorgeous," he whispers.

Who knew that just waking up in the morning could feel so damn good?

His mouth lowers to mine for long, lazy kisses as his fingertips journey over my skin to my breast, and he gently teases my nipple into a firm point.

There's no urgency in him this morning, nothing quick or fast in his movements. Instead, as the rain falls around us on this gray day, Wolfe takes his time.

And when he finally pushes into me, links our fingers, and presses our joined hands against the mattress near my head as he moves in long, languid strokes, he keeps his gaze locked on mine.

"I can't get enough of you," he murmurs against my lips. "It's never enough."

"I'm right here," I assure him and raise my legs high on his hips, inviting him to come even deeper. He fills me so completely it always takes my breath away. His body, so tight and firm with muscles for days, is a wonderland for my fingers, and when I grip firmly onto his ass, he groans.

What started as lazy and sleepy turns greedy in the blink of an eye. His mouth no longer tickles mine, but rather, he claims it as if he's making sure that I understand, without words, that I'm *his*.

It's the most intoxicating aphrodisiac there is.

And when he whispers my name, everything in me contracts, and the Earth falls away as we tumble into the bliss we made.

He rolls to the side so he doesn't crush me, and I sigh in contentment. "Coffee."

He snorts and pushes out of bed, then pads into the bathroom. A few moments later, with gray sweatpants hanging low on his hips, he emerges with that cocky grin that I love so much.

"I'm going to fetch your coffee, Your Royal Highness," he says and reaches for a T-shirt.

"Maybe don't put the shirt on," I suggest as I prop my head on my hand and watch him as I lie on my side.

"Why?"

"Because the view is damn good without it," I reply. "You know what they say about men in gray sweatpants."

He blinks. "No. What do they say?"

I grin and then fall back onto the pillow. "Let's just say it's a *really* nice sight. Like, really good."

"Women are weird," he mutters as he pads out of the room toward the kitchen.

While he's occupied, I handle my business in the bathroom and then pull on some black yoga pants and a sports bra with a cozy sweatshirt.

With as nasty as it is outside, today is all about comfort.

I reach for my phone and smile when I see messages from Cordelia, confirming our appointment for tomorrow morning when I plan to accept their offer to buy the kitchen portion of the B&B.

"Coffee," Wolfe announces as he returns to the bedroom, carrying two mugs and a brown paper bag under one arm. "And fresh marionberry scones from Three Sisters."

"How did you manage that?"

He smiles proudly as he passes me my mug and then sits next to me on the bed. "I have connections in this town, sweetheart."

"Oh, is that right?" I laugh and peek inside the bag, then grin when the smell hits me. "And they're still warm from the oven."

"Good connections," he adds. "It's nasty out there."

"I know. That's the Oregon coast for you. Mostly rainy and moody with moments of sunshine mixed in just enough to make you want to stay."

"There are a few reasons to stay," he says thoughtfully.

"Besides the stunning views?"

"Sure." He pops a bite of a scone into his mouth. "There's a fun Halloween party every year."

"True."

"And I own a business here."

"There is that."

He leans over to kiss my temple. "And the most amazing person I've ever met in my life is here."

"Really? Who's that?"

He grins and sips his coffee. "This girl I know. Best sex I've ever had, too."

"Well, that's definitely worth sticking around for," I agree and happily munch on my scone.

"I think we should build a house."

I choke and have to set my coffee aside so I don't spill. "What?"

"A house. You know, for us to live in."

I look around the room and back to Wolfe. "I thought we were living in a house already."

"We are. Hear me out, okay? I think we should choose a spot on the property and build a new house for the two of us. You could incorporate this house into the business. People would pay a lot of money to bring their family to stay in a lighthouse, not to mention, you could use it for events. And in the process, we could join our two properties together."

I'd actually thought the same thing in the past, that guests would probably love an opportunity to rent out the entire house.

"But I already have so much on my plate, Wolfe. We're finally moving forward on the B&B now that they repaired the roof and can get on with things, and it's just a *lot*. Let's table this conversation for now."

"But to be clear, you're not against it?"

"No." I retrieve my coffee and take a sip. "It would be fun to build something new with you, but I don't have the brain space for it yet."

"I get it," he assures me. "No rush."

I smirk. "Right, Mr. I Only Have One Speed And That's A Million Miles A Second."

He narrows his eyes at me. "I can be patient."

"Okay, good." I look him over, taking in his naked torso, and feel myself go just a little gooey inside.

"What?"

"You were always a good-looking guy. Even as children, I remember people saying that you were a handsome kid."

"Okay."

"But, damn, Wolfe, you got *hot*. And it's not just because you can drive a car the way you do—although watching you shift gears does things to me."

"It does?"

"Well, yeah. But you're...*hot*. I know I said that already, but I said it again because it's true. Handsome? Yes. Attractive? Definitely. But it's more than that. The sexy factor is off the damn charts."

"Sexy factor?" he asks as he calmly sets the coffee and scones aside.

"Yeah. On a scale of one to ten, you're like a twenty-six. And I know I'm babbling, and it's not as though I didn't notice this before, it's just that there are moments, like right now, when you're sitting next to me, half-naked, and we're just innocently talking about stuff and eating scones that it hits me."

"What hits you?" he asks as he slowly lowers me down to my back.

"That you're the sexiest human in the universe. And you're here with *me*."

His lips tip up into a small smile, and his eyes, so full of emotion, soften. "That's impossible. I can't be the sexiest in the universe."

"Why?" It's a whisper.

"Because that title belongs to you, sweetheart." With his lips on mine, we forget all about the coffee and scones. Instead, consumed by each other, we let the storm surround us in a soothing cocoon as we make love.

* * *

"I'm going to run out to the B&B and see how things are going," I announce several hours later.

"I'm headed to the garage in town," Wolfe counters and wraps his arms around me so he can kiss me senseless. "I'll see you later."

"Bye." I watch him jog through the mud to this Porsche and then wave him off. Before I can trudge over to the old barn to see June, my phone rings.

Speak of the devil... It's June.

"Hey, I was just going to come out and see you. Want a sandwich or anything?"

"Actually, I'm not there," she says. "I won't make it over today, but my crew's there, and they have everything handled."

"Okay." I walk back inside the house. "What's wrong?"

"Well, I'm trying to get some things packed up because it looks like I'll be living with my grandma for a while."

"What? Why?"

"Mold." She blows out a breath in disgust. "I found some mold in my basement, and I have to vacate while it's inspected and cleaned properly. Why did I rent this shithole?"

"Do you need help?"

"Nah, I can't take much with me. No furniture or anything because it could have mold in it."

"I'm coming," I reply and grab my purse and keys.

"Don't argue. You wouldn't let me do that alone. I'll be there shortly."

"Okay," she replies, and I can hear the relief in her voice. "Thanks."

After a quick call to Sarah, I learn that she's free today, as well, so I drive over to the garage to pick her up. I wave to Wolfe, and then Sarah and I head over to June's rental house on Starfish Lane.

"Mold is scary," Sarah says with a concerned frown. "It has to be from all of this rain and humidity over the past few days. It's unrelenting."

"I know," I agree as I pull into June's driveway. "There's so much moisture in the air, I'm surprised we don't all have mold."

"Don't say that," Sarah replies. "You just take that right back out of the universe."

"You're right. I take it back."

We hurry through another downpour to the front door and barge inside without knocking.

"I'm in the bedroom!" June calls out. "Unless you're an ax murderer, in which case, I'm not home!"

"I missed her sense of humor," Sarah says with a happy smile as we hurry down a long hallway. June's suitcases are on the bed, open, and clothes are haphazardly strewn around the room. "Did a bomb go off in here?"

"How many pairs of jeans do you own?" I ask at the same time.

"I'm not organized," June admits. "And I'm in a hurry because I don't want to die from mold inhalation."

"You won't die," I assure her. "What are you taking?"

236

"All of this." She makes a swiping gesture with her arm. "It's all of my work clothes and stuff."

"Do you own anything other than steel-toed boots?" Sarah wants to know.

"Why would I?" June asks. "I work *every* day."

"I dunno. Because you're a girl," Sarah says as she folds a flannel shirt and tucks it into a suitcase. "And sometimes a girl needs a pair of pretty shoes."

"Ew," June says with a scowl. "No. No pretty shoes."

"June doesn't like girl clothes," I inform Sarah and turn to June. "You can just stay with me, you know."

"And be stuck watching you snog Wolfe all the damn time? No, thanks. I'll take my chances with Annabelle."

I snort and turn back to the clothes.

"So, nothing's changed since we were in high school," Sarah says with a nod. "You went to the prom in slacks and a blue smock thing that you borrowed from your grandmother."

"So?"

"Okay, let's focus," I suggest and toss a pair of jeans into the suitcase. "This one will be jeans and underwear. That one is tops and bras. We'll put the boots in a tote or bucket since most of them are muddy."

"It's been rainy," June mutters. "Of course, they're muddy."

"Hey, I'm not judging."

We work quickly, and in less than thirty minutes, we're lugging the heavy luggage out to June's truck and setting it in the back seat where it won't get wet.

"We'll follow you up to your grandma's and help you

unload," Sarah says. "Don't argue. We're going no matter what you say."

"Fine," June says, rolling her eyes. "But you really don't have to."

"See you soon," I reply with a happy wave, and June can't seem to contain the pleased smile as she gets in her truck and starts the engine.

"She's not as grouchy as she wants everyone to believe she is," Sarah says. "And, of course, I'm going to give her a hard time about her wardrobe. She still has a sweatshirt that she wore in high school. *Before* I left, Luna."

"I know. Fashion just isn't her jam, you know?"

"I'm not even talking about *fashion*. I'm talking about regular wardrobe staples. I know she works a lot but come on."

"I did find some cute summer things in the mix," I tell her as we pass Lighthouse Way, headed toward Annabelle's house. "But, yeah, she could use a makeover."

"She would rather poke her eyes out than let us give her a makeover."

"Maybe that's why I want to do it so badly," I reply with a laugh. "Come on, let's unload."

"There's my girl," Annabelle says as we all get out of the cars and start to help June inside with the luggage.

"Wow, all of the decorations are already gone," I say in shock. "How in the world did you manage to do that so quickly?"

"Why, magic, of course," Annabelle says with a wink.

"Now, come in out of this rain. I've got some hot chocolate simmering in the kitchen, and I just baked some cowboy cookies."

"Thanks, Grandma," June says. "I'll take these bags up to my room later."

"We might as well just do it now," I urge June. "Then you won't have to later when you're full of chocolate, and all you want to do is crash."

"Good idea," Sarah agrees, and the three of us muscle the bags up two flights of stairs to June's old bedroom at the top of the turret on the side of the old Victorian house. "I always loved this bedroom."

It's round with a queen-sized, four-poster bed and a long dresser with an attached mirror.

"It still looks the same," I add and set the bucket of boots—that have to weigh at least sixty pounds—at the end of the bed. I cross to the window and look out, smiling when I see the lighthouse in the distance and the ocean beyond, raging in the storm. "It's the best view in Huckleberry Bay."

"No, yours is," June says as she joins me, and then Sarah comes up on my other side.

"No, this is," I counter. "You can see the lighthouse and the ocean. And I know that at night you can see the lights from town. It's magical up here, just like Annabelle said."

"What she *didn't* say was that she has a team of about fifty people who came up here the next day after the party and put everything away."

"Well, that takes the fun out of the illusion, doesn't

239

it?" Sarah says with a smile. "Someday, I'd love to have a place with a view like this. I love the ocean."

Sarah rests her head on my shoulder, June takes my hand, and the three of us just stand there, watching the storm.

"I dreamed of this," June whispers. "Of the three of us being together again, just like this. I didn't think I'd ever see the day it would happen."

"And yet, here we are." I smile at her. "We should go down for hot chocolate and cookies."

"I brought them to you," Annabelle says from behind us and sets the tray on the dresser. She wipes a tear from the corner of her eye. "Seeing the three of you like that took me back twenty years to when you were just young girls, thick as thieves, daydreaming up here in this tower together. My sweet girls."

She sighs happily and then points to the tray.

"Enjoy a treat and each other's company for a while. It's not as though there's a lot to do in this weather otherwise."

"Thanks, Grandma," June says as Annabelle leaves, closing the door behind her. "You know, even if they do get all of the mold out of that house and it's safe to live in again, I don't think I'll move back there."

"Why not?" I ask her as I reach for a cookie. Scones *and* cookies in the same day probably isn't the best idea, but I'll take a walk on the beach later and work it off. "The house isn't that bad."

"It's not great," June replies and pours the hot chocolate out of an old-fashioned silver teapot.

Annabelle always served us with fancy things like this. She said it made everything taste better.

"It's not my home," June continues. "I've known it for a while, but I've been too consumed with work to really take the time to do anything about it. But this was a good push to find something else."

"Will you rent again?" Sarah asks and sips her hot chocolate. "Whoa. Sidebar, what does she do to this to make it so damn good?"

"There's probably extra sugar in there," June says. "Or, you know, crack."

We laugh, and then June sobers.

"I don't really want to rent again," she continues. "I'd really like to buy something, but with the influx of out-of-towners moving in, the prices have gone sky-high. I don't know what I'll be able to afford."

"The right thing will come along," I assure her. "Probably when you least expect it."

"In the meantime," Sarah adds, "you can live here in this gorgeous room and let Annabelle spoil you."

"It's not a hardship," June agrees with a small smile. "Not at all."

November 1, 2008

Dear Diary,

Well, I'm finally over 21, so I got to go to the Halloween party that Annabelle throws every year! Holy crap, it was so fun! The theme this year was Dr. Seuss, and I went as Thing 2. June was Thing 1.

We had a great time dancing and playing games, and then, when the party was finished, June didn't want to go home, so we decided to make a spooky night of it and go to the cemetery behind the Little White Chapel.

*I don't know why, exactly, because I know precisely where to find a **real** ghost, but it was still fun. We giggled and had a good time walking around town after dark. It wasn't raining for once! I guess this is one of the good sides to living in a small town, feeling safe enough to walk around whenever you want to.*

Anyway, I need a nap now.

Love,

Luna

Chapter Seventeen

Wolfe

"I need an oil change," Apollo announces from the doorway and grins at Zeke and me.

"You're in the right place," I reply as I wipe my hands on a rag and cross to him. Zeke's head down in the business end of a Toyota, so I tap the keys on the laptop that sits on the counter, ready to help Luna's brother. "I have some information to get from you on this first visit, but then you'll be in the computer, and we won't have to do it next time."

"Cool." As I type, Apollo glances at the papers on the desk. "Who's building a house?"

I have some floor plans spread out that I was looking at earlier.

"No one. Yet," I murmur, frustrated because I can't type so I have to peck at the keys with two fingers. "I want to, but Luna's too busy to start thinking about it yet."

There's a heavy silence, and I look up into Apollo's sober face.

"You want to build a house *with* her?"

"Yes, I do."

"Are you planning to *marry* her, or are you just going to shack up with her forever?"

Forgetting all about the fucking computer, I lean on the counter and answer the other man truthfully.

"Oh, I'll be marrying her. I just haven't asked her yet."

"Why not?"

"Well, it's only been a few months, and like I said, she has a lot on her plate right now."

"No woman ever has so much on her plate that she can't accept a proposal. And it seems to me, that if a man has been living with a woman for a few months, one he's known for his whole life, he'd know whether he wants to put a ring on that girl's finger."

He smiles innocently, and I can't really argue with him.

"I told you I'm going to marry her."

"Okay, then. And regarding the house? I know she's busy with the B&B, but maybe you could take over the house project yourself. Have her choose some plans, and then *you* take it on. She'll be relieved."

"You think so? Don't women want to be involved in all the details when there's a project like this, though?"

"I think it's reasonable," Apollo says, shaking his head. "You want to get started on a house, and you have the time to dedicate to it. Relationships are a partnership, right? You're taking on this portion of the partnership. That's all. I know my sister, and I think she'll be happy with this arrangement."

"It makes sense to me," Zeke says as he joins us. "Your other place is finished. This place is finally in its groove. I don't see why you can't at least get started on a new house since there will be lots of work to do before you actually break ground. Things like hiring the contractor, making decisions, and all of that stuff. Get it out of the way. You'll be ahead of the game."

"Exactly," Apollo agrees. "She'll be excited about it."

"Okay, I'm going to do it. Thanks, guys."

"We're always here to help," Apollo says. "So, when are you going to propose?"

I laugh, but then an idea sets up residence in my head, and I know exactly what I'm going to do.

"Actually, Zeke, can you handle things here for a while? I need to run an errand."

"Sure thing," Zeke says. "Oh, and we should probably hire some part-time help. We're getting busier."

"Yeah, let's do that," I reply, already switching gears in my head. "I'll be back as soon as I can."

I hurry out of the garage and jog down the street to where Hart Jewelers has been for as long as I can remember.

When I walk in, the bell rings above the door, and Mr. Hart himself looks up with magnifying glasses on his face that make his eyes look huge.

"Well, hello there," the old man says with a polite smile and pulls the glasses off. He's holding a ring in his hands. "I'm just fixing this ring for Annabelle Snow. How can I help you, Wolfe?"

"You remember me?" I ask with a smile.

"Of course, I do. Watched every race I could get on television, too. We're really glad to have you home."

"I'm happy to be home. Mr. Hart, I need an engagement ring."

His wrinkled face creases into a wide grin. "Is that so? Well, you came to the right place."

I think about the flashy, expensive shops I could purchase a ring from in the big cities. Shops with blue or red boxes that many women would expect, especially from someone with my status.

But I think that a ring made here in Huckleberry Bay would mean more to Luna.

I look down into the glass case and see plenty of diamond rings on little round stands, but Mr. Hart doesn't pull the tray out of there.

Instead, he walks back to a big safe, spins the dial for the combination, and pulls out another black tray that he brings out to me.

"I keep the extra *good* stuff tucked away," he says with a wink, and I stare down at diamonds that would rival anything I'd find anywhere else in the world.

"This is impressive," I say after a moment.

"Engagement rings are my specialty," he says kindly, gently running his fingertip over the diamonds. "They're my favorite part of this business, just like they were my father's. He designed some of the rings you see here.

Ones that just haven't found the right homes yet. Most of them, though, are my work."

I point to a vintage-looking ring that looks like it belongs in the 1920s, and Mr. Hart smiles.

"My grandfather designed this one in 1925," he says and pulls it off the clip. "It's the last one in the shop that he designed."

"It's so classic," I murmur. "How did no one snatch it up before this?"

"Well, that diamond is rather large," he says slowly, "and the style is dated, although vintage rings have recently come back in style."

"So, you're saying it's expensive, and no one else wanted to splurge on it because it's old?"

He just smiles again. Mr. Hart is the most laid-back, patient man I've ever met in my life.

"I guess that's one way to put it."

"Would it be difficult to pair it with a wedding band?"

He frowns, narrowing his eyes. "I don't think so. I have one that would look just right with it. Here, let me grab it."

He opens another drawer and pulls out a band that looks like it was made for the engagement ring.

"It's always amazing to me when two pieces, built so many years apart, fit together so well," he says softly as I nestle the two rings together and immediately know, down to my marrow, that this is it.

These are Luna's rings.

"I'll take them."

Mr. Hart's eyes brighten, and he immediately shakes my hand. "Well, that's wonderful. Miss Luna's a lucky woman."

"No, I'm the lucky one. Hell, it'll be a miracle if she says yes."

"With a ring like this? You can't go wrong. Just let me know if it needs to be sized after you pop the question."

I pay for the rings and understand immediately what Mr. Hart was talking about regarding the price, and then, rather than return to the garage, I walk over to Three Sisters and flag down Cordelia.

"I need a favor," I begin.

"Tell me everything," she says.

"No one else is here," Luna says with a frown as we step inside Three Sisters Kitchen. "And it looks...*different.*"

Cordelia and her team came through for me big time with pretty little twinkle lights hung everywhere, flowers on *our* table, and the playlist I gave her softly drifting through the speakers.

It's exactly as I pictured it in my head yesterday when I spoke with Cordelia about it.

"Good evening," Darla says with a soft smile. "Please, follow me to your table."

Luna raises a brow at me, but I just shrug and follow both ladies to the table by the window that gives us an excellent view of the ocean.

She gives us menus and then winks at me before walking away.

"What's going on here?" Luna asks.

"We don't get to have special date nights, not like we would if we lived in a city. So, I spoke with the girls here, and we put together something special."

She's quiet for a moment, just watching me, and then a smile slowly spreads over that gorgeous face. "That might be the nicest thing anyone's ever done for me."

Buckle up, baby, because it's only going to get better.

She orders the salmon, and I opt for a steak.

She tells me about the tile she's chosen for the backsplash in the B&B's butler's pantry and how each guest room will have its own theme, all nautical based but not gaudy with it.

"Every single bathroom will have a deep, soaking tub. And I think I want to have different scents made for each room to really give my guests a different experience with each suite so they want to return again and again but try a new space in the inn. What do you think of that?"

I take a bite of my steak and nod. "I love it. I think that's a great idea. And like you said, it will entice people to come back."

"June's starting to move faster and faster with the build now, and I can finally see it starting to take shape. It's exciting, you know? Of course, you know. You just built an incredible garage on steroids."

I laugh and then reach for her hand, unable to keep myself from touching her.

"I do get it. And you *should* be excited, sweetheart. This is a very big deal, and I know it's going to kick ass."

"How is the garage doing?"

We settle into a nice conversation about work, the town, and people we know.

And when they take our clean plates away, and one of my favorite songs comes on, I take Luna's hand and lead her to the middle of the floor. I pull her into my arms, and we start to sway. She rests her hand on my shoulder, and I tuck our linked hands against my chest. I can't look away from her as we move slowly over the floor as the band in the speakers sings about tequila and flying over Colorado.

"This has been absolutely wonderful," she says softly, her eyes moving to my lips. "Thank you for making me feel special."

"You *are* special," I whisper before kissing her forehead, and as I turn her gently in a circle, I glance over her head to where about six women are huddled in the kitchen, watching us with soft, dreamy eyes.

I wink at them, and Cordelia responds with a big thumbs up.

"How do you feel about chocolate cake and champagne?" I ask Luna.

"I have very strong feelings about both of them."

"Oh?" I grin down at her. "And those feelings are?"

"Love. I'd say they land squarely in the love category."

"Excellent." Before we return to the table, I tip up her chin and take her lips with mine, softly. Sweetly. And with a slight nudge of my nose against hers, I lead her back to the table where the sweet dessert and bubbly wine are waiting for us.

I hold my glass up. "To the woman of my dreams. You're incredible, Luna. I love you so much, it steals my breath away."

Her mouth drops open. "What?"

"What part didn't you understand?"

"You *love* me?"

"Of course, I do. Babe, I—" I pause, and it hits me then that I've never said that to her before. Jesus, I've felt it. Sometimes, it hits me so hard it almost sends me to my knees.

But I've never said the words.

"Christ, Luna, I'm sorry. I'm completely in love with you. Irreversibly."

Tears fill her gorgeous brown eyes. "I love you, too."

I hear a sigh come from the kitchen but choose to ignore it. At least I know I'm not completely fucking this up. Only sort of because I'm ready for marriage, and I haven't even told her that I'm in love with her before this.

"But do you love me as much as you love chocolate cake?"

She laughs and sniffs away the tears, then takes a bite of the cake with a nice amount of chocolate frosting and sighs in happiness.

"Oh, it might be close."

I take a bite of my own. "Hmm. I don't know, maybe yours is better than mine."

"It's likely cut from the same cake, Wolfe."

I crook my finger at her. "Let me try it."

She giggles and holds her loaded fork up to my lips.

"Yeah. Yeah, I see what you mean." My eyes are on hers as I lick my lips. "That's pretty good. Probably because it's on your fork."

"Right," she says and sips her champagne. "How could I not love you? You always make me laugh."

"It's a skill that I've honed over the years," I agree.

After one more glass of champagne for Luna, and all the cake is gone, I nod to Darla, who's been hovering not far away while trying to look as if she's *not*.

"I think we're done here," I tell her. "Thank you for everything. It was perfect."

"Oh, I'm so glad," Darla gushes. "It was truly our pleasure. I hope you enjoy the rest of your evening."

"Thank you," Luna says as Darla hugs her. "Everything was wonderful. Even the music."

"Oh, that was all Wolfe, as well." Darla winks at her. "He knew exactly what he wanted for tonight."

With a wave, I lead Luna out to my Porsche, and as we drive home, she reaches over to take my hand in hers, holding on tight.

"Thank you," she says again. "That was fun."

"We're not done yet," I reply and turn onto Lighthouse Way, headed toward the lighthouse. We pass the new garage, and I slow down, making sure that everything looks as it should there. When I'm satisfied that it's all good, I keep going.

"We could stay there tonight. Or anytime really," Luna suggests. "It shouldn't stay empty all the time."

"Not tonight. But maybe sometime," I agree as I drive around the bend, and Luna's property comes into view.

Including the gazebo.

"Oh, my," she breathes as I come to a stop. We don't get out of the car quite yet because Luna's eyes are fixed on the lights in the gazebo. "Oh, it's so pretty. Are there even *more* candles than before?"

"Maybe one or two. Come on, let's go look."

I'm not even nervous when I take her hand, and we walk toward the place that's come to mean so much to the two of us. I knew, without a shadow of a doubt, that when I asked Luna to be mine forever, I wanted to do it here, in this place.

In addition to the candles, Mira and Cordelia snuck over to hang more twinkle lights.

It looks like something out of a fairy tale.

But before we reach the steps that lead inside, a car comes screaming up the road and screeches to a stop just a few feet away from us.

"Wolfe!" Apollo hurries out of his car, his face full of fear. "Hurry. Your garage is on fire."

Chapter Eighteen

Luna

I've never seen him this intense. This *angry*.

Wolfe's hands tighten on the steering wheel as he expertly takes us back into town. He's driving fast, taking the corners tight, but I know he's in complete control of the car.

That's not something I ever have to worry about.

"Sarah," I murmur and wring my hands, as anxious to get there as he is. "And...oh, God, her new cat. I've never seen Apollo look that scared."

He doesn't say anything at all, just tightens his jaw and turns onto the road where fire trucks, the police, and an ambulance block the way to Wolfe Automotive.

He parks, and we burst out of the car, running the rest of the way and moving through the crowd that's gathered to see what's going on.

"You can't go in there," Cullen Snow, June's older brother and one of the cops here in town says as Wolfe starts to hurry around a barricade.

"I own that place," Wolfe counters, but Cullen shakes his head.

"You have to stay back and out of the way so the fire-fighters can do their job.

"Sarah," I blurt out. "Cullen, Sarah lives in the apartment above."

"I just saw her," he says, scanning the crowd, and I follow suit, my heart lodged in my throat as I look for my friend.

"There," Wolfe says, relief in his voice. "She's there with June."

We run over, and I throw my arms around Sarah.

"Oh, my God! I was so worried about you!"

"We're okay," Sarah says, but her eyes are wide and glassy as she clings to Petunia and stares at the flames that reach high into the sky. "Scared, but not hurt. But—"

"What?"

She leans in and whispers in my ear. "My divorce papers were in there, Luna."

"Shit."

"What happened?" Wolfe asks, his voice completely calm and kind, in direct contrast to the intensity of his eyes.

"I heard a crash," Sarah says. "Petunia started to act funny, wouldn't let me sit, wouldn't leave me alone, and then I smelled the smoke. I grabbed her, came out here to the street, and called nine-one-one. I don't know what caused the fire."

"It's okay," I assure her as Sarah kisses Petunia on the

255

head. The cat is surprisingly calm in Sarah's arms, not trying to get away at all.

"SARAH!"

We all look around for the sound of the scream. Tanner comes running from out of the crowd, his face ashen with fear.

"SARAH!"

"Here!" I call back, waving. "We're over here!"

Tanner runs to us and simply scoops Sarah into his arms, holding both her and the cat close, rocking them all back and forth.

I look over to June, who shares a glance with me. And we know.

They belong together.

"Jesus Christ, I've never been so fucking scared," Tanner says and kisses Sarah on the forehead. "Are you hurt? Do you need the EMTs?"

"I'm okay," she assures Tanner. "We're not hurt."

"I could see the flames from my house," Tanner says as he turns to the rest of us and swallows hard as if his heart's lodged in his throat. "And when someone said it was the garage, I—"

He can't complete the thought, and Wolfe pats him on the shoulder as Apollo joins us.

"I heard Cullen say something about arson," June says, shaking her head. "Of course, there will be an investigation, but who would want to do something like *this*? It just doesn't happen in Huckleberry Bay."

"Kids?" I ask as I turn to the garage and watch as the firefighters shoot a huge stream of water into the building.

"Maybe some kids thought they'd play a trick, and it got out of hand."

"It could be anything," Wolfe says flatly. "And so many things in there are flammable. It wouldn't stand a chance. Shit, we had two cars in there that we were working on."

"Insurance will take care of it," June says.

"Yeah, well, still."

"Holy fuck," Zeke exclaims as he joins us. "What the hell?"

"That's what we're all wondering," Wolfe says. "But no one was hurt, and that's the most important thing. Where were you?"

"I was at home," Zeke says and clears his throat. "Busy."

I look at June and Sarah. *Busy?* I mouth.

Both of them shrug.

Who's Zeke been seeing? It's a small town. These kinds of secrets don't last long.

For a long while, we just stand on the street and watch the firefighters do their job, systematically putting out the flames until it's mostly just smoke.

"My paintings are all gone," Sarah says with a sad sigh. Tanner's still holding her, his arms wrapped around her from behind. "I know it's silly, but damn it, I worked hard on them."

"You'll paint more," Tanner assures her. "Wait, I didn't know you were painting again."

"It's just a hobby," Sarah says with a shrug, but her eyes are sad as she stares up at what was once her apartment.

A place of her very own after breaking free from a horrible marriage.

Suddenly, I notice that Daisy, the owner of The Grind, is passing out coffee and hot chocolate to everyone.

Harvey and Susan, the owners of Lighthouse Pizza, are making the rounds through the crowd, handing out slices of pepperoni and cheese.

"That's the thing about small towns," Wolfe says. "People rally."

"Oh, honey," Cordelia says and reaches out for my hand. Her thumb brushes over my fingers, and her face falls. "I don't want any of you to worry about breakfast tomorrow. We'll bring it to you, no matter where you are."

"Thanks," I reply with a grateful smile.

"Here's a little carrier for Petunia," Dr. Stevenson says as he opens the door of the small pet carrier, and Sarah urges the cat inside. "There's a blanket in there. And some water, too."

"Oh, that's awesome," Sarah says with a sigh. "She's wonderful, but she was getting heavy."

The owner of a new little boutique in town offers for Sarah to come and pick out some clothes for free. Suddenly, Scott, Sarah's younger brother, appears out of the crowd and hugs his sister.

Sarah goes still for a second, and then her arms encircle him, and she starts to cry.

"I'm sorry," she says as Scott hugs her tighter. "For everything. I'm so sorry."

"We'll worry about it later," Scott replies. "You can stay with me if you need to."

"She'll stay with me and my grandmother," June interrupts with a wink. "We have too much space for just the two of us."

Tanner's jaw tightens. I know he'd like to insist that Sarah go stay with him, but he doesn't say anything. He just rubs his hand over his hair and looks like he wants to punch something.

I cross to him and pat his arm.

"Give it time."

He simply nods as Wolfe crosses to me.

"You should go ahead and go," he says. "I'm going to stay here with Zeke until the fire's all the way out and we have some more information. You should help June get Sarah settled at her place."

"Okay." I take a deep breath and cup his face in my hands. "I'm so sorry, Wolfe. So, so sorry."

He closes his eyes and kisses my palm, then squeezes my hand.

"Me, too. I don't know when I'll get home, so don't wait up."

He hurries away, and I turn to June.

"Should we go?"

"Yeah, let's get out of here," June agrees. "Maybe that'll urge some of the others to leave and get out of the way, too."

We walk about a block over to June's truck, and when

we're all settled in, she pulls away from the curb. She has to take the long way through town as most of the main roads are blocked because of the fire trucks, but we're eventually headed out of town.

"Cullen looks great," I comment.

"He loves the job," June agrees.

We fall quiet again. Finally, I say, "Do you guys really need me? I mean, I'm happy to go help, but it's also totally fine with me if you just drop me off at home."

"You should go home," Sarah says. "Honestly, there's nothing to get settled. It's just me, Petunia, and the clothes on my back. Go on home and decompress a bit."

"Thanks. But if you need *anything*, just call me. I can be up there in just a few minutes."

June turns onto Lighthouse Way. When we stop by the house, I'm surprised to see that the candles and pretty lights on the gazebo are all out.

Someone must have come up to take care of it while we were in town.

"Thanks for the ride," I say as I hop out of the truck. "Call if you need me."

"We will. Same goes," June says through the window.

"Love you guys."

"Love you, too," Sarah calls as June turns around, and they drive away.

I should go inside, but I take a second to just breathe in the night air. I can still smell the smoke, and as exhausted as I am from the whole ordeal, I'm not sleepy.

So, with a quick look around outside, I head inside and straight back to the bedroom for a shower, to wash my hair and get rid of the smoke. Once I'm all clean and in comfy sweats and a T-shirt, I make a pot of tea and settle in my chair by the fireplace with Rose's diary in my lap.

Before I open the book, I take a sip of tea and smell Rose in the room with me.

"Tonight was bad," I say softly. "Poor Wolfe. He and Zeke put so much work into that garage. And in the span of just a few hours, it's all gone."

I shake my head sadly.

"What if he decides that all of this isn't worth it and leaves? The way your DP left you?"

A door closes, and it makes me smile.

"Yeah, I'm being dramatic. Okay, I'm going to read through some more of this until Wolfe gets home."

I crack open the diary and start to page through. I see mentions of a harsh winter, losing some animals to the cold, and then I turn to a page where she's drawn some hearts and written her name.

With a man's.

Rose Winchester loves Daniel P. Snow.

Rose Snow.

Rose Elaine Winchester-Snow.

It's the doodles of a young woman in love and pining for the man she's lost.

Except now I have a *name*.

"Who is Daniel Snow?"

I look up and blink.

"June's last name is Snow!"

I glance at the time and decide to wait to call her

until tomorrow. At past one in the morning, they're probably all asleep.

But I'm excited to ask June and Annabelle some questions, and maybe solve the mystery of Rose's first love.

I set the book aside and snuggle into the chair. I should go to bed, but I want to wait up for Wolfe and be here in case he needs anything.

Even if it's just to talk.

* * *

"Come on, baby," Wolfe whispers as he lifts me out of the chair and into his arms. "Let's go to bed."

"I'm sorry I fell asleep," I reply and rest my cheek on his shoulder. "Tried to stay up."

"You should sleep."

I feel him walking down the hall, but I can't open my eyes.

"Time is it?"

"After four," he says and kisses my hair. He always kisses me. I can smell the smoke on him as he lowers me to the bed and tucks me in.

I hear him rustling about the room a bit, and then I hear the shower.

I doze, falling in and out of sleep, but when Wolfe returns to the bed and slips between the covers, I instinctively scoot to him, and he pulls me into his arms once more. My head rests on his chest as he kisses my forehead.

"I'm so fucking glad you're here," he says softly. "So damn glad."

"Are you okay?" I open my eyes and frown up at him in the darkness. "Is your head hurting?"

"Surprisingly, no," he says. "I'm just coming off the adrenaline, and it's sinking in that some bastard set my business on fire."

"It's for sure that it was on purpose?"

"Oh, yeah," he says with a deep sigh. "They're still investigating, and probably will be for a while, but it was no accident. Fuckers."

"I'm so sorry." I drape my leg over him, trying to get even closer.

"Did you turn everything off in the gazebo?" he asks.

"No, it was already done when I got home. Someone must have come up while we were occupied with things in town."

"Hmm," he says.

After a few minutes, I feel his breathing slow and know he's fallen asleep.

I want to ask so many questions and make him reassure me that he won't leave for good.

But he's exhausted, and now isn't the time for that kind of conversation.

Instead, I keep my head pressed to his heart and let the sound of his breathing and his heartbeat lull me to sleep.

* * *

Rather than call up to June's place, I decided to just go up to visit. June texted and told me that they were all getting a slow start to the day, so I know they're home.

And I'd really like to talk to Annabelle, as well, so this works perfectly.

I park in the driveway, then walk up to the door and ring the bell. Just a few seconds later, June answers.

"Well, hey," she says.

"Hi. I have some questions for your grandma, so I thought I'd just come see how you're doing in person."

"We're good," June says as she steps back to let me in. "How are you? How is *Wolfe*?"

"He's...distraught. He and Zeke are already down at the garage, taking a look around with the arson investigator. He's mostly mad that someone would set the place on fire, especially with Sarah being upstairs."

"I get that," June says and leads me back to the kitchen where Annabelle and Sarah are eating scones from Three Sisters. "Did they deliver a big spread to your place, too?"

"Yeah, they did," I confirm with a smile. "It's nice that so many people want to help."

"That's what we do in Huckleberry Bay," Annabelle says. "How are those nice boys today?"

"They're going to be okay. Besides, I heard you didn't like Zeke so much."

"Oh, I like him just fine. I have to give him a hard time since he's new in town and all. But he's a good kid. Come in and sit down. Have a scone. There are at least a thousand of them here."

Before I sit, I cross to Sarah and hold her close, kissing her cheek. "You okay?"

"Better today," she confirms. "Petunia is still asleep upstairs, but we're going to be just fine."

"Good." I take a seat and reach for a scone. I might have a dozen of my own at home, but who can pass up this deliciousness? "Annabelle, I have some questions for you."

"I'm an open book, honey. Shoot."

"Well, I've been digging into my great-great-grand-mother, Rose Winchester. I found a bunch of her stuff recently and discovered that she was in love with a man who left town on a ship. One she thought was gone for good. She ended up marrying the man who would become my great-great-grandfather, but I'm really curious about that other man.

"At first, I only had the initials DP. But, last night, I found a page in her diary where she'd written out his name. Daniel P. Snow."

June and Sarah both gasp, but Annabelle just smiles. "That's right. What would you like to know?"

"*Everything*. Why did he leave? How long was he gone? Why did she think he was dead? I want to know everything. She's not very forthcoming in her notes. It's almost as if she were trying to hide it or something."

"She likely was," Annabelle says thoughtfully. "Boy, this is ancient news. Daniel Snow was my great-grandfather."

"But...wait," Sarah says, holding up her hand. "How

is Snow June and her siblings' last name? Wouldn't it be whatever their father's name was?"

"We changed it," June mutters. "For...reasons."

"That's another conversation for another day," Annabelle agrees. "According to family lore, Daniel was deeply in love with Rose. Why, he lived right here in this house. And he'd steal away to go see her at the lighthouse whenever he could, which was often. It was very romantic, really."

"What happened?" I ask, leaning forward in anticipation.

"He left for work. His father was wealthy, but Daniel was determined to make his own way. So, he said goodbye to Rose and promised to be back soon. I don't remember where he was off to. If you ask me, you can't make much money in just a few months' time, but he was young. Painfully so. And so was she. He never made the ship in time to get his ride home. Back then, you didn't fly or even ride in cars. You went by boat. It took a long time to travel.

"By the time he returned home, Rose had agreed to marry Lucas Winchester. He was a good man and eager to run the lighthouse. Rose's family approved, and Daniel came home too late to stop the wedding."

"How sad," June murmurs.

"Not at all, my darling girl," Annabelle says, waving June off. "If they'd married, the three of us would be *very* different than we are. We might not be here at all."

"True," June says. "Did Daniel pine for her for a long time?"

"He did, from what I heard," Annabelle confirms. "But, about a year later, he married my great-grandmother and moved on with his life."

"Wow," Sarah says. "And still lived just a stone's throw away from his first love."

"It's been said that Rose and Daniel maintained a relationship long after they both married and had children," Annabelle says, leaning forward to whisper loudly. "That they just couldn't stay away from each other. But that could just be gossip."

"I think that would be hard to do in such a small town," I speculate.

"You're probably right," Annabelle agrees. "But I did hear that he once gifted her with a car after her husband died."

I stare at her and then look over at June and Sarah. We all smile.

"I think I still have that car," I tell her and explain about the Ford we found in the barn.

"That could be it," Annabelle says. "Isn't that romantic? I mean, if they carried on while they were both still married, he was a cheating bastard, but still. It's a little romantic."

"Wow, all this time, this was the history, and I had no idea. I've been up to this house countless times over the years, and unbeknownst to me, it belonged to my great-great-grandmother's first love. It's just crazy."

"There's so much history here in Huckleberry Bay," Annabelle says. "Many tales similar to this one. The roots run deep in this community. Perhaps, before I die, I should write a book about it all."

"Oh, you absolutely should," Sarah agrees.

"I'd have to keep it unpublished until after my demise so no one could get mad at me while I'm alive. I know too many juicy secrets."

Annabelle laughs in delight, and I pull the photo of DP that I found in the trunk and pass it to her.

"Well, look at him." She presses her red lips together and examines the picture. "I've never seen an image of him this young. He was a handsome young man."

"He was hot," June says, looking over her grandmother's shoulder.

"Yeah, I see what Rose saw in him," Sarah adds, joining them. "Do you have photos of Lucas?"

"I do. I found a whole photo album full of old pictures. Some are even made of tin."

"That's a treasure," Annabelle says with a smile. "How lovely. Now, what are some other fun little tidbits of gossip I can tell you? Oh, yes. Let's talk about the Hart family and how they *used* to come into all the gold they used..."

* * *

"That's a lot of gossip," Wolfe says. It's later in the day, and we decided to come to the public beach in town and go for a walk on the sand together. "But I'm glad you were able to get some answers about Rose and DP."

"Me, too." I step around a washed-up jellyfish. "I

know I'll come up with more questions as I dive deeper into the family tree and Rose's things, but I'm happy to have that chapter closed. Oh, did I tell you that I went to see Cordelia and her sisters?"

"I don't think so. What happened?"

"I accepted their proposal to own the kitchen side of Luna's Light. They were so excited, and we spent about an hour going over some things, like menus and kitchen ideas. I'm *so* relieved that I made that decision, Wolfe. It takes a huge amount of stress off of my plate."

"I'm glad you did, too."

I grin and take Wolfe's hand, link our fingers. "Do you remember when Tanner was out here surfing when he was a senior and ended up getting hit in the head with his surfboard?"

"Yeah, there was blood everywhere, and June screamed that it would lure in sharks."

"I mean, in her defense, it could happen."

"Has anyone seen a great white shark off the shore of Huckleberry Bay?" he asks me.

"Uh, yeah," I say and laugh at him. "You know there are. They hunt the sea lions."

"Oh, yeah."

"Anyway, Tanner might have bled a lot, but he walked away from it pretty much unscathed."

"He always did have a hard head," Wolfe says. "Do you remember when our dads tried to build us a tree-house one summer, but the tree was old and fell apart?"

"They were so defeated." I lean over and kiss Wolfe's biceps. "But it all worked out. We were probably too old for a treehouse then, anyway. It wasn't long after that we started not hanging out as often."

"Kids grow up and don't play outside as much," he agrees.

We walk along the shore in silence for a while, watching a man fly a kite and kids building sandcastles.

It's a nice, sunny day today, but winter is just around the corner, and I can feel the nip in the air.

"You know, I just realized that you haven't mentioned having a headache lately," I say. "Have you been feeling better?"

"I haven't had one in a couple of weeks," he confirms. "And I won't complain about that. I hope that as time goes on, they become rarer. But it could be a fluke. Who knows, right?"

"Well, I'm glad you've been feeling better." I take a long, deep breath and smile as a big, yellow dog chases a tennis ball on the firm, wet sand. "Have you heard anything else about the fire? About who started it?"

"No. The investigator said it could take several months to piece it all together."

"Bummer." I brush a lock of hair off of my face. "Maybe we should get a dog."

"Yeah? What kind of dog?"

"I don't know. I like the big dogs like that one," I say, gesturing to the yellow dog. "Maybe after the B&B is up and running, and life calms down just a smidge, we can look into it."

"Sounds good to me. It could go to the shop with me sometimes, too."

"Maybe we should get a llama," I suggest and bite my bottom lip.

"That seems extreme but sure. Whatever you want."

"You don't want a *llama*," I say with a laugh.

"If it's what *you* want, we'll make it happen."

"So, you're just going to indulge me, no matter what?"

"Haven't you figured it out?" he asks, looking down at me with so much love, it steals the breath from my body. "I'll give you anything you want. You're the only one who matters, Luna."

"You're just a sweet talker."

"No, I'm just telling the truth."

June 20, 2005

Dear Diary,

We graduated! Thank God school's over because it was SO HARD to concentrate the last few months! But we're done, and now, I'll have one last summer with June and Sarah before I go off to college in the fall.

June says she's going to a trade school to learn welding and woodworking, and I think that's pretty cool. She loves to do that kind of stuff and has worked construction during the summer for a few years now.

I don't know what Sarah will do. Honestly, I worry about her. Her parents SUCK. They're just horrible people. They didn't even come to graduation, but my parents and Annabelle made it special for her, just like they do everything else. Sarah thinks she'll just stay here and work. I wish I could take her to college with me!

Some of us are going to Gordy's tonight for some burgers, and then tomorrow, my parents are throwing a huge party here on the property for my whole class and their families. We'll have games and music and lots and lots of food. I can't wait!

Love,
Luna

Chapter Nineteen

Wolfe

"I'd like to propose a toast," I announce, getting the attention of everyone here at Lighthouse Pizza. The place is packed, full of the members of my community who have been an incredible help to Zeke and me over the past two weeks. "To all of you and the few who couldn't make it here tonight. I always knew that Huckleberry Bay was a special place, but boy have you guys reminded me just how important it is to have a community rally behind you during a hard time."

I let my eyes drift over the room. When I come to Luna, I smile softly.

"Thank you for helping Zeke and me these past couple of weeks to clean up after the fire. Because of your help, we'll be ready to start rebuilding the garage very soon."

"You're going to rebuild?" someone calls out.

"Oh, hell, yeah. We're not going anywhere."

The room cheers, and I take a sip of my beer as I turn

to Harvey, the owner of the joint. "Everything tonight is on me. For the whole place."

"Susan told me," Harvey replies with a wink. "My wife might have a crush on you."

I laugh and glance over to where Susan and Luna are chatting at the end of the bar.

"I'm quite sure that's not true. I'm just spending some money in here tonight, that's all."

"Hey, let's play some pool," Tanner suggests, catching my attention.

"You're on," I reply and follow him to where Apollo and Zeke already have the balls racked and ready to go.

Sarah and June walk over to join us after making some song selections from the jukebox in the corner.

"Hey, Sarah, how's it going over at Annabelle's house?" Apollo asks her.

Sarah pastes a bright smile on her pretty face. "It's great."

"Liar, liar, pants on fire," Tanner mutters, but June just smiles in satisfaction, and the two women start playing a game of darts.

"When are you going to make a move there?" I ask him quietly.

"It's complicated," he says with a shrug, watching as Zeke breaks the balls. "And may not happen at all."

"The way you two watch each other? Circle around each other? Come on, man."

But he shakes his head again and glances over at Sarah, who's laughing and pointing at her bull's eye.

"There's history there," he says. "And she's still recovering from the asshole she married."

"But she's not now," I remind him.

Just then, Indigo Lovejoy walks over to Sarah and June and asks if he can join in on their game.

"You might want to move in before someone else does."

Tanner's jaw tightens, and his eyes narrow as he watches Indigo shoot darts with the girls. When Sarah laughs at something the man says and lays her hand on his arm, Tanner swears under his breath.

Just then, Indigo takes a call and walks away from Sarah, and Tanner sighs in relief.

"Think about it," I suggest.

"Damn it, your turn," Zeke says after he misses a shot.

Zeke likes to lose as much as I do. Which is to say, not at all.

"Prepare to get your ass handed to you," I tell him with a cocky grin.

But just as I'm about to sink the third ball in a row, Luna walks past and completely destroys my concentration. I miss.

"Damn."

"I don't think I've ever seen you lose it over a woman," Zeke says thoughtfully. "And I've known you for a damn long time."

"I don't know what you're talking about." I sip my beer and keep an eye on my girl as she throws a dart, and it bounces off the board and onto the floor.

So, darts aren't her strong suit.

Maybe I should give her some pointers.

Suddenly, a dance song comes on through the speakers, and June, Sarah, and Luna scream in excitement.

"I guess they like this song," I say.

"Oh, God. Here they go," Apollo says with a grin, and the three women begin to dance a routine they've clearly known since they were teenagers.

They wiggle their hips, fling their arms over their head, and then squat like they're dropping it like it's hot.

It's fun and oddly sexy.

"They remember the moves," Tanner says with a grin.

"Are you kidding?" Apollo asks. "They did this dance every damn day the summer before their sophomore year. I got so sick of this stupid song."

When the song ends, and the women strike a pose, all in different degrees of height, we break out in applause.

Luna takes June's and Sarah's hands, and they bow to their audience and then laugh. I can't help myself. I stride over to Luna, take her face in my hands, and kiss the fuck out of her, right in front of most of Huckleberry Bay.

There are whoops and hollers and one request for us to get a room before I pull back and smile down at her.

"God, I fucking love you."

Luna laughs. "Because I can do a silly dance?"

"Because you're amazing."

"Okay, break it up, you two," June says, clapping her hands. "I haven't had enough shots to witness this kind of PDA."

"You haven't seen anything yet," I warn her, but I just continue grinning down at the woman I love. "Let me know when you're ready to get out of here."

"No. Absolutely, not," June says, pulling Luna out of my grasp. "You're not going to steal her away just because you want to...*do things*. We're having a party here, in case you missed it."

"Honey, I *planned* it."

"Exactly," Sarah jumps in. "So, it's rude to leave early. Let us have some fun before you whisk her off to engage in your sexy ways."

Luna's been giggling this whole time.

"But the sexy ways are something to write home about," she declares.

"I don't want to know," Apollo decides and returns to the pool table. "I actually want to poke my mind's eye out to erase that image from my brain."

We return to playing pool, and the girls play their darts, and before I know it, the whole place is pretty much empty, and it's past midnight.

"One hell of a party," Indigo says as he walks over to shake my hand. "You didn't have to foot the bill."

"Yeah, I really did. Thanks for all your help, man. I appreciate it."

"I'm around if you need more."

As Indigo makes his rounds through all the guys to say goodnight, I cross to Luna. She, June, and Sarah have been sitting at the bar, chatting and laughing, for the past hour.

"Are you ready to head home?" I ask her.

"Yeah, my lips are numb," she says and blinks her glassy eyes. "And I'm tired. Too much tequila."

"You're impressive," I tell her. "No salt and lime?"

"Who needs training wheels?" June asks and then laughs. "Boy, we're drunk."

"I'll drive you home," Apollo informs her.

"No," she says, shaking her head. "I'd rather walk."

"I wouldn't," Sarah says. "So, yes, Apollo, you may escort us home in your chariot."

"I should have stayed sober," June mutters as I help Luna to her feet, take her purse and jacket, and help her out to the car.

"So fun," she says with a happy sigh as she sinks into my leather seat. "I don't remember the last time I had that much fun."

"I agree." I turn onto Lighthouse Way, and when we pull up to the house, Luna's already asleep.

Her soft skin looks like glass in the moonlight. I want to ask her, right now, to marry me.

I've wanted to ask her many times over the past couple of weeks, but the moment was never right.

It's been damn frustrating.

I push out of the car and manage to wake her enough to lead her inside, and when we get to the bedroom, I gently pull her out of her clothes and get her into our bed.

Within two minutes, she's snoring.

* * *

"What are you doing?" I ask as I plop a waffle fresh from the waffle maker onto a plate.

"I'm making a list," Luna says and chews on the end of her pen.

"What kind of list?"

"A list of the lists I need to make."

She slathers butter on her waffle and then dumps so much syrup on it I wince.

"Holy shit, babe, you'll go into sugar shock."

"I like a little waffle with my syrup," she says with a wink. "Anyway, I have so much to do this week, I have to make a list of lists."

"It's too early for this." I sip my coffee and then pour batter into the maker for my waffle. "How can you even be in productivity mode already?"

"It's morning," she says as if that says it all. "I have shit to do. I have to talk with Dotty at Books on the Bay about helping me with the library in the B&B. I have to go over potential menus with Darla. I have to choose from floor samples, paint colors, light fixtures, and a million other details. Then I have to make a list of things I need to get done for the lighthouse. And *then*, I need a list for—"

"I get it." I hold up a hand and pluck my waffle out of the maker, shaking some powdered sugar on top before taking a bite.

We settle into silence as we both eat. My eyes are hot on hers as my mind drifts to this morning in bed.

Let's just say we worked up an appetite and earned these waffles.

"Do you have a few free minutes before you dive into your lists?" I ask her.

"Sure." She finishes her waffle and takes her plate to the sink. "What's up?"

"I want to show you something. Grab a jacket."

She pulls on a jacket and slips her feet in her golashes, and I lead her outside.

It rained a bit last night, so we have some mud. We squish our way to the spot I like, and I stop.

"I think this is a great spot," I inform her.

"Okay, for what?"

"For our future house."

She narrows her eyes and looks around. We're still near the cliffs, on the other side of the lighthouse from the B&B, so it's private.

"We would have a view of the water *and* the lighthouse, so you'd know if anything was ever wrong, but we're tucked away from the prying eyes of guests at the B&B."

"Okay, I can see that. It really is a good spot. And you'd be close to your new garage." She nods slowly, taking it in. "Yeah, I like it. Good idea."

She turns and smiles at me but then notices the stakes in the ground.

"Why are there pink ribbons on these stakes?"

"That's from the surveyor. I already contacted the county, and they came out for permit stuff. I have a couple of different plans for you to choose from, but I think the main bedroom should be right here."

I stand near the cliffs and gesture with my arms wide.

"It'll have the best view. And if we put it on the second floor, we can have a killer balcony for sunset watching."

"Wolfe."

I turn and see that she's lost her smile.

"Yeah?"

"We already discussed this. I don't want to talk about building a house right now. I just told you in the kitchen that I have a million things on my plate."

She walks back to the house, and I hurry after her.

"But that's the beauty of this," I say as I walk next to her. "You don't have to do *anything*. I'll handle all the details so you can still concentrate on the new business."

She shakes her head and walks through the front door of the house and back to the kitchen.

"I don't want you to just take over," she says, her voice rising. "If we're going to build a house, I want to be a part of it."

I drag my hand through my hair in frustration.

"But you just said that you're already busy."

"I am. Very busy."

"Then I don't see why I can't just take over this project and get it underway."

She looks like she wants to scream.

"Because I don't want you to do that, Wolfe. Besides, why would you want to start this *now*? Your garage just burned down, and you have to rebuild there. You're also still rebuilding classic cars in the other garage down the road. We're both stupidly busy right now, and the thought of adding another thing on top of it gives me freaking *hives*."

"I can do it."

"Do you hate this house so much?" she demands. "I know it's not new and super fancy, but it's nice, and it's plenty big enough."

"It's not that," I insist. "I like it just fine."

"We don't even always have to stay here every night," she continues. "If you want to stay down at the fancy barndominium, I'm down for that. It's a cool space, and we should use it."

"That's not the point. I just want to get the other house *started*. I want to move forward with it."

"Well, I'm not ready."

We stare at each other, both angry and frustrated, and I shake my head.

"I'm going to take a walk and clear my head," I say, turning for the door. "Before I say something that I can't take back."

"Good idea," she fumes. I close the door behind me, headed straight for the path down the cliff to the beach below.

"Fucking stubborn woman," I mutter, making my way down the rocks. It looks like the tide is going out, which is good.

I need a nice, long walk.

I love her more than anything. I want to give her *everything*. I just want to move forward with our lives together. To build something wonderful with her. Something that's not just mine or hers but...

Ours.

I want that house so badly, pieces of each of us together in one space, in a home we build together. I want to make a family with her there.

I want it more than anything I've ever wanted before.

It's not just a matter of marrying her. I want it all. And I'm anxious to get started as soon as possible.

Why doesn't she see it that way?

Just as I'm almost to the sand below, the headache hits.

"Fuck."

It's like I'm immediately in a dark hole. I can't even hear the water or see anything at all.

I drop to a rock and sit, hoping that this one will subside after just a few minutes.

But pain spears through me, stealing my breath, and then there's nothing at all.

Chapter Twenty

Luna

"Why is he so insistent?" I shake my head and pace the kitchen. "He told me he could be patient, but here he is, pushing. Because he goes from zero to sixty in one-point-six seconds, and I just *knew* he wouldn't be able to go slow on this. I just knew it."

I smell Rose and try to ignore her. I'm not in the mood to have a conversation with a ghost.

"I think he doesn't like this house because it's not fancy enough."

I walk into the living room and look around.

The house is nice. It's the biggest home attached to a lighthouse on the west coast, with almost three thousand square feet of living space, and I have plenty of guest rooms and just...*space*.

"Sure, it's a hundred years old, but it's not awful. It's certainly adequate to live in for a couple more years while I get the business going, and he finishes rebuilding the garage, and *then* we can build something else."

I think I sound perfectly reasonable. So why won't he just *listen* and take what I say at face value?

"What woman wants a house to be built without any input from her?" I ask, getting even more worked up. "For God's sake, I need to choose all of the things, and I'm already choosing a lot of things, and it makes my head pound."

Rose slams a door.

"I know, you don't want me to leave the damn lighthouse, but it's not like I'm going far, Rose. It's a hundred yards south, that's all. I'm sure you can still look in on us over there when you're not busy haunting whoever has rented out this place. You'll be a busy ghost."

I blow out a breath, but Rose slams another door.

"Great, now you're throwing a fit. There's only enough room for one woman to lose her shit at a time here. And that woman is me today. Sorry, not sorry."

Suddenly, a wind blows through the room, and the window facing the gazebo flies up. I can only gape at what I'm seeing.

"Oh, God. You're not just freaking out with me, are you?"

Another door slams, and I run out of the house toward the cliffs and look over the side.

"Shit. Shit, shit, shit."

Wolfe is almost to the bottom, and it looks like he's slumped over.

"The tide's coming in. Oh, God. JUNE! JUUUUUNE!!!!"

I scream June's name until I see her come running out of the B&B.

"What? What's wrong?"

"Wolfe." I point over the cliff. "He's down there, and the tide's coming in. If he's passed out, I won't be able to get him up."

"I'm calling the police," she says, immediately reaching for her phone. "I'm all over it, Luna."

"I'm going down there. Tell them to hurry!"

The rocks are slippery from last night's rain, so I have to move much slower than I want to. It feels like it takes me *hours* to reach him, and when I do, I almost have a panic attack.

He's definitely passed out.

"Did you fall?" I ask, looking around him. "There's no blood on your head. I don't think you fell. Shit, a migraine? Damn it, Wolfe, wake up and tell me what to do!"

I cup his face and realize that the water is lapping at my feet.

"The water's rising, Wolfe. Come on, baby, I need you to wake up."

His eyes flutter open, but he moans and slumps again.

"No. Damn it, we're not doing this today. You're not leaving me like this. Also, this is the last time you walk down here."

I blow out a breath and look down. My knees are wet now.

"Why does the water seem to rise so quickly? And it's damn cold."

"LUNA!"

I look up and see several people looking down at us. There are men in uniform, and they're securing ropes of some kind.

"Help is here," I tell Wolfe. "But it would be better if you could wake up and help me. I have to keep your head above the water, and it's coming in fast. The waves are going to wash up to us in a minute."

Terror has me in its icy grip as I watch two men hurry, carefully making their way down the rocks to us.

"We're getting a board secured to bring down for him," Cullen says to me. "What happened?"

"I'm not sure, but I think it's a migraine. They hit hard and fast and take him out."

Cullen's face is grim as he turns to his coworker.

"He's out of it. We need the board. Let's get them out of this water."

The next twenty minutes feel like hours as they secure Wolfe to the board. He opens his eyes briefly and winces when he's touched, but we're soon climbing back up to the top. They transfer Wolfe to a gurney for the ambulance.

"You scared me," I say as I press my face to Wolfe's once we're in the rig and racing to the hospital about thirty minutes away.

"Luna?" Wolfe asks and squeezes his hand over mine.

"You're going to be okay." I kiss his cheek. "Damn it, we can live wherever you want as long as you don't leave me."

He licks his lips. "Not going anywhere. Fucking headaches."

The EMTs get fluids going and monitor his vital signs.

"Slightly hypothermic," one mutters. "Temp is ninety-six-point-one."

"How is that even possible?" I demand. "He wasn't in the water that long."

"Wind," the same one says briskly. "The cliffs are cold, and he's not wearing a coat. That water is frigid, and every minute counts in moments like that. He's damn lucky you found him when you did."

My throat closes. Dear God, I could have *lost* him.

"I'll warm him up." I snuggle up to him and press my body to his as best as I can on the narrow cot. "I'm sorry if this hurts you, but we have to warm you up, Wolfe."

"'s okay."

When we finally arrive at the hospital, they take Wolfe to a room and move him to a bed, covered in a warming blanket. Amaryllis Lovejoy hurries into the room.

"I got the call that he was on his way in," she says as she quickly examines him. "What happened?"

"I don't know for sure—"

"Fucking migraine," Wolfe says weakly. "Hit out of the blue. Knocked me out. That's never happened before."

"He'd just climbed down the cliff to the beach. He didn't know that the tide was coming in."

Amaryllis's blue eyes go wide in fear.

"Oh, God."

"Exactly."

"Stop hovering," Wolfe says. "I'll be fine. Just get rid of this bitch of a headache."

With her mouth set grimly, Amaryllis shakes her head. "I can't. I wish I could."

Several hours later, once Wolfe's warm and the worst of the headache is gone, they discharge him from the hospital.

Apollo and June are waiting to drive us home.

"You came...*together*?" I ask in surprise.

"You couldn't keep either of us away," June says and hurries over to hug me. "That was damn scary."

"Let's not do it again," Apollo agrees. "Come on, let's go home."

* * *

"I'm sorry," Wolfe says a few hours later. We're settled in at the house, sitting by the fire and just trying to calm our nerves after what happened this morning.

"No, *I'm* sorry," I reply. "I overreacted."

"No, you didn't," he says and takes my hand in his. "I need to learn how to be patient. It's just that I'm excited to start our lives together, and the house feels like a big piece of that. I'm excited to carry you over the threshold one day."

"I get it. I'm excited for all those things, too." I brush my fingers down his cheek. "It's just a lot right now. Maybe a month from now, it won't feel like so much, but I'm not ready for the house-building thing. Not yet. Let me get the B&B finished, and then we can move on to the next project."

"We balance each other," he says softly. "And that's a good thing."

"I meant what I said earlier, in the ambulance. We can live *anywhere*, Wolfe, as long as I'm with you. If Rose hadn't alerted me today, I might have lost you, and that's completely unacceptable."

"I want to live here," he says. "And, eventually, we'll build the house. I can rein it in for a little while."

I snuggle up to him and thank God that he's okay. As long as we're together, we can figure everything else out.

* * *

"How do they do it?" I ask as Wolfe drives us home from dinner at Three Sisters Kitchen.

"What's that?"

"How is it that literally everything they cook is *amazing*? And the restaurant itself is just so *pretty*. I love being in there. They do such a good job, and I'm so relieved that they're going to run the kitchen in Luna's Light."

"My chicken was great," he agrees and turns into the driveway.

I grin at the sight of the gazebo.

It's all lit up with candles and twinkle lights.

"I feel like we've been here before."

Wolfe looks over at me and smiles before kissing my hand gently.

"We're going to try this again, hopefully with no interruptions this time."

Without another word, he climbs out of the car and walks around the hood to open my door for me. Then, with our hands linked, he leads me into the gazebo.

Red, pink, and yellow blooms of all different kinds and varieties are in vases and laid on every surface, making the gazebo smell like heaven.

And sitting on the table is a simple, black box.

Wolfe walks over and picks it up. "Come have a seat, sweetheart."

I do as he asks, and to my delight, Wolfe lowers himself to one knee.

"If I've learned one thing over the past few weeks, it's that you and I can survive just about anything. Whether it's a fire or my stupidity, there isn't much of anything that we *can't* get through together."

He swallows and looks down at the box that he's rolling between his hands, and then he looks up at me with so much love it shines brighter than the candles around us.

"I think I've been in love with you since I was nine," he says, and it surprises a giggle out of me. "No, really. And I hate that it took something bad to drive me back home to you, but I'm also so damn grateful for it. I thought I'd lost everything when I found out I couldn't race anymore, but little did I know that my life was truly just beginning."

I can't help myself; I reach out and cup Wolfe's face in my hand.

"I'm also grateful for what racing did for me. I wouldn't have been a good husband to you if I hadn't gone and lived that life. I know that deep in my bones. I wouldn't have appreciated you the way I do now. I love you so much."

"I love you, too," I whisper and brush a tear off my cheek.

"I hope so because I'm asking you, here and now —*finally*—to marry me."

He clicks open the box, and a diamond ring winks up at me. The center diamond is bezel set and looks...vintage.

"Wow."

I look up into his eyes and smile.

"Of course, I'll marry you. I can't imagine spending my life with anyone *but* you, Wolfe Conrad."

He helps me slip the ring on my finger, and then he lets out a loud whoop and scoops me up into his arms, swings me around, and kisses me senseless.

Suddenly, all the people we love surround us. Even my parents are here, and I can only stare at Wolfe in shock.

"How?"

"It doesn't matter," he says. "It's all for you. Because I knew you'd want to share this moment with them."

"Congratulations, my darling girl," Mom says as she kisses my cheek.

"When did you get here?"

"This morning," Dad says and hugs me. "We've been planning this for a couple of weeks now."

I look at Wolfe, but he's already been swept up by the others, laughing with Apollo.

"I think he'll have lots of surprises in store for me over the years."

"I hope so," Mom says, just as a light breeze blows through, carrying the special scent of Rose with it.

Even she's giving us her blessing.

When Wolfe makes his way back to me, he kisses me once more, not at all worried about the public display of affection.

"Yuck," I hear June say.

"We have cake," Cordelia announces. "And coffee from Daisy."

"Will every moment always be a community event?" I ask with a laugh.

"That's how we do things in Huckleberry Bay," Annabelle reminds us all.

July 1, 2021

Dear Diary,

Wolfe's home. He's here for a charity race, and I haven't seen him in many years. The man looks better in person than he does on TV.

He looked me right in the eyes today before his accident, and it was like something deep down in my soul stirred. Woke and recognized him. Which I know is ridiculous. HB isn't his home anymore, and I'm sure that once he recovers from that horrible crash today, he'll be off to somewhere else in the world to race cars and meet exotic women.

But for just that moment earlier, something in me shifted.

Love,
Luna

Epilogue

Sarah

Fifteen Years Ago

"God, you're worthless."

Mom spits the words as I hurry to grab my jacket and leave the house for the night.

"I want you to stay here and take care of me."

"You're not sick," I tell her flatly. "You're drunk. And I don't want to take care of you when you're like this because you're mean."

"Oh, baby." Her face transforms from mean to sugar-sweet, just like that. "You know I don't mean it. It's just that I'm so lonely because your daddy's been gone for a few days, and you're never home. Why don't you stay here? We'll watch a movie. I'll make your favorite popcorn with extra butter."

"We don't *have* popcorn. Or butter." I shake my head and walk to the door. "Sleep it off, Mom."

"You ungrateful bitch!" she screams, and something smashes against the door as I close it.

Thank God Scott's sleeping over at a friend's house tonight, and I can escape with Tanner.

I've never brought Tanner home to meet my parents, even though we've been dating for more than a year. There's no way in hell I want him to meet them.

It's just so embarrassing.

My mom is a drunk, and my dad sleeps around with just about anyone and everyone. We've moved four times this year alone because they keep skipping out on the rent.

I'm shocked that people will even rent to them anymore. Huckleberry Bay is small, and I know that people talk.

I hurry down the street to Gordy's, where I'm supposed to meet Tanner for dinner, and smile when I see that he's already sitting at our usual booth.

"I'm *so* glad you're home," I say with excitement as I slide onto the bench next to him and hug him tightly. Tanner's a sophomore at Oregon State, and he hasn't been home in more than three months.

The worst three months *ever*.

"Yeah, it's good to be here."

But he doesn't smile at me in that special way he usually does. And he doesn't kiss me.

A ball of dread forms in my belly.

"What's wrong?"

"Shit, this sucks," he mutters. "Listen, Sarah. I think that maybe we should take a break."

I move away and slide into the booth across from him so I can look him in the eyes.

"Why?"

He swallows hard and shakes his head, not meeting my gaze.

"It's just too hard, you know?"

"Look at me, Tanner."

He does, and the sadness in those green orbs makes me want to scream.

"Did you meet someone else at college?"

"What? No." He shakes his head, and I believe he's telling me the truth. "No, it's not that at all. It's just that being away from you is hard, and I can't concentrate because I'm worried about you, wondering if you're okay. And I really need to work hard at school, Sar. My parents are paying for me to be there, and I don't want to screw it up."

"I won't call you as much," I promise. "I know I call too often, but it's just because I miss you so much. But I'll stop. I'll just see you when you're home."

But he's already shaking his head.

"It's just a break for a while," he repeats. "Let me get through another semester to see where I am. You know?"

"No." My world is shattering around me. "No, I don't know at all. I love you, Tanner."

"I love you, too," he whispers and closes his eyes. "But this is for the best right now."

"Are you going to see other people?"

"I...I don't know."

"Oh, my God, Tanner."

"That's what people do when they break up, right? They see other people. Don't wait around for me, Sar. You're a senior, and you should go to prom and do all the things."

"School's almost over," I remind him. "I'm graduating in a few months, and then I can move to Corvallis with you. We won't have to be apart anymore."

"I don't think that's going to happen," he says flatly. "And I hate that this hurts you. I hate it so much. But we're young. We should live apart for a while. I'm sorry, Sarah."

He offers me a brief smile, and then he's gone, and I'm left alone in the booth, wondering what in the hell just happened.

What am I supposed to do now?

Are you excited for Sarah and Tanner's story in Fernhill Lane? You can preorder it here: https://www.kristenprobyauthor.com/fernhill-lane

From Wall Street Journal Bestselling author Kristen Proby comes a small town, second chance romance! Fernhill Lane is the newest installment in the Huckleberry Bay series!

. . .

She didn't think she'd ever come home again.

When Sarah Bitterman left Huckleberry Bay at the tender age of nineteen, newly married to a much older man, she had every intention of coming home to visit. Sadly, she quickly learned that was out of the question.

Until her husband throws her out with only the clothes on her back and finally sets Sarah free.

Coming back to the small seaside town has been the hardest thing she's ever done. Facing those who loved her the most and think she turned her back on them is almost unbearable. But she *needs* her two best friends, and she's longed to make amends with her little brother.

Huckleberry Bay is like the art in her soul. And now she can put down roots and begin to heal.

Tanner Hilleman knew it was a mistake to let the love of his life go all those years ago, and he's never stopped thinking about her. Now that she's home, while he's giving her the space she needs, he's also determined to make Sarah see that they belong together.

. . .

Unfortunately, Sarah's past has followed her to Huckleberry Bay and threatens to destroy everything she loves. Will she and Tanner survive it? Or will it tear them apart for good?

About the Author

Kristen Proby has published more than sixty titles, many of which have hit the USA Today, New York Times and Wall Street Journal Bestsellers lists.

Kristen and her husband, John, make their home in her hometown of Whitefish, Montana with their two cats and dog.

f facebook.com/booksbykristenproby

▢ instagram.com/kristenproby

BB bookbub.com/profile/kristen-proby

g goodreads.com/kristenproby

Newsletter Sign Up

I hope you enjoyed reading this story as much as I enjoyed writing it! For upcoming book news, be sure to join my newsletter! I promise I will only send you news-filled mail, and none of the spam. You can sign up here:

https://mailchi.mp/kristenproby.com/ newsletter-sign-up

Also by Kristen Proby:

Other Books by Kristen Proby

The Single in Seattle Series
The Secret
The Scandal

The With Me In Seattle Series

Come Away With Me
Under The Mistletoe With Me
Fight With Me
Play With Me
Rock With Me
Safe With Me
Tied With Me
Breathe With Me

Also by Kristen Proby:

Soaring With Fallon

Big Sky Royal
Enchanting Sebastian
Enticing Liam
Taunting Callum

Heroes of Big Sky
Honor
Courage
Shelter

Check out the full Big Sky universe here:
https://www.kristenprobyauthor.com/under-the-big-sky

Bayou Magic
Shadows
Spells
Serendipity

Check out the full series here: https://www.
kristenprobyauthor.com/bayou-magic

The Romancing Manhattan Series

All the Way
All it Takes
After All

Also by Kristen Proby:

Check out the full series here: https://www. kristenprobyauthor.com/romancing-manhattan

The Boudreaux Series

Easy Love
Easy Charm
Easy Melody
Easy Kisses
Easy Magic
Easy Fortune
Easy Nights

Check out the full series here: https://www. kristenprobyauthor.com/boudreaux

The Fusion Series

Listen to Me
Close to You
Blush for Me
The Beauty of Us
Savor You

Check out the full series here: https://www. kristenprobyauthor.com/fusion

From 1001 Dark Nights

Also by Kristen Proby:

Check out the entire Crossover Collection here: https://www.kristenprobyauthor.com/kristen-proby-crossover-collection

CPSIA information can be obtained
at www.ICGtesting.com
Printed in the USA
LVHW051921290422
717487LV00004B/122